I Think I'm A Monster

Bloodlines & Chains
Book 1

by

Catherine M. Clark

Wylde Publishing

Copyright © 2024-25 Catherine M. Clark

All rights reserved. ISBN: 9781919227603
The characters and events portrayed in this book are fictitious. Any similarity to real persons, living or dead, is coincidental and not intended by the author.

No part of this publication may be reproduced, distributed, or transmitted in any form or by any means, including photocopying, recording, or other electronic or mechanical methods, and not to be used for AI training without the author's prior written permission, except in the case of brief quotations embodied in critical reviews and certain other non-commercial uses permitted by copyright law. For permission requests, please get in touch with the author.

2nd Edition

Content Warning

Within this story, there is a scene of self-harm and a suicidal act that some may find challenging to read.

Chapter 1:
1998

Devika

My desk is a warzone. A chaotic landscape of stray pencils, half-empty paint tubes, and teetering stacks of inspiration. The afternoon sun bleeds through the window, casting a warm, honeyed glow over everything as it begins its slow descent.

It's hard to believe I'm officially sixteen. Friday marked the big day, an event I'd been anticipating with a nervous flutter for months. Among the gifts was a treasure trove of new art supplies, and my heart actually did a little flip-flop when I unwrapped them. The highlight was a set of coloured pencils nestled in a sleek wooden box that smelled like cedar. The weight of it felt like a promise. There were shades I'd never even seen before—electric blues that hummed with energy, velvety purples that whispered of twilight—all just waiting.

And yet.

As my birthday got closer, the familiar weight in my chest returned, a cold counterpoint to the vibrant new pencils. It's a shadow that clings a little tighter with each passing year, a trend that started when I was twelve after a routine check-up went sideways. Amidst the sterile scent of antiseptic, I was handed a diagnosis—some rare genetic disorder that basically hijacked my life. The medication I have to take, a daily ritual of chalky pills, is supposed to help. Instead, I got a whirlwind of unexplainable pains. Sometimes it's a sharp sting, like fire ants marching under my skin. Other times it's a deep, throbbing ache in my joints that makes zero sense.

It feels like my own body is a traitor, and every year, it finds a new way to remind me how fragile I am.

To keep my parents from worrying, I've mastered the art of the cheerful façade. Bright laughter that doesn't quite reach my eyes. A light-heartedness that feels rehearsed. Leading up to my birthday, I felt like two different people—one was desperate to celebrate, to just feel *normal*, and the other was dreading the inevitable pain that came with another year of... well, of this. But I resolved to make the most of it. I clung to the genuine smiles of my three closest friends, Clare, Liz, and Tom. They're the only ones who get to see me without the mask.

My birthday is the one day a year I'm allowed to venture out with them. A rule that chafes, but I've learned to live with it. We dove into the blissful anonymity of the cinema, the smell of buttery popcorn a familiar comfort. Afterwards, we hit the bowling alley, our shouts and the satisfying clatter of pins a temporary shield against the turmoil inside me. I savoured every second of that fleeting freedom.

But even with them, an ache of isolation throbbed under the surface. As I blew out my candles, I couldn't shake the pang of missing out on what other teenagers have so effortlessly. Still, I gathered the happy moments like jewels, pushing the darker thoughts away. If only for a little while.

Now, as twilight melts into a cool Sunday evening, I lose myself in the lines on the page. Moonlight streams through my window, casting long, dancing shadows. I pick up my favourite graphite pencil, its wood worn smooth in my hand, and apply the finishing touches to one of my favourite scenes: unicorns in a sunlit meadow.

The grass is dotted with wildflowers in shades I've only imagined—vibrant violet, sun-kissed yellow, deep crimson. I can almost feel the warmth of the sun on my skin, see the shimmering coats of the unicorns as if they're cloaked in a magical aura. Their manes flow like silk in a breeze I can't feel but can perfectly picture.

My pencil glides across the paper with a soft *shush*. I pour all my focus into the delicate spiral of their horns, the powerful curves of their bodies, and the sweep of feathered wings folded against their flanks. Yes, mine have wings. It just feels right. My mind drifts to a world where anything is possible, a place far more real than the homework and chores that are my actual life.

My parents don't get it. Not really.

"I just don't know where you get it from, darling," Mum often says, her voice full of loving confusion. They can't grasp how this world in my head is as real to me as the desk under my hands. It's my escape. When I was little, they tried drawing with me, their stick figures so hilariously bad I'd laugh until my sides ached. It's a warm memory, but their interest faded as my skills outgrew their scribbles. It's okay. I'm content in my world.

With each stroke, it feels like I'm peering through a veil into another reality. The completed image is so lifelike it feels like I could reach out and touch the soft mane of a unicorn. The sensation is a sudden rush that makes my fingertips tingle, as if I'm not just looking at a drawing, but witnessing the real thing through my window. I've tried to explain it to them, that electric hum when a piece comes alive, but I see the faint, puzzled line between Mum's brows and know they don't understand.

"Devika!"

An internal groan rips through me. Mum's bedtime call. A spark of rebellion ignites, and I pretend I haven't heard, shading a delicate shadow beneath a unicorn's leg.

"Devika, don't ignore me. School tomorrow." Her voice is closer. The third stair tread creaks. I sigh, giving in, and start packing away my precious pencils just as she appears in the doorway.

"Come on, love. It's late," she says, her voice soft as she leans over my shoulder. Her hair, smelling of lavender, brushes my cheek.

"Oh, honey. That's amazing." Her admiration is a warm balm. "What's that on the side?"

I hadn't even realised I'd started sketching it. A house and a shimmering lake. In my head, it's already a cheerful yellow with grey shutters.

"A farm," I explain, my voice a little quiet. "A safe place for them."

She smiles, her eyes crinkling at the corners. She leans down and kisses the top of my head. "You have such a skill, my little miracle," she says, her voice thick with affection. "But you'll have to finish it tomorrow. Why are they different colours, though? I always thought unicorns were white."

Her hand rests on my shoulder. As always, it's unusually warm. A deep, penetrating heat that seeps right into me.

"I don't know, Mum," I say honestly. "They just… are. These ones must be special. Besides," I add, a small smile playing on my lips, "variety is nice, isn't it? A white one, a midnight-black one, and a dappled brown one. They're all just as stunning."

"You're right about that," she concedes. "Anyway. Bedtime."

I huff out a theatrical sigh. "I know, *Mother*," I drawl. "I just like to finish while it's fresh in my head." I give her a hug, inhaling her familiar, comforting scent.

"I know, hun. But it's late," she murmurs against my hair. "We'll get in trouble with the sleep police."

I roll my eyes. It's her standard line. "Fine. I'll go brush my teeth."

"Good girl. Don't forget your tablets. Dad's coming up to say goodnight."

She heads downstairs, and I turn towards the bathroom. After splashing my face with cool water, I hear him. Heavy footsteps on the stairs, quickening in a playful challenge to beat me back to my room.

A thrill zips through me. I let out a surprised squeak of laughter and sprint down the short hallway. I dive into my room a second before he reaches the top of the stairs, hurling myself onto the bed and pulling the duvet up like a shield, giggling breathlessly. His rich, booming laughter echoes from the hallway, a sound that always makes my heart feel full.

"Wow, you're getting fast, speed machine!" he exclaims, his face radiating amusement as he appears in the doorway.

"Maybe you're just getting old and slow, Dad," I shoot back from my duvet fortress.

He clutches his chest in mock horror. "Is that so? I'd better start heading up five minutes earlier then."

"No! That's cheating!" I laugh. "Just accept it. I'm faster now."

He concedes with a proud nod. "It seems you are. And Mum says you're still one of the fastest runners at school. When's sports day?"

"Next month." Excitement bubbles up inside me. "Don't tell me you forgot? Is your memory going along with your speed?"

That's all the invitation he needs. His fingers are suddenly wiggling under the duvet, finding my ribs. I squeal, dissolving into helpless laughter. "Stop! I didn't mean it!"

He lets me go, his face alight. "I just let you win nowadays," he says, his voice warm. "I'm excited to see you run your heart out, my little speedster."

I roll my eyes, but a warm feeling spreads through my chest. I *am* good at running. Despite being slim and tall, not muscular like the other athletic kids, I have this strange stamina that always surprises people. My PE teachers push for team sports, but I prefer running solo—the cross-country or the 100-metre dash.

That way, I don't have to hear the hurtful names some of the other kids aim my way when they think I can't hear.

A cold shadow briefly dims the warmth of his praise, and I shove it down, hard.

Catherine M. Clark

Chapter 2: Bloodlines

After my father bids me goodnight, his voice a low rumble of affection, he ensures I take my nightly medication – the small, chalky tablets that are a constant reminder of my supposed frailty. He then tucks me in snugly, the familiar ritual of him adjusting the blankets around me a comforting weight. As I nestle into my favourite position—curled up on my side, cheek pressed against the cool cotton of the pillowcase—my eyelids grow undeniably heavy. After what feels like only a short amount of time, a pleasant lassitude steals over me, and I feel myself slipping into the welcoming darkness of sleep… or at least, I think I do.

This doesn't feel like any other time I've fallen asleep. It's an entirely unusual sensation, like being gently set adrift in a vast, silent ocean of ink. The darkness envelops me, complete and profound, yet it's oddly calming, devoid of menace. Time itself feels irrelevant in this velvety void, stretched and meaningless. Though I float untethered in its depths, fear, quite inexplicably, eludes me. After what feels like an eternity compressed into a moment, or perhaps a moment stretched into an eternity, the formless abyss begins to shift and swirl, the inky blackness coalescing, morphing into something more tangible, more defined.

I open my eyes—or at least, I perceive the act of opening them, to find myself standing in an unfamiliar room, a stark, almost shocking contrast to the anticipated comfort of my bed. The very walls seem to pulse with a subtle, contained energy, their perfectly circular shape creating a surreal, almost dizzying sense of confinement. In the centre of this strange chamber, a luxurious black leather sofa immediately catches my attention, its sleek, inviting surface beckoning yet simultaneously enigmatic, like a panther coiled in shadow.

As I slowly take in these peculiar surroundings, my gaze wanders to the walls, which are adorned with strikingly unusual paintings. Each piece is a masterpiece of the bizarre. Some depict angels with incredibly expressive, almost painfully beautiful features, their vast wings unfurling with a grace that seems to defy the canvas. Juxtaposed with these are other forms—creatures I can't readily identify, some looking like hideous, nightmarish monsters, their eyes glinting with a palpable, evil intent. The colours swirl and bleed together, vibrant and electric yet also haunting and melancholic, creating a dreamscape that is both breathtakingly beautiful and deeply unsettling. I can't help the thought that surfaces, clear and distinct. *'This is quite an unusual dream,'* a sentiment that echoes in the silent caverns of my mind as I try to grasp the significance, if any, of this strange new world.

"Do you admire them?"

The voice, cool and melodious, from the other side of the room makes me jump, my heart leaping into my throat. I whirl around to face its source. Once again, I'm taken completely aback, my breath catching, as I behold the most exquisitely beautiful woman I have ever seen. She is tall and slender, with hair like spun moonlight and eyes the colour of amethysts. Uncertain how to respond, another thought forms, sharp and clear, *'This is unlike any dream I have ever experienced.'* I remain silent, simply watching her, my feet seemingly rooted to the spot.

"Hello. You are Devika, correct?"

The unexpected, casual recognition of my name sends a tiny

spark of surprise, almost a shock, through me. In the surreal landscape of this vivid dream, it feels strangely fitting, almost preordained, that she would know who I am. Yet, I can't shake the nagging, insistent thought that I should know her too, baffled by the startling clarity of her presence not just in the room, but in my mind.

"For now, you may refer to me as Cat," she declares, her tone laced with an alluring, unshakeable confidence as she watches me fidget nervously, shifting my weight from one foot to the other in this ethereal, strangely charged space we occupy.

"Cat," I test the name on my tongue. "Your name is Cat. I don't believe I've ever met anyone by that name… or at least, I don't think I have." My voice wavers, the words tinged with a profound uncertainty that mirrors the churning in my stomach.

"You have never encountered me before this moment, Devika," she replies, her voice smooth and undeniably calming, reminiscent of a gentle summer breeze that somehow, impossibly, manages to ease the frantic edge of my anxiety, even as my heart continues to race in bewildered confusion. Her enchanting, almost preternatural presence is a curious juxtaposition to the mounting, undeniable unease I feel.

"This is truly a peculiar dream," I manage to say, my brow furrowing as I grapple with the sheer strangeness of it all—the unnerving vividness, the razor-sharp clarity of every detail, the almost tangible warmth that seems to emanate from her gaze.

A soft, knowing smile dances on Cat's perfectly shaped lips, illuminating her striking features as she regards me with a mixture of what seems like genuine understanding and a touch of sympathy. Then, she speaks again, her voice low and enigmatic, each word imbued with a strange weight, "This isn't your typical kind of dream, dear."

Her words hang in the air, heavy with unspoken implication, and I feel a fresh wave of unease wash over me, cold and prickling. I can't help but question, with a sudden lurch of my stomach, whether I am truly asleep, or if I have somehow been pulled into this room against my will, a rabbit caught in a curious, shimmering snare.

"This *isn't* a dream, Devika. You are still nestled safely in your bed at home, though," Cat continues, her amethyst eyes sparkling with a sincerity that both intrigues and frightens me in equal measure. "I wanted to introduce myself to you because you are an incredibly special individual." Her voice softens. "By now, you should have begun to sense some… changes within yourself, changes that might unsettle you. There will be more on the horizon—more that you might find even harder to accept and navigate through. However, I am here for you. I can offer support throughout this challenging period, if you'll let me."

Her words float through the air, seeming almost nonsensical, like phrases from a forgotten language. "What are you talking about? What do you mean, *changes*?" I say, confusion draping over me like a heavy, suffocating blanket. Yet her voice, so soft and melodic, possesses an almost magical quality that keeps me anchored to the moment, preventing me from dissolving into sheer panic.

"Since your twelfth birthday, Devika, have you not felt a little strange? As if there might be something… not quite right within your body?" she asks, her gaze steady, unwavering, and strangely inviting. As I absorb her question, a profound sensation of unease stirs deep within me, a cold dread unfurling. I want to spiral into a panic, to scream or run, but there is something so preternaturally serene and calming about her presence that it steadies my racing heart, tethers my scattering thoughts. The gravity of her words slowly, inexorably, dawns on me—they resonate with a deep, undeniable truth I've tried to ignore. She is right. I *have* been grappling with unsettling, inexplicable sensations ever since I turned twelve. It's the very reason I find myself dependent on the array of medication cluttering my nightstand.

"My parents… they told me I have a genetic disorder. Why?" I manage to ask, my voice barely above a whisper, raw with a sudden, unexpected vulnerability.

Cat gently shakes her head, her long, silky, moon-coloured

hair cascading around her shoulders like a waterfall as she makes her way to the large, inviting sofa that sprawls in the corner of the room. The couch seems to sit in a pool of warm, golden light, adding to its undeniable allure. Instead of collapsing into its plush cushions as I might have expected, she conjures, with a mere flick of her wrist that I almost miss, a sleek, dark wood chair. As she settles into her seat with a graceful, fluid ease that speaks of innate power, she extends an open-handed invitation for me to sit on the sofa.

A wave of uncertainty washes over me, leaving me momentarily frozen, my feet feeling like lead weights. The utterly surreal nature of the situation makes it incredibly hard to ground myself, to feel any sense of normalcy. I instinctively pinch the skin of my left hand hard with my right fingers, expecting the sharp sting of pain as a wake-up call, a jolt back to reality. But I'm surprised, then bewildered, to discover that it doesn't hurt at all. There's no sensation, nothing. This realisation hits me like a trickle of icy water down my spine. I can only conclude that I must be truly, deeply caught in some bizarre, elaborate dream. Suddenly, my previous fears, the anxieties about school and my health, appear trivial, almost insignificant, dissolving like mist in the morning sunlight.

With a newfound, if somewhat fragile, clarity and calm, I slowly approach the sofa. My fingers tentatively graze the luxuriously soft leather material, which feels almost like a gentle, living caress against my skin. There is an undeniable allure to this sofa, a silent promise of profound comfort, a potential refuge from whatever turmoil might lie outside this strange, circular room. Without further hesitation, I sink into the inviting embrace of the cushions, letting out a sigh of relief that I hadn't realised I was holding. The extraordinary softness envelops me, seeming to melt away the last tenacious remnants of my anxiety. Everything about it feels impeccable, perfect, almost like I'm being cradled in a cocoon of impossible warmth and serenity.

As I sink deeper into the plush cushions, it feels like the single most comfortable thing I have ever experienced—like being enveloped in a warm, secure, comforting embrace. The fabric is impossibly soft against my skin, and for a fleeting, blissful moment, I forget entirely about the world outside, about Cat, about everything. I instinctively draw up my legs and curl into a cosy, foetal position, leaning back to fully appreciate the way the sofa cradles and supports me. It is, without a doubt, even better than my beloved bed, and I can't help but fantasise about having a miniature version of it in my bedroom, a personal sanctuary where I could retreat whenever I needed comfort or peace.

Just as I am about to lose myself completely to the blissful warmth and drift off into a deeper, more conventional sleep, Cat's voice, though still gentle, slices through my reverie like a silver knife, pulling me sharply back to the peculiar reality of our situation.

"Devika, I am sorry to interrupt your… comfort, but we don't have much time." The quiet urgency in her tone startles me, shattering the peaceful, warm bubble I had so quickly wrapped myself in.

A flush of embarrassment washes over me as I quickly open my eyes, my cheeks feeling slightly warm from having been caught in such a moment of pure, unadulterated indulgence. "What do you mean we don't have much time?" I reply, my voice still laced with a lingering confusion, the remnants of my blissful near-slumber. "This is a dream, isn't it? It can last as long as it wants to."

Cat's next words send an unexpected chill down my spine, chasing away the last vestiges of warmth from the sofa. "That's true, to an extent. But as I've already said, this isn't *a* dream, Devika. Time moves much faster with the way I brought you here. By my reckoning, it's almost morning in your world." The gravity of her statement begins to sink in, and I feel an unsettling mixture of shock and profound disbelief reflect on my face, which I'm sure she can see.

"Wait… I don't understand." I stammer, my mind struggling to grasp the surreal, almost paradoxical nature of our conversation. "What other type of dreaming *is* there?" Every instinct screams at me that I'm caught in some sort of elaborate fantasy, a product of an overactive imagination or perhaps a strange fever. Yet her serious, unwavering demeanour makes it impossible to dismiss her words entirely.

"Have you read any books about the paranormal and the supernatural, Devika?" Cat asks, her gaze piercing, as if she were attempting to assess the very depth of my understanding, the limits of my world view.

I hesitate, a pang of regret, a familiar sense of restriction, tightening in my chest. "My parents... they haven't let me read many books like that so far," I admit, my voice small. "I've only been allowed to read a few about... well, about witches, and even then, they say such stories are a waste of my time. Why do you ask?" I reply, honestly confused by the sudden shift in topic.

Her sigh is heavy, laden with a frustration that seems almost palpable in the still air of the room. It's as if my ignorance, my sheltered upbringing, weighs heavily on her mind. She takes a deep, steadying breath, gathering her thoughts before dropping what feels like an earth-shattering bombshell. "The Paranormal and Supernatural world is real, Devika."

For a long moment, I am rendered utterly speechless. My mind goes blank. *Is she joking? Is this part of the dream's strangeness? Or does she genuinely believe what she is saying?* Silence envelops us, stretching into what feels like an eternity, until I finally let out a nervous, shaky laugh, a desperate attempt to ease the suffocating tension with disbelief.

"It's true, Devika. And I am a paranormal being," she asserts, her expression entirely grave, her tone reminiscent of one of my teachers explaining a particularly complex and non-negotiable scientific principle. "I have the ability to enter certain people's minds while they sleep. Under the right circumstances, I can even send messages, impressions, while they are awake, if my connection to them is sufficiently strong."

Her words hang in the air, heavy, surreal, and utterly bewildering, as I try desperately to process the whirlwind of impossible information. The room around me, with its pulsing walls and strange paintings, feels both intimately familiar and profoundly foreign, caught in some liminal, shimmering space between dream and an unthinkably altered reality. I start to feel a terrifying surge of panic building within me as her words truly begin to sink in. My breaths come in quick, shallow gasps, my chest tight. I frantically look around the circular room, my eyes darting from one painted angel to the next monstrous creature, searching for a means of escape, a door, a window, anything. When I glance back at Cat, I see that her exquisite expression is one of genuine concern. She shifts to the very edge of her conjured chair, tentatively reaching out her right arm towards me, her fingers long and elegant.

In a state of utter, mind-numbing panic, I attempt to slip away, to scramble off the sofa, but my body feels as though it's glued to the spot, immovable and heavy with a dread that paralyses my limbs. My eyes dart around the dimly lit room again, desperately seeking an escape, but I am met only with the suffocating enclosure of solid, seamless walls that seem to press in on me, the air growing thick and hard to breathe. The shadows in the corners of my vision dance ominously, and a disorienting wave of drowsiness washes over me, like I'm falling back into that initial inky darkness.

Then, out of nowhere, I feel a gentle, unexpectedly warm touch on my knee, jolting me from my frantic, spiralling thoughts. My heart still racing, I turn my head to see Cat now beside me on the sofa, her hand resting reassuringly on my knee. Surprisingly, a wave of profound calmness washes over me, as tangible and immediate as a warm tide sweeping across a cold beach, pulling me back from the precipice of terror and settling me into the plush, secure embrace of the sofa once more. The soft, luxurious fabric envelops me, grounding me amidst the swirling chaos of my thoughts.

Despite being on the verge of sleep again, that familiar, heavy drowsiness creeping back in, a strange duality of consciousness envelops me. I can't shake the peculiar sensation that radiates from

I Think I'm A Monster

Cat's touch. My gaze drops to her hand, and for a fleeting, almost imperceptible moment, I swear I see a faint, ethereal glow pulsing softly beneath her fingers where they rest on my knee. It's almost like some hidden, gentle energy is transferring from her to me, illuminating the small space between us with a soft, pearlescent light.

I jerk my head up to meet her gaze and find her wearing a concerned, yet somehow reassuring, smile. There is an undeniable intensity in her amethyst eyes, a depth of sincerity that seems to bypass all my fear and doubt.

"I'm sorry if I've alarmed you, Devika," she says, her voice gentle yet firm, like velvet draped over steel. "I was hoping for a… more positive reaction. Given your amazing drawings, the worlds you create on paper, I expected you to be more open to the reality of the paranormal world. But I see now that I misjudged the situation." Her voice softens further, a hint of genuine vulnerability breaking through her composed exterior. "During a recent search for someone else, I stumbled across your essence, your light, and I sensed then that you were in potential danger. Once I had located the person I was looking for, I returned to see if I could help you out of this predicament, honey."

As her words begin to slice through the thick, clinging fog of my residual panic, I feel my mind slowly uncoil, like a tightly wound spring gradually releasing its pent-up tension. Thoughts, questions, and nascent fears surge forward in a chaotic torrent, each one clamouring for attention. The sheer weight of her concern, the sincerity in her voice, seeps through the layers of my anxiety, igniting a flicker of bewildered urgency. I find myself blurting out, the words a jumbled mix of confusion and a desperate need for answers, "How do you know what I've been drawing? And… and why do you think I need *saving*?" The question hangs heavily in the air between us, thick with implications and unspoken, terrifying fears.

"When I first came upon your essence, Devika," she replies, her gaze steady and intense, holding mine captive, "I felt the immense, raw power coiled within you, like a sleeping dragon. But whatever drugs those people – your parents – are administering are actively stifling it, suppressing who you truly are. The medication they've been giving you is beginning to lose its grip, its efficacy is waning, and that's why I can finally reach out to you now, why you can perceive me." She pauses, and a glimmer of what looks like pride, or perhaps admiration, shines in her eyes. "I visited you in your sleep, in the mundane world, and I saw all your drawings. They are not just sketches, Devika. They are extraordinary. You possess a rare, vibrant talent, and those images… they reveal so much about your inner world, your true nature."

    I furrow my brow, the complexities of her statement swirling in my mind like a kaleidoscope. "But… how is it possible that I didn't see you? Or that my parents didn't notice you when you were in our home?" The thought of a stranger, however beautiful, moving unseen through our house sends a fresh shiver of unease down my spine.

    "I have the ability to cloak myself in invisibility, to evade the notice of most mortals," she explains, her voice soft yet firm, imbued with an undeniable authority. "Now that the medication's hold on you is weakening, you are finally able to see me, to perceive beyond the veil. I can appear to you like this, without fully revealing my true self in the physical realm. If I did that, those people, your 'parents,' would be able to scent me too, as paranormal beings give off a unique, identifying scent, a scent that others can detect. If you agree, Devika, I would like to visit you in the physical world when it's safe, when I can. Then, I can begin to guide you through what lies ahead and help you navigate the considerable challenges you're going to face. I believe we have a little time before you are in any real, immediate danger, so I will try not to overwhelm you with too much information at once." She leans slightly closer, her amethyst eyes searching mine. "You feel… different to me, Devika, unlike any I have encountered. Yet, there's an undeniable similarity too, a resonance that marks you as truly one of a kind."

    As I gaze intently at Cat, I can see an unshakeable resolve

etched in her exquisite features. Yet, an overwhelming wave of utter exhaustion suddenly sweeps over me. My earlier panic, though dampened by her presence, begins to return, a cold tide rising within me, and I feel myself being inexorably pulled back towards that inky, formless darkness from which I first emerged. She seems eager, almost anxious, for my response, her expression a captivating blend of hope and keen anticipation. Uncertainty clouds my thoughts, thick and disorienting. I question the very nature of her words, battling the nagging, insidious thought that this might all just be an elaborate figment of my exhausted imagination—a mere, albeit incredibly vivid, dream.

Just before Cat's luminous form begins to fade entirely into the encroaching, velvety darkness, I manage a slow, almost hesitant nod. Her warm and incredibly reassuring smile blossoms in response, her amethyst eyes crinkling at the corners, and it is the very last thing I see before I jolt awake. I inhale sharply, a ragged gasp tearing from my lungs, my heart pounding against my ribs like a trapped bird, as the familiar reality of my bedroom rushes back to envelop me in its mundane, comforting embrace.

Catherine M. Clark

Chapter 3:
Nightmares and Lies

"Devika, it's okay, shhh, it's okay," my mother soothes, her voice a low murmur beside my ear. Her arms are wrapped around me, a firm, grounding presence as she sits on the edge of my bed. A thick fog of confusion clouds my mind as I try to recall the events that have just unfolded, my heart still thumping a frantic rhythm against my ribs. "What's... what's going on?" I ask, my voice raspy and shaky, barely a whisper.

"I think you had a nightmare, honey," Mum explains, her hand stroking my hair back from my forehead. "You cried out in your sleep – a short, sharp sound – and it woke me up. When I came to check on you, you were thrashing around quite a bit. I've been trying to comfort you, hoping my presence would calm you down." Her gentle touch, though always so intensely warm against my skin, is undeniably soothing to my frayed nerves.

I struggle to bring the details of the supposed nightmare to the forefront of my mind. It didn't *feel* like a nightmare, not in the way I've read about them. And I've never, ever thrashed in my sleep before; I'm usually a very still sleeper. But as I concentrate, pushing through the lingering drowsiness, the memories start to flood back, vivid and startlingly clear. Then, it hits me like a tidal wave, a jolt of recognition so strong it makes me gasp. "Cat!" I exclaim, the name escaping a little too loudly, my head snapping up as I frantically scan the dimly lit room for her. But, of course, she isn't there. She was only present in my dream. *It was just a dream, nothing more.* My mind chants the words, a desperate litany. It *seemed* so real, so tangible, but it was just a strange, incredibly vivid dream… right?

"Who's Cat?" my mother inquires immediately, her brow furrowing with concern, her hold on me tightening almost imperceptibly. "Is she a girl from school? Has she been bullying you, Devika?"

I instantly understand why her mind would leap to that conclusion. I have been bullied, picked on with varying degrees of cruelty, since I was about eight years old. They target me because I look different. My eyes are a unique, almost luminous silver, and my hair is an unusual, natural blend of fiery red and shimmering silver that looks for all the world like I've had it professionally dyed some outlandish colour. My parents even had to obtain a formal letter from our doctor to prove to the school that my features were entirely natural, as the strict school rules prohibited artificial hair colours and custom contact lenses. This whole business, of course, just caused more issues at school, and now I'm firmly labelled as the 'Weird freaky girl.' It's the primary reason why my social circle consists only of Clare, Liz, and Tom.

"No, Mum, she isn't a girl from school," I reassure her quickly, forcing a small, hopefully convincing smile. "Don't worry. It was just a strange dream, that's all. But thank you for coming in." I lean into her embrace, trying to convey reassurance I don't entirely feel. Her body, as always, feels like it's radiating an intense heat, almost like she's running a constant fever, but I'm so used to it now after all these years that I barely register it consciously.

"Are you sure, poppet?" a man's voice, deeper and laced with a similar worry, asks from my open doorway. I turn my head to find my dad standing there, his silhouette framed by the hall light, his gaze fixed on us.

"Just a weird dream, Dad. Nothing bad, I promise." I try to sound more certain this time.

"I'm glad to hear that, honey." He takes a step into the room.

"We've never known you to cry out in your sleep before, so it worried us. I'm relieved you're okay."

My mother slowly releases her grip on my shoulder and rises to her feet. She gazes down at me one last time, her expression still etched with a lingering concern. Then, with a gentle reminder, she makes her way towards the door where Dad is waiting. "You only have about twenty minutes before your alarm goes off," she cautions, her voice practical now. "If you lie back down and nod off again, you'll struggle to wake back up properly and you'll be groggy all morning." With those words, she and my father exit my room, their soft footsteps fading as they return to their own.

Collapsing back onto the bed, I find myself staring up at the familiar, textured landscape of my ceiling, lost in contemplation of my dream – or whatever it was. Gradually, my racing heart slows its frantic pace, fading to a tranquil, steady rhythm, eventually becoming so quiet that I can no longer feel its distinct beat against my ribs. Was the dream truly *just* a dream, a random firing of synapses? Or did it hold some deeper, more profound significance? It seemed as though I had scarcely closed my eyes after Dad left last night, yet it felt like I had slumbered through the entire night, deeply and exhaustively. Opting to set these troubling thoughts aside for the time being – or at least attempt to – I muster the will to rise from the bed and make my way to the bathroom. The solitary nature of my morning routine is, on days like this, a distinct blessing. Given the luxury of a little extra time before my alarm is due, I indulge in a long, refreshing shower, knowing that my parents' ensuite means I have this space entirely to myself.

After completing my morning ablutions, I return to my room and feel an odd compulsion to glance around carefully before shutting the door. I find myself searching for Cat in the corners and shadows of my room once again, a foolish, hopeful little flutter in my chest, but as expected, she is nowhere to be found. *Of course, she isn't.*

With a sigh, I reach for my school uniform from my chest of drawers and wardrobe and get dressed before sitting down to brush my hair at my vanity table. As I gaze into the mirror, I can't help but fixate on my unique features, the ones that set me so obviously apart. My hair, that unusual blend of red and silver, glistens and shimmers under the electric light, almost like spun metal. I then turn my attention to my eyes, which, unlike my parents' warm browns and blues, are a captivating, clear silver. Upon closer inspection today, leaning right into the mirror, I notice something new – or perhaps something I've never paid enough attention to before. Tiny, almost infinitesimal pink or light red specks are scattered like delicate dust around the outer edge of my iris. It's a detail so subtle that it could easily go unnoticed from a distance, almost invisible unless one were looking for it. As I ponder whether this change is genuinely new or if it has always been there, hidden in plain sight, I can't help but let out a small, dry chuckle at my own intense introspection. *You're seeing things, Devika.*

    I grab my school backpack, already heavy with books, and head downstairs. I find my parents already seated at the kitchen table, engaged in the quiet ritual of breakfast. They have both decided on cereal this morning, their spoons clinking softly against ceramic bowls. I decide I'm in the mood for toast, so I take a couple of slices of bread from the loaf and place them in the toaster. Then, I gather a plate, a knife, some strawberry jam, and butter from the fridge, along with a carton of orange juice. After pouring myself a generous glass of juice, I place the carton back into the fridge.

    As I turn toward my parents, taking a tentative sip from my glass, I notice my mother watching me intently, her cereal spoon paused midway to her mouth. My father is absorbed in the morning newspaper, a rustling shield between him and the world, while he eats his breakfast. I set my glass down at my designated seat, and, with perfect timing, my toast pops up, golden and ready. After buttering the toast and adding a thin, glistening layer of strawberry jam, I put everything away neatly and finally sit down at the table. My mother's gaze remains unwavering, still fixed on me.

"What?" I ask, perhaps a little more sharply than intended.

"Are you absolutely *certain* you're okay, darling?" she asks again, concern deeply etched on her face, making her look older. "Hearing you cry out like that this morning... it really frightened me."

My father, lowering his paper slightly, turns his gaze from it to my mother, a look of shared worry passing between them. "I didn't catch any of that, you know," he admits, his brows furrowing slightly. "I only woke up when you got out of bed. Did it really sound that distressing?"

My mother gives a solemn, almost imperceptible nod, her eyes never leaving my face as she continues to assess my expression, searching for any sign of lingering distress. My father then shifts his attention back to me, his voice softer now but still filled with an underlying urgency. "Are you sure everything is truly okay, Devika? Is there something on your mind that's troubling you? Something at school, perhaps?" His inquiry feels genuine, as if he's hoping to uncover some hidden worry, perhaps fearing that there's something deeper, something more significant, behind my silence.

"I'm fine, Dad, honestly, I promise. I'm not worried about anything," I lie, the words feel foreign and heavy on my tongue. It's the first deliberate lie I think I've ever told them about something that feels important. "I don't even really remember the dream now, so it couldn't have been anything important. It was just a... a silly nightmare. Have you ever had any like that before?" I ask them, a desperate attempt to change the subject, to deflect their intense scrutiny.

My parents exchange a look, a silent conversation passing between them. After a moment, the worry visibly begins to recede from their faces, replaced by a more relaxed understanding. "You're right, honey," Dad says, a small smile touching his lips. "I have had a couple of nightmares like that before, especially when I was a kid. Can't remember for the life of me what they were about anymore, but you're right, they fade quickly. I'm sure your mother has, too."

    I look towards her just as she nods in agreement. "He's right, I have," she confirms, her voice lighter now. "But remember, darling, if there is ever anything you *are* worried about, anything at all, you can always talk to us about it, okay?" She studies my face intently, clearly looking for confirmation that I would, indeed, go to them. So, I nod, agreeing, a small, forced smile on my face. The lie makes them both visibly happy, their relief evident, but it sits like a cold stone in my own stomach. I'm lying again. I haven't told them I've been feeling 'off,' truly unwell, for years now. And since my birthday last Friday, I've been feeling even worse than ever before. A dull ache is already settling behind my eyes as I sit there, mechanically eating my breakfast, a fervent, silent prayer echoing in my mind that I won't actually be sick at school. If I am, I'm absolutely certain the school nurse will call my parents and rat me out, and then this whole charade will unravel.

Chapter 4:
The Emergence

I walk to school, much like any other day, the strap of my backpack digging comfortably into my shoulder. This time, though, my mind isn't on the usual anxieties about lessons or avoiding the notice of certain classmates. Instead, I'm lost in a vivid daydream, replaying every detail from my encounter with Cat over and over again. My thoughts churn. I *should* have been terrified by the implications, by the sheer strangeness of it all. But why would I be, when it was surely just a dream? A peculiar one, yes, but still just a figment of my sleeping mind. It *felt* incredibly real, though, and she hinted at things, whispering possibilities that made absolutely no logical sense. I think… I think she was trying to tell me that I was somehow paranormal. The thought sends a tiny, illicit thrill through me. I've always wondered what being a witch or a shifter, or something equally fantastical, would actually be like. It's precisely why I love to lose myself in drawing things related to myth and fantasy, like my absolute favourites, the graceful unicorns and mischievous, glittering fairies.

I am so lost in these swirling thoughts, utterly engrossed in my internal landscape, that I suddenly collide with a solid form. The impact is surprisingly forceful, causing me to stumble backwards a step, while my best friend, Clare, yelps and tumbles to the pavement, landing with a distinct *thump* on her bottom.

"Woah, Dev! How fast were you actually going?" Clare exclaims, her hand instinctively going to rub the left cheek of her bottom, her face a mixture of shock and pained surprise. "It felt like I just hit a brick wall!" Her reaction takes me aback; her words echo strangely in my ears. I was sure I had been walking at a leisurely, thoughtful pace, certainly not sprinting. Despite my confusion, I quickly reach down to help her up, my own heart giving a little jump of alarm.

"Oh my gosh, Clare, I'm so sorry!" I explain, mortified, as I check her over to make sure she isn't truly hurt. "I was totally lost in my thoughts, completely oblivious, and not paying a shred of attention to where I was going." Luckily, after a moment of wincing, she seems okay, brushing herself down.

"It's alright, Dev," Clare says, managing a slightly strained smile. "I'll let it slide *this* time, seeing as it's still technically your birthday week. But next time, I won't be so forgiving, mark my words," she jokes, her usual playful smile finally breaking through.

"I'm really, *really* sorry," I repeat, my cheeks still warm with embarrassment. "I had this incredibly strange dream last night, and it's just been stuck in my head, on a loop, all morning."

"Ooh, what was your dream about then?" Clare teases instantly, her eyes lighting up as she nudges me conspiratorially with her shoulder. "Any cute boys involved? Was it steamy?" I just roll my eyes in response, a small smile playing on my lips despite myself.

"What cute boys?" Clare and I both jump in surprise as we turn to find our other friend, Tom, has somehow managed to sneak up silently behind us. I'm so startled that my hand flies out, and I end up playfully slapping him on the arm.

"Hey! How many of your friends are you planning to assault today, Dev?" Tom jokes, grinning as he narrowly avoids a retaliatory slap from Clare as well. "I witnessed you take down Clare just now. That was quite a feat of brute strength! Anyway," he continues, his gaze flicking between us, "which cute boys are you two dreaming about?" He sounds, and looks, just a little bit jealous.

I shake my head again, a genuine laugh escaping me this time. "We are *not* talking about cute boys. That's all Clare's department, as that's pretty much all she ever thinks about. I had the craziest, most vivid dream last night about this tall, incredibly beautiful woman. It was just so… weird."

"Dev, how are we ever going to go out picking up boys together when we're older if you've suddenly changed teams on me?" Clare says with mock horror, then chuckles to herself. "And no, before you ask, you can't practise your new moves on *me* either." Liz, our third companion, can't help but join Clare's laughter as she catches up to us just in time to hear the tail end of Clare's pronouncement. Tom, however, looks even more jealous now, but also a little worried that I might genuinely have changed teams.

I glance around cautiously, my heart giving a little flutter of unease as I ensure that no one is eavesdropping on our increasingly loud conversation. The very last thing I need is more teasing at school, especially about my already strikingly unusual hair and eyes. And being one of the top students somehow only seems to add fuel to that particular fire for some people. "Shh, you lot! Don't say things like that out loud," I whisper urgently, my eyes darting around. "I already get enough flak as it is. And just for the record, no, I haven't switched teams."

Liz raises an eyebrow, her curiosity clearly piqued. "Okay, okay. So, what was so strange about this dream, then? And who was this mysterious woman?"

"I honestly have no idea who she was," I reply, my mind drifting inexorably back to the circular room and Cat's luminous presence. "She claimed her name was Cat, and she said… well, she said she was essentially paranormal—like some kind of spirit, or being, that could visit people in their dreams." I study their expressions closely as I speak, bracing myself for disbelief or ridicule, hoping to gauge their reactions accurately.

To my utter surprise, they exchange quick, loaded glances, a flicker of something I can't quite decipher – intrigue, perhaps? – dancing in their eyes before they turn back to me in perfect, almost unnerving unison.

"Wow, Dev, that's actually really cool! Do you think it was real?"

I am completely taken aback by their synchronised response, accompanied by a shared expression of wide-eyed, almost breathless disbelief. It feels utterly uncanny—like a scene from a badly scripted movie rather than a casual chat among friends on the way to school. I had braced myself for scepticism, for them to laugh it off, perhaps even engage in some light-hearted teasing, given their similar interests in all things paranormal usually led to them trying to spook each other. Instead, they seem genuinely, intensely fascinated, and that unexpected reaction leaves me pondering if I'm the one over-analysing the whole situation. Perhaps I should simply relish the bizarre dream experience for what it was... but that eerie, sudden synchronicity is nagging at the back of my mind.

"How... how did you both manage to say the exact same thing, at the exact same time, like that?" I ask, genuinely bewildered, my brow furrowed.

Once again, they share that quick, knowing look before turning back to me in perfect, disconcerting harmony. "Because we have a psychic link, of course!" they declare in unison, their voices playful and undeniably mischievous.

A fresh wave of confusion washes over me, and I stare at them in complete, dumbfounded shock, seriously questioning whether I am still caught in the lingering grip of that strange dream. But just as I begin to contemplate this bizarre idea, they both burst into peals of laughter, nudging each other.

I cross my arms, adopting a mock-serious expression, though a smile is tugging at my own lips. "Alright, what's so funny then? Spill."

"Sorry, Dev! Your mother texted us this morning," Clare explains between giggles, her cheeks flushed with amusement. Liz and Tom nod along, trying to suppress their own laughter. "She asked us to keep an eye on you today because you apparently had a really bad nightmare last night and seemed a bit… off, before you left for school. She just wanted us to look out for you, make sure you were okay. So, we thought playing a little prank on you would be a funny way to cheer you up. Did it work?"

They all wear proud, expectant grins, their eyes sparkling with shared mischief. I have to admit, there *is* something undeniably amusing about their little ruse, but I'm not about to let them know that just yet. Instead, I raise an eyebrow and issue a playful warning, my voice low and theatrical, "Just watch your backs, all of you. I will get you back one day. Revenge will be mine."

"Yeah, yeah, Devvy, I'm quaking in my boots, watching my back," Clare says with a teasing smile, nudging me again. "So, your mother claimed it was 'just a bad nightmare,' but *you* insisted it was merely a 'weird dream.' Please explain yourself, madam?"

As she speaks, Liz nods in eager agreement, her eyes glimmering with curiosity. Tom leans in too, his earlier jealousy seemingly forgotten in favour of intrigue. I take a deep breath, feeling the weight of their collective anticipation. I slide my arms into Clare's and Liz's, positioning myself in the middle, and gently pull them towards our school gates, eager to avoid another late arrival.

Once we start moving at a brisker pace, I feel a surprising compulsion to share the details of my bizarre dream, or at least, some of them. "Alright, so here's how it went," I begin, my voice slightly hesitant at first, but gaining confidence as I recount my adventure in the circular room.

However, the moment I finish my carefully edited story, just as we arrive at the school gates, they bombard me with questions, each one more intense and rapid-fire than the last. "What colour was the woman's dress? Was it floaty?" Liz shoots out, her face alight with genuine intrigue. Clare chimes in immediately, demanding to know exactly how I *felt* during the dream – scared, excited, calm? – and whether the setting, the room itself, was familiar in any way. Tom just walks with us, listening intently.

But there are a few crucial, unsettling details I don't reveal—the most haunting being the question the woman, Cat, had posed just as I jolted awake. *Could she visit me in the real world?* The words had lingered in my mind all morning, heavy with an eerie, almost threatening significance. I also carefully skirt around the truth of what Cat had actually said, fabricating a few more colourful, fantastical details about the dream to keep them entertained and on a less alarming track, deliberately avoiding the parts where she said I was powerful, or that she believed my parents were drugging me. So, I make up some random, innocuous crap about ancient prophecies and hidden treasures instead.

In the end, they seem enthralled by my embellished tale, though they playfully critique its finer points. "It would have been *way* cooler if a super hot guy had shown up instead of some random woman, though," Clare giggles, her eyes narrowing with that cheeky, appraising glint she often wears when discussing potential romantic interests. The idea sends an involuntary shiver down my spine, making me profoundly thankful it *wasn't* the case. I can't help but feel a strange sense of gratitude for the bizarre, beautiful woman instead—a strange comfort in an already deeply unsettling experience.

As we arrive at school properly, the crisp morning air, still holding a faint chill, is filled with the sounds of laughter, shouted greetings, and animated chatter that surround us. We find a vacant spot at one of the outside picnic tables, conveniently located near the edge of the playground, where we can watch our fellow students of all ages swing, chase, and play before the bell. As we settle in, our conversation flows effortlessly, revolving around my birthday celebrations and the enjoyable trip out we'd had on Saturday. We exchange stories, laughter punctuating the air regularly, creating a comfortable, familiar cocoon before the inevitable structure of the school day begins.

Suddenly, the shrill, piercing sound of the bell rings out, slicing through our moment of camaraderie, signalling the official start of the school day. We quickly gather our bags and half-eaten snacks and make our way towards our form room for registration. Unfortunately, as we navigate the bustling, crowded hallway, a few students hurl the usual unkind names in my direction. *"Freakshow!" "Silver-eyes!"* I clench my jaw tightly, trying to ignore the barbs, and focus on my friends walking beside me, determined not to let their taunts dampen my spirits. After all, I often feel almost invincible, or at least significantly braver, as long as I have my friends by my side.

Entering the familiar classroom, however, a sudden wave of profound unease washes over me, cold and prickling. An uncomfortable, tingling sensation prickles down my spine as a dull ache begins to spread insidiously across my back and shoulders, even sending sharp, unexpected pangs through my teeth. The world around me blurs for a fleeting, terrifying moment, and it feels as though everyone, every single person in the room, is bathed in a soft, pulsating white glow. Just as quickly as it came, the disorienting haze lifts, and I find myself standing at the door, momentarily frozen, my breath caught in my throat. Liz glances back at me from a few paces ahead, sensing my hesitation, she looks concerned. I quickly try to mask my discomfort, feigning a sudden thought, muttering something about thinking I had forgotten something important in my locker. She seems to accept this flimsy explanation, or at least doesn't question it, satisfied enough to head to her usual seat.

I take my place next to the window, where the early sunlight streams in, its warmth a welcome sensation on my face. Tom takes his seat right in front of me, while Clare prefers her spot next to him. She often claims that it's better for her neck, jokingly lamenting about the awkward angles we sometimes find ourselves in during class discussions when trying to see the board or the teacher. But I know, deep down, she really sits there because Liz always, without fail, takes the seat next to me. For some strange, unspoken reason, Liz won't let

Clare sit next to me, which, to be honest, I would actually prefer, as I generally get on better with Clare and consider her my absolute best friend. I learnt years ago not to bring the subject up again, as Liz would get funny and defensive about it and somehow make us all feel bad.

Our school has a slightly unique structure that sets it apart from most others in the area. Instead of the usual method of students moving from class to class for each lesson, we remain in our designated form classroom for about half our lessons, and the teachers rotate depending on the subject matter. The only exceptions to this routine occur during our science labs, art and design, music, drama, and PE classes, when we venture off to different, specialised rooms. This year holds a particular significance—it's our last one within these familiar, comforting walls. After the long summer holidays, we will transition to De Burgh Secondary School, as we have decided to stay on for sixth form. However, to do so, we must attend De Burgh for our sixth form years instead of following the traditional path to college. The thought of such a significant change looms ahead, filled with both a nervous excitement and a definite hint of apprehension.

I take the books I need for the first few lessons out of my backpack, then lift up my desk's hinged lid and place the books neatly inside, preparing for the day. Afterwards, I hang my bag on the hook on the back of my chair. My friends do the same, a familiar, synchronised rustling of bags and books, just as our form tutor, Miss Evans, walks in and begins to take the registration.

The day begins on a relatively positive note. Although I still feel those persistent, nagging twinges of pain in my body – a low, humming ache in my back and shoulders – I manage to make it all the way to lunchtime with no more strange visual incidents. The weather outside is beautiful—clear, azure skies and a gentle, refreshing breeze—so once we've collected our meals from the canteen, we decide to take our trays outside. We find an empty table under the cool shade of a large, ancient oak tree at the edge of the field, and the four of us settle in, eagerly digging into our food.

I have barely taken a few bites of my sandwich when that deeply unsettling wave washes over me again, stronger this time. It starts as that familiar dull ache in my back and shoulders, but it rapidly, progressively intensifies until a sharp, almost blinding pain radiates through my teeth, prompting me to let out a soft, involuntary whimper. For a moment, my vision blurs again, far more intensely than before, and this time, I am absolutely *sure* I spot a strange, ethereal glow emanating from my friends, almost like a soft, coloured light surrounding each of them – Clare a pale green, Tom a gentle blue, and Liz a faint orange.

With concern instantly etched on their faces, Clare leans closer, her own green aura seeming to waver. "Dev, what's wrong? You've gone completely pale! Tom, go get a teacher, quickly! Something is definitely wrong," she urges, her voice laced with a genuine urgency that cuts through my daze. Liz and Tom are calling my name repeatedly, their voices sounding distant and muffled, their eyes wide and filled with intense worry.

Tom scrambles up from his seat and glances around frantically, searching for a teacher on duty, but just as suddenly as the discomfort enveloped me, it abruptly ceases. The pain recedes, the glows fade, and my vision clears. I take a deep, shaky breath and manage to signal for Tom to come back, reassuring him and the girls that I'm okay now, though I still feel decidedly far from normal; a strange, vibrating sensation thrums beneath my skin.

"Dev, I really think you should go and see the nurse. This doesn't seem right at all. Something is clearly wrong with you today," Clare insists, her concern still evident in her voice and the tight line of her mouth. Tom returns to the table, his expression troubled and deeply anxious, hovering uncertainly.

Liz, ever practical, though perhaps trying to lighten the tense mood, asks teasingly, though her eyes are still worried, "Dev, is it... you know... have you started your *monthly thing*?" This unexpected comment takes me completely by surprise, instantly transporting my thoughts back to our awkward sex and health education class from last year, where the topic had been thoroughly, and rather clinically, covered. A wave of intense embarrassment washes over me, and I can feel my cheeks flush a burning hot crimson. My mother had also taken the time to explain it all to me, in her own gentle way, but her words had only added to my overall discomfort with the subject—especially with Tom sitting right there, looking as concerned and bewildered as ever. I feel a horrible mix of vulnerability and awkwardness, desperate to shift the focus away from my inexplicable pain and the very personal implications behind Liz's blunt question.

"I... I don't think so, Liz," I reply, trying to keep my voice steady, though it comes out a little breathless.

"Are you absolutely certain? Because if not, I really, *really* think you should go and see the nurse," Liz suggests again, concern clearly etched on her features now, her earlier teasing gone.

"What... what are you two talking about?" Tom interjects, his brow furrowed in utter confusion as he looks back and forth between Liz, Clare, and me.

"Periods and cramps, Tom," we all three chime in unison, exchanging knowing, slightly exasperated glances.

"Um... right. Okay." Tom stammers, his eyes widening slightly with a mixture of alarm and discomfort. "So... should I go get the nurse then? Does she need to go to the hospital or something?" We all roll our eyes, though affectionately this time, trying to suppress our amusement at his earnest, if clueless, concern.

"It's a girl thing, Tom. Don't worry your head about it," Liz reassures him, a hint of fond exasperation in her voice.

Tom scratches his head, still looking completely perplexed. "Right. I *know* it's a girl thing. Girls can be... well, weird sometimes," he mutters, as if attempting to make sense of the entire confusing conversation by categorising it.

"So can boys, Tom, believe me," Liz shoots back, a teasing

smile finally breaking across her face. "Just count yourself lucky you're not a girl and don't have to deal with it." She then turns her focus back to me, her expression clouding over with worry once more. "But seriously, Dev, what's really going on? You've had this super strange dream, and now you're acting like you're in serious pain. Something just isn't right today."

"Don't worry about it, Tom, honestly," I say, pointedly trying to get everyone off the subject of my health, or lack thereof.

"Yep. Girls are definitely weird," he reiterates with a firm nod, as if that single pronouncement explains everything in the universe he doesn't understand.

We share a brief, collective chuckle at Tom's endearingly awkward demeanour and his utterly bewildered expression. "I think I might have just done something to my back while I was asleep, you know, during that nightmare Mum mentioned," I explain, grasping for a plausible excuse. "My mother said I was thrashing about quite a bit in my sleep, and I think ever since then, I've just been feeling these sharp, odd pangs in my back and shoulders. If it keeps bothering me, I'll either go see the nurse later or talk to Mum about it properly after school," I explain, hoping against hope that this will satisfy their curiosity and finally put an end to the topic for now.

Catherine M. Clark

Chapter 5: The Hidden Truth

I manage to navigate through the rest of lunchtime without any further strange incidents, a small, internal victory for which I am genuinely grateful. As the shrill bell rings, signalling the end of our break, we all gather our discarded sandwich wrappers and empty juice cartons, making our way back to our form room for the next lesson, which, unfortunately, is maths.

About halfway through the class, as Mr Harding is patiently explaining some particularly complex algebraic equations at the blackboard, his chalk squeaking rhythmically, I feel a peculiar sensation wash over me. Unlike the sharp, localised pain I had faced earlier during lunch, this is something entirely different—a sudden, overwhelming wave of dizziness that strikes me completely unexpectedly, leaving me momentarily disoriented, the numbers on the board swimming before my eyes. I shake my head sharply, trying to clear the sudden fog in my mind, and focus intently on the fifth question Mr Harding has written on the blackboard, determined to keep up with the lesson.

As I lift my pencil to write down my answer, it happens. The pencil, a sturdy wooden one, snaps cleanly in half between my fingers with a loud, sharp *crack* that resonates unnervingly through the otherwise quiet room. The unexpected sound seems to vibrate off the walls, drawing every single pair of eyes in the classroom directly towards me. I can see a few eyebrows raise in genuine surprise, while Penny, one of my chief tormentors, lets out a startled, theatrical squeal, her hand flying dramatically to her mouth.

This sudden moment of inexplicable chaos immediately sets off a ripple of muffled laughter among my classmates, the focused tension of the maths lesson forgotten in an instant. I glance over at Penny, who is now shooting me decidedly dirty looks, her expression a familiar, unpleasant mix of annoyance and thinly veiled disbelief. Her overt irritation only seems to fuel the general amusement, making it feel like I'm the unwilling star of some ridiculous comedic show that I certainly hadn't signed up for. Despite the surrounding laughter, I feel a deep, burning flush creep up my cheeks, and I wish desperately for the floor to open up and swallow me whole.

Mr Harding, ever observant, swiftly gets up from his neatly organised desk at the front of the room and approaches me, a clear sense of concern in his kind, crinkly eyes. "Is everything okay, Devika?" he inquires, his voice quiet but filled with genuine worry, cutting through the subsiding giggles.

I quickly respond, my voice a little shaky, "Yes, sir. My pencil… it just snapped. It must have already been broken, and I just didn't realise." I hastily shove the two broken pieces into the clutter of my desk and reach into my pencil case for another one, avoiding eye contact with anyone.

"Okay, Devika. Not to worry. Carry on," Mr Harding says reassuringly, giving my shoulder a brief, comforting pat before he turns and heads back to his desk. I've always admired Mr Harding. He's one of the oldest teachers in our school, with a gentle stoop and a halo of white hair. He's also not a very tall man; well, to me, he isn't particularly tall, standing at about the same height as my mother, who is approximately five feet five inches. Rumours have been circulating for a while now that this might be his last year teaching at this school before he retires. Whether those rumours are true or not, I know I'm going to miss him deeply if he does go, as he has always made it a quiet priority to ensure that no one bullies me, at least not overtly, in his classroom.

I get distracted for a moment, my thoughts drifting, and start worrying about the kinds of teachers I might have at De Burgh next year. I am concerned that they might be like many of the other teachers here, who either fail to notice or choose to ignore the bullying that occurs in class. I find myself glancing out of the window, my mind wandering, and look over the empty expanse of the playground. As I start to turn back to get on with my maths work, something catches my eye. I snap my head back to the playground.

There, seated at one of the weathered wooden picnic tables, the woman from my dream – Cat – sits. She is facing away from the table itself, her back leaning casually against its surface, and her legs are tucked in under the bench, crossed neatly at the ankles. She holds both of her hands clasped together in her lap and is looking straight at me, directly into the classroom window. She *smiles* when she sees I have noticed her, a slow, enigmatic smile that sends a shiver down my spine. I am so utterly shocked to see her there, in the solid reality of the school playground, that I feel frozen to the spot for what feels like hours, though it can only be seconds. I study her intently the whole time, my mind racing, trying to make sure I am correct, that this is truly the Cat from my dream. Finally, with an enormous effort, I manage to pull myself together and slightly turn my head towards Tom, who sits in front of me. Making absolutely sure I can still see her sitting at the table out of the corner of my eye, I whisper, "Tom… Tom, who do you see sitting out in the playground?"

Tom turns in his seat and looks at me, appearing confused for a moment by my urgent, hushed tone. "What's up, Dev?" he asks, his voice low.

"Please, Tom, can you just tell me who you see sitting in the playground?" I plead with him, my gaze finally flicking away from the playground to look directly at Tom, willing him to understand.

"Okay, okay, calm down," Tom replies, then turns in his seat and looks out at the playground. I watch his face intently as his forehead scrunches up into deep frown lines. I know, with a sinking feeling in my stomach, that he doesn't see her. When I look back out onto the playground myself, my heart lurching, I see no one out there at all. The table is empty.

"Sorry, Devvy. I don't see anyone out there," Tom says, turning back to me, his concern now clear as day on his face. I look around me at my other friends; Clare and Liz are looking equally concerned as Tom, having obviously picked up on our hushed, urgent exchange.

I quickly look away from my friends' worried faces and pretend to carry on with my work, my hand trembling slightly as I pick up my new pencil. When I'm sure my friends have stopped staring at me, I sneak another peek back out over the playground, but she is still gone. Had I really, truly seen her? Or had my overactive imagination, fuelled by the vividness of the dream, conjured her up simply because the last thing she had asked me was if she could come to see me in the real world? I shake my head again, more forcefully this time, and get back to work, trying as hard as I possibly can to put it, and her, out of my mind.

I somehow manage to make it through the rest of the school day without any more major incidents—mercifully, I reach the final bell without any further dramatic confrontations or strange visions, aside from Penny's relentless, targeted taunting during the last few lessons. As if her direct verbal jabs aren't enough on their own, her cruel remarks invariably draw in the usual crowd of onlookers, their snickers and whispered laughter echoing in the background like a malevolent soundtrack. Each snicker feels like an icy dagger, twisting deeper into my chest and amplifying my already profound sense of isolation.

As the final bell rings, its shrill sound signalling both an end to the school day and a new beginning of sorts, I don't linger for my friends. Having already prepared to leave early during our last class, discreetly packing my bag under my desk, I slip out the door with a determined purpose, desperate to be the first one out of the classroom.

My heart races as I quickly make my way down the bustling, noisy corridor, brushing past other students who are chatting cheerily about their plans for the evening, their carefree voices a stark contrast to the turmoil inside me. For a fleeting moment, I think I hear my friends calling out my name from behind me, but I brush it off, choosing to ignore them as I focus solely on reaching the liberating exit.

I push through the heavy school gates, feeling a strange, unsettling mixture of relief and residual tension wash over me. It isn't until I stand by the pedestrian crossing, waiting for the little green man to signal it's safe, that I hear someone behind me calling my name clearly and with unmistakable concern. I hesitate for a second, then start walking as the light changes, pretending I can't hear them over the noise of the traffic.

"Dev! Dev, wait up! Don't let those horrible girls get to you," Clare's familiar voice rings out, filled with genuine, heartfelt concern as she finally catches up to me, slightly out of breath. "I know it's hard, believe me, I see it. But just try to think about it—soon, we'll be changing schools. Hopefully, most of them will be in different classes, or even different schools altogether, and then all of this awful name-calling will finally, *finally* come to an end."

Her mention of changing schools strikes a raw chord within me, suddenly igniting a fresh wave of anxiety. Uncertainty, cold and sharp, courses through my veins. I take a deep, shaky breath, attempting to push the nagging, fearful thoughts aside. To distract myself as much as her, I decide to share a little of what has been weighing so heavily on my mind. "Yeah, I know, Clare. It's just… it's so hard to cope with sometimes, you know? I don't really get what I've ever done to deserve this kind of treatment. It feels like it's been going on forever, and I'm just so incredibly glad I have you guys in my corner," I confess, my voice laced with a hint of vulnerability that I rarely allow to show.

Clare offers me a warm, reassuring smile, her eyes glistening with sincerity. "You will *always* have us, Dev, no matter what," she promises, her words enveloping me like a comforting, protective blanket. Liz and Tom, who have caught up by now, stand nearby, nodding in solemn agreement, their expressions reflecting the same unwavering support. I feel a genuine wave of relief wash over me, and a small, grateful smile creeps onto my face. I can see the undeniable truth of their words shining in their eyes, grounding me in a reality where, at least with them, I'm not entirely alone.

The daily trek to and from school leads us past an expansive, dense wooded area, vibrant with unseen life, that eventually opens up into a lively, well-used playground and a bustling skate park located at the far end of my street. I usually have the option to walk around the perimeter of the park or take a shortcut directly through its heart. Typically, I choose the latter, unless I see large, boisterous clusters of other schoolmates already occupying the space, in which case my route immediately shifts to the longer, less confrontational path.

Today, as we stroll along the road that runs adjacent to the woods – known ominously by local legend as 'Bloodwood' – the air is thick with the rich, loamy aroma of damp earth and the sharp, fresh, clean scent of pine needles from a recent shower. The late afternoon sun filters weakly through the dense canopy above, creating dappled, shifting shadows that dance almost ominously across the path, sending an involuntary shiver down my spine. My senses feel strangely heightened, making me acutely, almost painfully, aware of every rustling leaf and distant, mournful bird call.

Despite the distinct chill of unease that hangs in the air around Bloodwood, there is also something undeniably enchanting about these woods, especially after a rain shower. The vibrant green moss that carpets the ground in patches shimmers in the scattered daylight, glistening like tiny, precious emeralds embedded within the dark soil, lending a magical, otherworldly quality to the forest floor that momentarily captivates my attention.

As we amble down the winding, slightly overgrown road, a profound sense of apprehension begins to creep up my spine, causing the fine hairs on the back of my neck and arms to stand at sharp attention. An irrational, gut-wrenching feeling settles deep in my stomach, whispering insidiously that we are being watched by unseen eyes lurking among the deep, impenetrable shadows of the trees. I cast a furtive, sideways glance at my friends, searching their faces for any sign of similar awareness, or at least hoping to find some comfort in their relaxed reactions. But they seem blissfully, frustratingly ignorant of the unsettling, heavy tension that has blanketed me like a dark, suffocating cloud. Their cheerful laughter and animated chatter echo in the still air, contrasting sharply with the profound disquiet that has wrapped itself tightly around me, making me feel like an isolated outsider even within my own small group.

As I cautiously edge closer to the roadside of the winding path, an icy shiver dances sharply down my spine, prompting me to peer intently into the dense, shadowy thicket of trees that looms ominously just to our side. Shadows flicker and writhe among the tangled branches, and an unsettling sense of heightened alertness fills the air, making my skin prickle. My friend Liz momentarily catches my eye, her gaze darting towards the woods for just an instant, a flicker of something I can't read in her expression, before she smoothly turns back to the animated chatter with Clare and Tom, seemingly unaffected by the eerie, watchful surroundings.

The three of them are now deeply engrossed in a lively, enthusiastic discussion about an upcoming blockbuster superhero film—the kind that always sparks considerable excitement and debate among our group. As they exchange passionate opinions on the cast, the potential plot twists, and the special effects, I find myself wrestling with a heavy, suffocating sense of foreboding that gnaws relentlessly at my insides. No matter how hard I try to engage in their spirited conversation, to offer my own thoughts on the film's trailer, my mind is clouded with an unsettling, unshakeable notion that something truly ominous looms just beyond our sight, hidden within the deepening gloom of Bloodwood.

Eventually, my friends say their goodbyes, their voices echoing with plans for the evening, and begin to head towards their respective homes as we reach the main gate to the park. A familiar pang of loneliness washes over me as I watch them go. I cherish these moments of easy camaraderie, but I can't quite shake the feeling that the day's underlying tension still lingers profoundly in the air. However, I can still connect with them online later during our scheduled gaming sessions, my persistent desire to have a mobile phone nags at me more strongly than ever. I had set my heart on a sturdy Nokia 3210 for my sixteenth birthday, believing it would bridge the gap between these moments of in-person contact with my friends. Yet, my parents remained firm, almost unyielding, in their stance that I was still too young for such a responsibility. When I pointed out that many, if not most, of my friends already owned phones, their response was an unwavering, slightly frustrating reminder that I needed to focus on my schoolwork and avoid unnecessary distractions.

This constant, underlying longing for easier connection is one of the primary reasons I pour so many of my emotions into my drawing, using my art as a vital outlet for my complicated thoughts and often overwhelming feelings. I'm allowed to spend some time on my father's laptop to play games and chat with my friends three times a week, just for a few hours. They don't really like me doing this, but they gave in when I kept nagging.

I finally arrive home. My heart feels a little lighter after walking with my friends, but the unusual, unsettling events from earlier in the day still cling stubbornly to the edges of my mind. The moment I close the solid front door behind me, the familiar, comforting scent of my mother's cooking fills my olfactory senses with herbs and roasting vegetables, wafting through the air and pulling me momentarily from my thoughts. I take off my blazer and school tie, hanging them up on the coat hangers by the front door, and leave my heavy school bag casually at the foot of the stairs. A moment of intense hesitation washes over me as I contemplate whether or not to share the strange occurrences, particularly the pencil incident and seeing Cat, with my mother. Despite my deep love for her and my father, they have a historical tendency to be somewhat dismissive, or overly pragmatic, when it comes to my more unusual worries or anxieties. As I make my way slowly towards the kitchen, I waver precariously between wanting to voice my concerns and my ingrained instinct to keep the profound unease entirely to myself.

As I reach the end of the narrow hallway, the familiar sights and sounds of home surround me. To my left, the wooden staircase ascends to the upper floor, its bannister polished to a warm, honey-coloured sheen from years of use. To my right, the inviting glow of the front room and adjoining dining room beckons, their doors slightly ajar, offering glimpses of familiar furniture and cherished possessions. I pause at the kitchen's threshold, the true heart of our house.

The air inside is rich with the layered aroma of fresh produce – onions, peppers, garlic – and gently simmering spices. Stepping inside, I spot my mother by the kitchen work surface, her hands moving deftly as she slices through vibrant red tomatoes and crisp green bell peppers, then slides them into the pan on the stove. They tumble with soft plops into a gleaming stainless-steel saucepan, which is already emitting a gentle, rhythmic hiss. She hums softly to herself, a tuneless, contented sound, completely absorbed in her task, the warm light from the window casting a golden, almost hazy glow around her as she prepares our dinner. I take a quiet moment to absorb the scene, the comforting normality of it all, and it's then that I decide to share only a carefully selected fraction of the truth about my perplexing day.

"Hey, Mum," I call out softly as I enter the kitchen properly, the comforting scent of spices and simmering vegetables wrapping around me like a familiar, reassuring hug. My mother turns from the stove, a warm smile instantly gracing her lips, though I can sense, with a familiar pang, the slight worry that always seems to linger in her eyes, a telltale sign that she almost always knows when something is weighing on my mind, even before I speak.

"Did you have a good day at school, honey?" she asks, stirring the contents of the pot with a practised, efficient hand while glancing my way.

I shift nervously from one foot to the other, suddenly acutely aware of her focused attention. My fingers intertwine before me—a nervous, fidgety habit I just can't quite seem to shake off, no matter how old I get.

Her keen gaze flicks down to my restless hands, and I notice her expression change almost imperceptibly as she sets down the wooden spoon she had just used to stir the colourful vegetables she had added to the pot. She turns to face me, her stance open and inviting. Her eyes lock onto mine, concern clearly etched into the slight furrow of her brow. "What's up, Devika?" she asks gently, the warmth in her voice barely masking the undercurrent of urgency beneath it.

I hesitate, my heart racing as I feel the heavy weight of my unspoken concerns, the things I *can't* tell her, pushing uncomfortably against my chest. "Erm…." The hesitation hangs palpably in the air between us, like an indecisive, hovering cloud, and I struggle to find the right words, the safe words, to break through the expectant silence.

My mother steps a little closer, her every move patient and deliberate, the familiar bustle and sizzle of the kitchen fading into the background. "Devika, what's wrong?" Her voice is soft yet undeniably insistent, filled with a nurturing, maternal urgency that makes it perfectly clear she won't rest, won't be satisfied, until I share whatever it is that's troubling me.

I know I have to tell her *something*. "Erm… I've been getting this strange feeling sometimes," I confess, the words tumbling out in a rush. "It's… it's made me feel dizzy a few times today." I pause, then add, "I thought at first it was just from eating too much sugar on my birthday weekend, you know, all that cake and sweets, but it's been happening more often now, even today." I watch as my mother's expression slowly turns to one of deeper, more pronounced worry.

After a brief, thoughtful pause, she finally responds, her voice laced with carefully controlled concern, "Okay, darling. Well, I will talk to your father about it when he gets home from work, and we'll see what he thinks. Then maybe we will call Dr. Evans in the morning to ask for some advice. As you said, it might just be that you overdid it a bit with treats, and it's just making you feel a little off. Or perhaps," she adds, her gaze becoming more focused, "your current medication needs a slight adjustment. It could even be something as simple as growing pains, you know. You've shot up this past year."

As she mentions my medication, a memory, sharp and sudden, comes into focus, cutting through my anxiety. During my dream, something Cat had said… something about the medication I was on… that it made it hard for her to find me, or something like that. I was so overwhelmed and confused at the time that I had completely forgotten all about it until this very moment. The implications of that statement now feel enormous, chilling.

"Right then," Mum says, her tone becoming more brisk, though the worry hasn't entirely left her eyes. "You head on up to your room now and try to relax a bit. Try to do any homework you have first, get it out of the way, then you can relax properly on your bed and listen to some music or read until dinner is ready. Then we can see how you feel later this evening and decide what's best to do." She still looks a little worried about the situation, a subtle tension around her mouth that, for some reason, makes no logical sense to me. *Why would simple dizziness worry her so much?*

I just say, "Okay, Mum," and then head out of the kitchen and up to my room, grabbing my heavy school bag from the bottom of the stairs on my way. Once I enter the familiar sanctuary of my room, I quickly change out of my restrictive school uniform. I put on a pair of comfortable, worn jogging bottoms and a soft, oversized T-shirt and pull my shoulder-length hair up into a practical, if slightly messy, ponytail. I much prefer wearing it down during school so I can hide behind its curtain in class if I want to, but for homework, up and out of the way is best. Then, with a sigh, I get on with my homework, the image of Cat sitting in the playground, and her words about my medication, replaying in my mind.

Chapter 6:
Breaking Hearts

The last math problem blurs into nonsense on the page. I shove the textbook aside. It's a shoddy effort, I know, but Cat's voice from the dream keeps echoing in my head, looping her words about my medication until they're a meaningless, terrifying hum.

You don't need it. It's poison.

Since I was old enough to understand, they've fed me the same line. *It's for your rare genetic disorder, Dev. It's why your hair and eyes are the way they are.* A neat, tidy explanation.

The explanation is full of holes as I rack my brain, digging through memories until my head aches, finding nothing. No sickness, no strange ailments before I was twelve. I've always had silver and red hair, as well as silver eyes. So why did the debilitating fatigue, the insidious ache in my back and the throb in my jaw only start when the daily pills did? It has worsened over the years. It doesn't track. The thought is a cold seed of dread planting roots deep in my gut. Could a woman from a dream be right?

I flop onto my back, pulling on my headphones and blasting music like Mum suggested. Anything to drown out the noise in my head.

A sharp rap on the door jolts me, my heart launching itself against my ribs. "Dev, honey, are you decent?" Dad.

I scramble to sit up, trying to wipe the turmoil from my face. "Yeah, Dad, come in."

He steps inside, his brow etched with deep lines of concern. He moves with a familiar weight, sinking onto the edge of my mattress and making it dip. "Your mum tells me you haven't been feeling well." He studies my face, his voice a gentle rumble laced with worry. "Can you tell me what's bothering you?"

I chew on my lip, the words I want to scream lodging in my throat. How much can I say? I settle for the vague story I gave Mum, a watered-down version of the truth. I can always add more later if needed.

"It's... hard to explain," I start, aiming for puzzled, not terrified. "I just get this weird, swirling tension inside. And earlier, I felt dizzy. Disconnected. I dunno." I force a sheepish shrug. "I probably just had too much sugar since Friday."

He doesn't buy it. I see it in the way his eyes hold mine, searching. He's looking for the cracks. After a long, tense moment, he speaks, his voice quiet but firm. "Maybe, poppet. But I'm not taking chances. I'm calling Dr. Evans tonight." A knot of ice forms in my stomach. "Is there anything else? About how it feels?"

I just shake my head, my throat too tight to speak. Revealing anything more feels like stepping off a cliff. He watches me for a few seconds longer before letting out a soft, defeated sigh.

"Okay." He leans in, pressing a kiss to my forehead. His lips are hot against my skin, a familiar comfort that now feels alien, a brand. The thought makes me flinch.

As he stands, the bed creaks. He pauses at the door. "You stay put and rest until dinner, alright? Hopefully, some proper rest will sort you out." He offers a small, tight smile that doesn't reach his eyes, and then he's gone, pulling the door gently closed behind him.

The silence he leaves behind is heavy, suffocating. A profound unease settles over me. I've always been honest with them, my life an open book. But now, a tiny, insistent voice in the back of my mind screams at me to keep quiet, to hide. The shadows in my room stretch into long, distorted fingers as evening bleeds through the window. I find myself desperately wishing for another dream, for another chance to see Cat. I need her to tell me what's happening, to prove that I'm not losing my mind.

My parents, bless their practical hearts, would laugh. They dismiss anything supernatural with a wave of the hand. Paranormal. That's what Cat called me. The word feels strange on my tongue, foreign, especially in a house built on logic and reason. Did I really see her at school, by the playground? The memory is a frustrating wisp of smoke.

I squeeze my eyes shut, focusing on the ache of wanting to see her, to talk to her, to demand answers.

And that's when it happens.

'Devika.'

Her voice isn't a memory. It's here. Now. Inside my head. It's rich and clear, a melodic intrusion that cuts through my mental static.

'If you want answers, you need to listen to your parents on the phone with the doctor. But you must not get caught. As you move, I want you to repeat this phrase in your mind. I must be silent. Over and over, until you are safely back in your room.'

The words vibrate through me, a tangible, humming power.

'I've cast a small ward on you,' she continues, her mental tone turning serious. *'It will help shield you. Just keep repeating the phrase to activate it.'*

A hysterical laugh bubbles in my throat. *I'm officially insane. Hearing voices. Fantastic.*

But some new, primal instinct uncoils in my gut. I slide off the bed. My hand hesitates on the doorknob. *This is crazy.* I chuckle, a dry, nervous sound in the quiet of my room, and then take a breath, a new resolve hardening inside me.

I must be silent. I must be silent.

I turn the knob. The familiar, tell-tale squeak I'm bracing for never comes. The door swings open in absolute, unnatural silence. My heart hammers against my ribs, a frantic bird in a cage. I step into the hall. My bare feet, which should make a soft thud on the carpet, make no sound at all. The world has gone mute, except for the low murmur of voices from downstairs.

I must be silent. I must be silent. The phrase is a lifeline. I creep to the top of the stairs, my pulse thundering in my ears. Leaning over the polished bannister, I try to catch their words, but they're muffled, indistinct. There's only one way.

With painstaking slowness, I lower myself to the floor, the carpet fibres pressing into my cheek. I lie flat on the landing, my ear pressed to the gap at the top of the stairs, the cool wood a shock against my skin.

Now I can hear them. Guilt, sharp and hot, washes over me. I'm spying on my own parents. But the desperate need to know what they're hiding eclipses everything else.

"John, do you… do you think the medication has finally stopped working?" Mum's voice is a raw whisper, frayed with worry. The faint rustle of her clothes tells me she's pacing. "Is she… starting to get her abilities?"

"I don't know, Sarah," Dad replies, his voice low and strained. "This has never happened before with any of the others. Typically, the plan holds until they're eighteen, for the integration."

Integration? Others?

The questions hit me like a physical blow, a flurry of punches to the gut. My breath catches. *Others?* Do I have siblings I've never met? Or are there other kids like me, subjected to the same… plan? The thought is a crushing weight. I grip one of the bannister spindles, the smooth, cool wood anchoring me as Dad's voice shifts. He's on the phone now.

"Sean? Yes, it's John. Look, we have a problem." His tone is clipped, clinical. "Devika's been feeling strange. Dizzy, disoriented."

A pause. I strain to hear the voice on the other end, but it's just a faint, tinny squawk.

"Are you sure increasing the dosage will fix it?" Dad's

scepticism is a blade. "We don't know what she is, not for certain. We don't know if the standard medication will have the same suppressive effect on her as it did the others, even with a higher dose."

What she is. Not *who.* The words detonate in the quiet space of my mind. The world tilts, spinning out of control. Panic, cold and sharp, claws its way up my throat. I have to get back to my room. Now. Before I fall apart right here on the landing.

Every movement is born from sheer terror. My limbs tremble as I push myself up. The silence ward still holds, but the pressure in my chest is building, a scream I can't let out. I stumble back into my room, my heart a painful, frantic drum against my ribs. I manage to close the door without a sound.

I scramble onto my bed, fumbling for my mp3 player, my hands shaking so violently I can barely work the buttons. I jam the headphones on my ears and crank the volume. Thrashing guitars and screaming vocals fill my head, a desperate, flimsy shield against the words that just shattered my world.

It's no use. The music is just noise. For the first time in my sixteen years, a true, full-blown panic attack seizes me. An invisible band clamps around my ribs, squeezing the air from my lungs. I'm drowning. I gasp, but my lungs won't fill. My heart hammers erratically. Black spots swarm my vision. The edges of my consciousness begin to fray.

Just as the darkness threatens to swallow me whole, Cat's voice cuts through the chaos, a beam of light in the storm.

'Devika, breathe. It's going to be okay. I will help you. I promise.' Her voice is a soothing balm on my frayed nerves. *'I didn't want to overwhelm you in the dream, but… we are related, Devika. You are of my blood.'*

The words are meant to be a comfort, but they only add to the dizzying confusion. *Related?* My mind flashes to Mum and Dad—to their clinical, detached voices discussing me like a lab specimen. A project. A terrifying chasm opens up between the family I've always known and the nightmarish reality crashing down around me.

I lie on my back, staring at the ceiling as the last of the daylight dies. I have to pull myself together before dinner. They'll know. One look at my face and they'll know something is broken.

An idea sparks. A desperate, wild hope. Can she hear my thoughts, too?

I take a deep breath, focusing all my energy, and push a thought towards her.

'Cat? Cat, can you hear me?'

The silence that answers is crushing. I try again, more forcefully this time, desperation colouring my mental voice.

'Cat, please! I need to talk to you!'

A silent, frustrated sigh escapes me. It's useless. Then, a faint whisper brushes against my consciousness.

'I can hear you, Devika. I can't always be listening; it takes a great deal of energy. But it's getting easier as the suppressants leave your system. What is it, little one?'

The casual confirmation hits me with the force of a physical blow—the *suppressants.*

'Are you saying... the medication... it isn't for a genetic disorder?' My thought is a trembling, terrified thing.

'In a way, it is,' she replies, her tone gentle but firm. *'If you consider what you are to be a 'disorder.' That medication's only purpose is to stop you from becoming who you were meant to be. To suppress your abilities. They don't want you to know you're a paranormal being. I am so sorry, honey. I know this must hurt.'* Her sorrow feels real, a tangible wave of emotion that washes over me.

I can barely think. Grief and fear are a thick sludge in my veins. Tears prick the corners of my eyes. I am so, so scared. I manage to push one more thought out, a broken whimper.

'What... do... I... do?'

'The truth always hurts most when love is involved,' she says softly. *'You are remarkably smart and mature for your age, Devika.*

It's part of our nature. Right now, the most important thing is to avoid taking that medication. Anyway you can. It will make it easier for us to talk. Eventually, it will allow me to visit you physically. The medication also suppresses 'the sight'—your ability to see beings like me. I cannot risk being seen by human eyes in your town. And Devika... you must tell no one. Not your friends. It's too dangerous.'

'What?!' The thought is a shout in my head. *'Not my friends? I need them. They wouldn't betray me!'* A new wave of despair crashes over me. How can I do this alone?

One more question burns in my mind, a question I'm terrified to ask.

'Cat?'

'Yes, honey.'

'What... what am I?'

The silence stretches, heavy and profound. Her reply is not what I expect.

'You, Devika, are unique, even among our kind. I'm not certain how you will evolve. But tell me... have you been feeling any new physical sensations?'

'Well...' I try to catalogue the strangeness. *'There's this feeling... it moves through me. It starts as an ache in my back, then it shoots up to my shoulders. It hurts. A lot. And my teeth ache, and my vision gets blurry. And I'm pretty sure people... they start to glow with different colours when it happens.'* The words rush out, a desperate plea for an explanation.

'I'm sorry to tell you this, Devika, but you are heading for a challenging, painful time as your body awakens,' she says, her voice full of sombre sympathy. *'Because the medication suppressed your development for so long, these changes will likely be more intense. The glows you see—that is your sight awakening. Soon you will see the auras of others. Their souls. The tooth pain... that means you'll be growing at least two new teeth. Fangs, most likely. When they come in, you must be careful not to smile too widely until you learn to control*

them. And be careful around anyone who is bleeding. Your instincts may be... strong.'

My mind short-circuits. *Fangs? Seeing souls?* I need to get to a library. I need books. Something, anything, to explain this. She hasn't mentioned the back pain, but before I can ask, another sharp, decisive knock sounds at my bedroom door.

The interruption is a jolt of ice water. The panic has receded, replaced by a strange, brittle calm.

Now I just have to act normal.

Whatever the hell that is anymore.

Chapter 7: Venom and Steel

I'm grappling with a suffocating sense of unease, desperately trying to hold together the façade of normalcy that was, until recently, my entire life. The carefully constructed calm shattered last night at dinner. Mum noticed me just pushing food around my plate and asked what was wrong. In a moment of raw vulnerability—and a desperate attempt to deflect from the betrayal echoing in my chest—I confide in them about Penny.

As I explain how her relentless bullying is getting worse, they offer their usual pragmatic advice: ignore her. They label her as jealous, insignificant, and destined for a bleak future of menial jobs and loneliness. I've heard it all before, but this time, their clinical dismissal, their utter lack of empathy, strikes a dissonant chord. It's not just about Penny. It's the chilling implication that anyone who deviates from their narrow definition of acceptable is doomed. Their judgment leaves me feeling profoundly misunderstood, the sting of it sharp and deep.

I manage to divert their attention, but the real challenge comes later. Dad walks in to say goodnight, his palm holding not two, but three white tablets. He usually just leaves them for me. Tonight, he sits on the edge of my bed, his gaze unwavering.

"Dr. Evans called back," he says, his voice carefully neutral. "He thinks we should up the dosage. Your 'condition' seems to be worsening with age," he adds, with a chilling casualness, that we'll find a new 'balance' soon, which my horrified mind translates to *more pills, forever.*

I feel utterly trapped. With him watching me, there's no escape. The pills feel like lead weights in my hand. I swallow them down with the water he brought, the act a bitter surrender.

Once the house is quiet, I wait, coiled with anxiety, listening for the deep, regular breathing from their room that signals sleep. Then, I creep to the bathroom, my heart pounding a frantic rhythm against my ribs. I repeat Cat's phrase over and over in my head, a desperate mantra against the silence. *I must be silent. I must be silent.* Is it magic? Another question for the list I may never get to ask.

Inside the bathroom, the cold tiles a shock beneath my bare feet, I do something I never imagined I would. My fingers tremble as I force them down my throat. My body heaves in wretched, silent convulsions. It's a vile, difficult process, and I keep chanting the phrase, praying I don't make a sound. Finally, I retch violently into the toilet bowl. Tears stream from my eyes, blurring my vision, but I see no sign of the white tablets. It's been too long. They've already dissolved. A wave of despair washes over me. I can only pray he doesn't watch me take them again. The failed attempt means one thing with an aching certainty: I won't be hearing from Cat today.

Despite the turmoil, a hot shower revitalises me, a small mercy considering the leaden exhaustion I wake with. I stayed up too late, lost in a fantasy novel, and now I'm on the verge of being late for school. Breakfast is a repeat of yesterday: two slices of toast. I devour the first, but the clock forces me to grab the second to eat on the way.

As I'm about to bolt, my parents stop me. Their morning routine feels more like an interrogation now.

"How are you feeling this morning, honey?" Mum asks. Her voice is warm, but her eyes have a new, sharp edge. Dad watches me from the dining table, lowering his newspaper, his expression unreadable.

"Fine, really. But I have to go or I'll be late," I say, trying to mask the desperate need to escape this house.

"Why the tearing hurry?" she presses.

An internal groan. I can already hear the tardy bell shrieking. I fabricate an excuse, the guilt a fresh pang. I've told more lies in the last twenty-four hours than in my entire life. "I promised Clare I'd help her with maths homework before the test today."

"Alright, sweetie. Have a good day," Dad chimes in, his eyes still assessing me. "If you feel unwell, make sure the school calls us immediately." The way he looks at me sends a chill down my spine. He doesn't believe me.

I nod, force a bright smile, and bolt out the door. The cool morning air is a welcome slap to the face. I take a deep, ragged breath, trying to steady myself for whatever comes next.

I stroll down Hollow Lane, the park across the road is usually a calming sight. Today, it's unnervingly deserted. The sun casts long, dancing shadows across the dew-kissed grass, but there's no laughter, no chatter of dog walkers. The silence is unnatural. Despite the prickle of unease, I cut through, needing to make up for lost time.

As I near the exit by Bloodwood, hesitation grips me. The memory of being watched yesterday returns—icy fingers on my spine. I'm about to turn back, to take the long way around, when I spot Clare waving energetically from the park gate. Her beaming smile radiates a warmth that travels across the distance and gives me the courage to keep going.

To my surprise, a sense of calm envelops me as I approach the woods. Birds chirp, sunlight filters through the branches in cheerful, golden patches. I feel no eyes on me. Nothing.

Maybe it was the increased dosage. The thought nags at me, a persistent voice of regret. I should have found a way to get rid of those tablets. A desperate part of me hopes yesterday's paranoia was just a side effect, a phantom of my own anxious mind.

But as I let my guard down, a premonitory chill slips through me. The day is young. I have a dreadful certainty that the strange sensations—the pain, the visions—will be back.

I'm about to find out just how terrifyingly right I am.

We meet Liz and Tom at our usual spot and arrive at school on time. No strange incidents, no odd feelings. They all ask if I'm okay, their concern genuine. The words burn on my tongue. I want to tell them everything. But Cat's warning echoes in my mind, and I just say I feel much better. As we navigate the crowded halls, Penny's predictable insults bounce off me. She's probably still mad I made her squeal when my pencil snapped yesterday.

First period is English. Usually, I love it. It's my chance to dive into worlds of my own making, worlds of magic and myth. Mrs Patterson, my teacher, often playfully questions my fascination with the paranormal. I always just say it's a realm I find captivating. But today, a heavy, impenetrable fog clouds my mind. The usual stream of ideas has dried up, leaving a barren landscape.

We're supposed to be crafting a narrative set in a world unlike our own. The prompt should be invigorating. Instead, my mind is sluggish, bogged down. I stare at the blank, accusing page, willing a single idea to spark. I can feel Mrs Patterson's expectant gaze from her desk. When she walks around the room, she pauses for a long time at my desk, my few disjointed sentences a testament to my failure.

Her brows furrow. "Miss Lorcan, are you perhaps experiencing a touch of writer's block today?" she asks, her voice gentle.

"It seems so, miss," I whisper, pushing my pencil aimlessly across the page. "I can't get my thoughts to flow."

She nods, a determined look on her face. "Wait there."

She crosses to the large storage cupboard, the familiar scent of old paper and ink wafting out as she opens it. She returns with a thick, sober-looking book and places it on my desk with a soft thud. The cover reads: Nineteen Eighty-Four by George Orwell.

"Why don't you read this for the lesson, Devika?" she encourages, her eyes bright with enthusiasm. "It's technically university-level, but I think you'd find it thought-provoking."

"So, just read it instead of writing the story?" I ask, my fingers tracing the raised letters on the spine.

"Yes. It might get your own creative juices flowing for next time."

"Alright, miss." A flicker of interest ignites within me as I open the book. But before I can start, a prickling on the back of my neck makes me look up. It's no surprise to see Penny shooting me a venomous glare from across the room. She mouths *'teacher's pet'* with exaggerated movements. I just shake my head, sigh, and lose myself in the book, determined to ignore her.

Next up is PE. I stick close to Clare and Liz as we head to the changing room. Ever since I got cornered by a group of older girls last year, I make sure I'm never alone. They pushed me around for what felt like an eternity, and I ended up hiding behind the equipment shed, crying, only for Liz and me to both get detention for being late, as it was Liz who came and found me.

On the field, Mr McGregor, a burly man with a booming voice, is already hyping up the inter-school sports day. The competition is fierce this year. He has high hopes for me; I'm in the 100, 200, 400, and the relay. Today, he wants me to focus on the relay and the tug-of-war. I'm secretly thrilled—Clare and Liz are on my team for both.

I take my position for the final leg of the relay practice, the weight of expectation settling on my shoulders. We're all determined to give it our best. Ben, the sixth-form TA, blows a piercing whistle, and the race explodes into motion. Joanne, our first runner, bursts from the starting line. She's a formidable sprinter, navigating the lumpy, uneven field with surprising grace. My heart races in sympathetic rhythm with her pounding feet. I cross my fingers, praying for a clean handoff.

Just before she reaches Suzie, she stumbles. Her reflexes keep her upright, but she loses precious seconds. The other team gains a significant lead. My stomach drops. Suzie grabs the baton cleanly, but she can't make up the lost time.

A flicker of hope ignites as Suzie makes a flawless handoff to Liz. It's a moment of perfect synchronisation. I see Mr McGregor shake his head, his disappointment clear even from here. Liz, her face a mask of determination, miraculously starts to narrow the gap.

Adrenaline, sharp and electric, surges through me as she gets close enough to pass the baton. I take it, my hand gripping it tightly, and push my body to its absolute limit. My legs turn to lead, burning, but I gulp in air, fighting to maintain my rhythm.

To my shock, the runner from the other team, once so far ahead, is slowing down. I can hear Clare and Liz yelling my name, their voices piercing the rush of wind in my ears. A sudden, inexplicable surge of raw energy floods me. It comes from some deep, untapped well inside. My legs pump like pistons. I don't just gain on the other runner; I fly past her.

The world blurs. My focus narrows to the white tape of the finish line. With one last, bursting effort, I cross it, my lungs on fire. I glance back. The other runner is still metres behind. I bend over, hands on my knees, chest heaving, trying to process what just happened.

Liz and Clare rush over, enveloping me in a sweaty group hug.

"Dev, that was incredible! You were so fast!" Clare exclaims, her eyes shining with pride.

"Yeah! How did you get so much faster all of a sudden?" Liz asks, her tone a mix of excitement and suspicion.

"They… they must've had a bad day," I pant, my mind racing. *Could this be my 'abilities' emerging?*

"They weren't having a bad day, Dev. You were having an

amazing day! You unofficially broke the school record for the 400 metres!" Liz says, her voice full of awe.

Clare pulls me into another hug. "We are totally going to crush them on sports day!"

As Liz's arm brushes mine, I realise with a jolt that she feels hot. Just like my parents. The thought is so distracting I stand there like a lemon, then I realise, *Oh, god. If I was faster because of the medication wearing off, my parents will find out from the school.* This is all too complicated. I might have to try and reduce my speed myself during the competition.

I have ten minutes to catch my breath before tug-of-war.

Our ten-member team assembles, a mixture of nervous excitement on our faces. I position myself in the middle of the line, Clare directly in front of me. We struggle into our thick gloves and lift the coarse, heavy rope.

Mr McGregor stands at the centre point, scrutinising both teams. "On your marks... get set... GO!" His shout startles me, my mind still reeling from the race.

The sun beats down as we brace for the pull. I dig my heels into the damp grass, summoning every ounce of strength. The rope jerks sharply—in our direction. The other team is caught completely off guard.

In our excitement, a few of our teammates behind me lose their footing, stumbling like dominoes. Clare yelps as she tumbles backwards, landing squarely on top of me. The impact knocks the breath from my lungs in a painful *whoosh*. Even as I fall, my hands maintain their grip. I give the rope one last, desperate tug.

Winded, I glimpse the opposing team surge forward, then collapse in a tangled, comedic heap.

"Phenomenal, girls!" Mr McGregor bellows, a wide, incredulous grin on his face. "Only five of you were actually pulling at the end! The rest fell, and you still managed to triumph over a full team of ten!"

His words fill me with an exhilarating disbelief. But a sharp, unpleasant voice cuts through the celebration.

"Mr McGregor, sir."

We all turn. It's Cathy Johnson, strutting toward our teacher, her posse of mean girls trailing behind her like vultures.

"Yes, Miss Johnson?" he asks, his smile fading.

"I have a serious concern," she says, a nasty sneer on her lips. "I suspect Devika Lorcan is using steroids." Her voice is dripping with malice. "It's not normal for someone to suddenly get so much better. How else do you explain her winning the relay when she was miles behind, and then this? It's not natural!"

Mr McGregor's gaze flicks to me, his expression suddenly serious. He signals for me to step aside. My heart races, but I'm grateful when Clare and Liz flank me, a human shield against the hateful glares.

"Girls, this is a private conversation," Mr McGregor says, looking flustered by their silent solidarity.

"Sorry, sir," Clare interjects, her voice surprisingly steady. "But those girls have been tormenting Devika for years. You're condoning their bullying by even entertaining this." She sounds like a lawyer from a courtroom drama. I'm floored. The teacher looks genuinely taken aback.

"Wow. That was… impressive, Miss Swanson," he stammers. He turns back to me. "However, I must ask you directly, Miss Lorcan. Have you taken any performance-enhancing medication?"

The unfairness of it all threatens to overwhelm me. "The only medication I take, sir, is for a diagnosed genetic disorder," I reply calmly, meeting his gaze. "The dosage was increased last night. I have to take it before bed." It's the truth. A carefully curated slice of it.

The tension shifts. "Okay, Devika. I'm sorry, but I had to ask," he says finally. "To be honest, I didn't think you had. You don't show any of the usual signs—no mood swings, no muscle growth. All I can say is well done. You performed exceptionally well today." He then gives a mischievous, conspiratorial smile. "Now, head back to the changing rooms, girls. I'll have Miss Johnson and her friends put away all the equipment."

Chapter 8:
The Reaper's Touch

After PE, we make our way, sweaty and buzzing, to the clattering chaos of the cafeteria. The large room echoes with the lively chatter of students. As we settle at our usual table by the window, Liz and Clare launch into an animated, theatrical recounting of the relay and the tug-of-war. Tom, who was off playing football, missed the entire spectacle. He leans in, elbows on the table, chuckling as Liz and Clare act out their impressions with exaggerated gestures. His loud, unrestrained laughter draws amused glances from nearby tables.

When their story reaches the part where Cathy Johnson accuses me of taking steroids, the mood at our table shifts. The levity evaporates. Tom's expression darkens, his jaw tightens. I see his fists clench under the table.

"I'll teach them a lesson or two," he seethes, his fury palpable. The intensity of his protective anger surprises me, a brief warmth touching my anxious heart. Despite the tension, I manage a small laugh at the more comical parts of their story, grateful for this small island of support amid the turmoil churning inside me.

Once we've cleared our trays, we head towards Mr. Harding's maths class. The hallway, usually filled with banter, feels oppressively heavy today. An unsettling, inexplicable dread washes over me as we approach the classroom door, sending cold shivers down my spine. It's like a dark cloud of foreboding has settled right over my head.

The feeling intensifies so rapidly that my legs turn to jelly. My hand trembles as I grip the cool metal of the door frame to steady myself. The room spins, the familiar posters blurring into meaningless shapes. I fight against a disorienting urge to faint, each breath feeling laboured and thin.

"Devvy! Dev, are you alright?" Tom's concerned voice breaks through the haze. His brow is furrowed with worry, his hand hovering near my arm, ready to catch me.

"I... I don't know. I just feel... really dizzy," I reply, my voice weak and distant. A plausible lie slips out. "Maybe I pushed myself too hard in PE." Regret washes over me. I yearn to tell them everything, to unburden myself of this gnawing terror. But some powerful, unexplainable instinct forces me to keep it all locked away.

"Come on, let's get you to the nurse," Clare suggests, her eyes wide with alarm. "You haven't been yourself since the weekend, Dev. You must be coming down with something."

"No!" The word is out too quickly, raw panic rising in my throat. If I go to the nurse, my parents will be called. I can't face their scrutiny right now. "I just need to sit down for a minute, honestly," I plead, trying to sound normal.

Reluctantly, they agree. I enter the classroom and a small wave of relief washes over me. The room is empty, the desks neatly arranged in silent rows. The quiet helps steady my frayed nerves. If Penny and her cronies were here, they'd have a field day with my obvious distress.

I sink into my usual desk by the window, the slight creak of the chair a mundane comfort. The dizziness persists, blurring the edges of my vision. I close my eyes, resting my head in my hands, trying to will away the disorienting sensation that's warping my reality.

As I focus inward, I realise the feeling isn't coming from inside me. It feels like an unseen energy is moving stealthily towards me from across the room. Its path is bizarrely precise: a straight line, then a sharp right angle, then another. It's floating towards Mr. Harding's desk like a tangible whisper.

I cautiously open my eyes. Standing in the very spot where the strange energy radiates is Mr. Harding himself, absorbed in a low-toned conversation with another teacher. He seems completely unaware of the invisible current that has captured my attention. The other teacher nods and walks off, leaving him alone.

My gaze darts around the room. Tom, Clare, and Liz are all focused on me, their expressions a blend of deep concern and unnerving curiosity. Their silent, intense staring only amplifies the charged energy in the room.

"What?" I ask, my voice sharper than I intend.

"Are you okay, Dev? You're acting… really strange," Clare says, her voice soft with worry.

I'd almost forgotten they just watched me stumble to my chair. I try to relax my posture, to arrange my face into something resembling normal. "Sorry, guys. I think a headache just came on. It's a really bad one. Maybe a migraine."

"Dev, if there's something wrong, you know you can talk to us," Liz says, her gaze direct, pleading.

"Honestly, everything is fine," I lie again, the words tasting like ash. "I just have a nasty headache. I didn't sleep well, and then PE must have been the last straw. That's all." I try to infuse my voice with an affection I hope they can feel, even through the deception.

The lesson begins. Mr. Harding's voice sounds strained as he calls the register. I try to focus on the geometry problems, but the unsettling energy, seemingly originating from Mr. Harding himself, hangs heavily in the air. A gnawing discomfort makes the back of my neck prickle.

About thirty minutes into the lesson, morbid curiosity compels me to glance at my teacher. At first, he seems normal, marking papers at his desk. But then I notice a subtle, peculiar movement—an almost imperceptible sway in his chair. For a split second, a disorienting visual trick makes me see two Mr. Hardings, one slightly transparent and overlaid on the other.

I can't look away. I realise with dawning horror how profoundly unwell he appears. Beads of sweat glisten on his pale, almost greyish forehead. His brow is furrowed in pain, the muscles in his face contorting involuntarily.

Then I see it again—that faint, shimmering movement surrounding him, more distinct this time. It's as if something ethereal is trying to break free from his body, a translucent wisp of smoke caught in a sunbeam.

His condition worsens dramatically before my horrified eyes. I raise my hand, my own body trembling. It takes him a long moment to focus on me, the effort painfully evident.

"Mi-ss Lo…can," he slurs, each syllable a laborious effort.

"Sir, are you okay? You… you don't look well," I say, my own voice shaking. He just stares blankly. Whispers ripple through the classroom as other students start to notice.

I turn to Tom, who sits in front of me. "Tom, go! Get the headmaster, Mr. Davies. And any other teachers you see. Quick!" I then turn to Clare. "Clare, call 999! Get an ambulance! I think… I think he's having a heart attack."

Girls gasp at my blunt words, but Clare, to her credit, fumbles for her phone, her fingers shaking as she dials. Tom is already out the door.

"Does anyone know CPR?" I ask the class, my voice louder than I intend.

A sea of scared, pale faces stares back. Then Aidan, a quiet boy, speaks up. "I… I think we need to get him on the floor. In the recovery position." He stands hesitantly, looking terrified as he tries to rally the other boys, but they're frozen.

It's too late. A sickening crash echoes from the front of the class. Mr. Harding has collapsed, his chair tipping over with a loud bang. He hits the floor hard, making a dreadful sound, and he ends up sprawled in front of the blackboard.

Clare's voice is high with panic as she talks to the emergency operator. Girls around me are crying now, soft, frightened sobs filling the air. A few let out small screams. I feel utterly paralysed, a chaotic mix of fear and nausea swirling inside me. As I try to take a step forward, that strange, invisible force pulls at me again, stronger this time, drawing me towards him.

Just as raw panic sets in, the classroom door flings open and the headmaster, Mr. Davies, storms in, his face grim. He makes a beeline for Mr. Harding, his abrupt entrance causing a few girls to scream again. At the same time, the distant wail of an ambulance siren reaches us, growing rapidly louder.

Overwhelmed, I feel tears welling in my own eyes. Liz places a steadying hand on my shoulder. I sink back into my chair, trying to control my breathing. Little does anyone know, things are about to get terrifyingly worse.

Mr. Davies positions Mr. Harding on his back, checking for breath. He shakes his head grimly and begins performing rescue breaths. As I watch, I can't shake the overwhelming, chilling feeling of death emanating from my teacher, a cold that settles deep in my bones.

The shimmering, translucent movement around him returns with even more force. Another Mr. Harding, a perfect, ethereal double, begins to slowly separate from the body on the floor. The spectral figure looks confused, then turns to gaze down at his own lifeless form with an expression of dawning, sorrowful acceptance.

Then, he looks directly at *me*. His ghostly lips move.

'Thank you, Miss Lorcan. Thank you for trying to help me.'

His voice is shockingly loud and clear. No one else reacts.

I sit frozen, a scream trapped in my throat. I bite it back, somehow managing to form a thought in reply. '*I'm so sorry, sir.*'

His spirit looks shocked that I can perceive him. He seems

about to say something else, but his ethereal gaze shifts to the side of the room, his expression changing from sorrow to awe. I follow his gaze and what I see leaves me breathless.

Near the classroom door, a faint, shimmering opening has appeared, a tear in the fabric of reality. Through it, I can see pristine white buildings, lush greenery, and serene-looking people walking about. Some of them, impossibly, have bright, feathered white wings.

A mysterious, imposing figure emerges from the opening, as ethereal as Mr. Harding's spirit. He is tall, grasping a long, dark wooden shaft with a wickedly curved, gleaming silver scythe at the top. He also has magnificent white wings, folded neatly behind his back. He's dressed like a Roman centurion: a short, white leather kilt, silver armour plates, a simple sleeveless tunic, and sandals strapped around his powerful calves. A billowy, hooded white cloak conceals part of his form, the deep hood shadowing his face. He advances silently towards Mr. Harding's spirit.

The last words I hear from my teacher's spirit are filled with peace and wonder. *There's... such a bright, beautiful light... it's calling to me.*

I want to scream, to warn him, but I can't make a sound. The winged figure lowers the scythe. When the gleaming blade touches Mr. Harding's spirit, his form begins to gently dissolve, breaking apart into motes of light that flow up into the blade. Within seconds, he is gone.

The figure turns back towards the shimmering opening. But he pauses. Then, to my absolute horror, he starts to turn his hooded head slowly, deliberately, in my direction.

Panic freezes my blood. It would not be good for this being to know I can see him. With a monumental effort, I wrench my gaze away, forcing myself to stare at Mr. Harding's physical body as the headmaster continues CPR, oblivious.

My hands are shaking so violently under the desk I'm surprised it's not rattling. *Is that the Grim Reaper?* The old stories flash through my mind—he could take your soul, even if it wasn't your time.

I feel like I'm going to pee myself from sheer terror.

Just then, I hear a soft *thump* and a faint suction noise. I risk a tiny glance. The shimmering opening and the reaper are gone.

And that's when the paramedics rush in, their faces grim and focused. They take over from the exhausted headmaster, who, along with other teachers, begins ushering us, shocked students, out of the room. It takes me a full minute to gather the strength to stand. When I finally do, my legs feel like lead, I realise the oppressive, weird feeling is completely gone. I feel... strangely normal again, just shaken. A profound relief, so potent it almost makes my knees buckle, washes over me as I follow my stunned friends out, taking one last, sorrowful look back at my favourite teacher.

Catherine M. Clark

Chapter 9:
Daughter in Disguise

We are all ushered into the vast, echoing space of the school hall. A pale-faced teacher informs us in hushed, serious tones that, due to the tragic circumstances, we are not allowed to leave yet. An announcement crackles over the internal system, instructing teachers to keep all remaining students in their classrooms. A heavy, shocked silence descends upon the hall, punctuated only by occasional sniffles and whispered questions.

Soon, teachers begin making hushed, grim-faced phone calls from the office. They are contacting our parents, one by one, to arrange for us to go home safely. Gradually, our numbers dwindle as students are quietly escorted out, carefully kept away from the corridor where my classroom is now a scene of tragedy. Clare, Liz, and Tom get permission to leave but choose to wait for me, a silent, supportive presence in the emptying hall. Their loyalty is a small, warm anchor in the cold sea of my shock.

When it's my turn, a subdued Mrs. Davison informs me that my parents have agreed I can go home and that my mother is leaving work to head home herself. Just as I'm about to leave with my friends, the headmaster, Mr. Davies, approaches, his expression drawn and weary. He stops me gently, requesting a private word. My friends nod, stepping back, though their worried eyes remain fixed on me.

"Miss Lorcan... Devika," he begins, his voice low and tired.

"Are you feeling... okay?" His brow is furrowed with concern as he scrutinises my face.

"I'm actually fine, sir," I reply, surprised by the steadiness in my voice. Strangely, despite everything, I'm not as shaken as I would have expected. A peculiar, unnatural calmness resides within me, an unexpected clarity, as if some subconscious part of me was prepared for this. The horror of what I witnessed is undeniable, but I try to mask it. I don't want to burden him further.

"I'm... relieved to hear that," he says, a faint, shaky sigh escaping his lips. "I heard from Miss Periwinkle that you were the one who took charge, who arranged for help so quickly."

"Um, yes, sir," I hesitate, a flicker of uncertainty creeping in. *Am I in trouble?* "I asked Tom to get you and requested Clare to call emergency services. I trusted she could handle it."

He regards me thoughtfully for a long moment. "That was very quick-thinking, very mature of you, Miss Lorcan," he finally says, his voice heavy with sincerity. "I wanted to express my profound gratitude. I'm... I'm incredibly saddened to inform you that despite our best efforts... we were unable to save him." His voice quakes on the last words, raw sorrow etched onto his features. "But I wanted to thank you for what you did."

"There's no need to thank me, sir," I reply softly, the finality of his words settling in the pit of my stomach like a cold stone. "He was my favourite teacher. I... I will miss him dearly."

As I say the words, the brutal reality of Mr. Harding's absence crashes over me like an icy tidal wave. The true weight of never seeing his kind, encouraging smile again sinks in. And suddenly, the tears I've been holding back flow freely, hot and stinging. It's not just the shock of his death; it's the gut-wrenching realisation that the gentle guidance and warmth he offered are gone forever. The thought truly breaks me.

Tears cascade down my cheeks in unstoppable streams. For once, I don't try to wipe them away.

Noticing my distress, Mr. Davies reaches out and gently,

almost awkwardly, brushes away my tears with his thumb. His touch is surprisingly comforting. Then, to my astonishment, he envelops me in a warm embrace. I stiffen for a second, but as I gradually sink into the unexpected comfort of his arms, I feel the faint tremor of his own suppressed sadness. I realise, with a pang of shared humanity, that he needs this as much as I do.

"I'm truly sorry if I've upset you further, Devika," he murmurs against my hair, pulling away slightly to make eye contact, his own eyes red-rimmed. He gestures for my friends, who are watching with deep sympathy, to join us.

"It's not your fault, sir," I manage, my voice thick with emotion. "I just… realised I won't ever see him again. I promise I'll be okay."

Clare approaches, her cheeks glistening with tears. "Is everything okay, Dev?" she asks, her voice quavering.

Mr. Davies gives a gentle, reassuring nod. "You can all head home now. Clare, could you please make sure Miss Lorcan is alright? If you could walk her home, I would be very grateful."

They all nod in immediate agreement. Together, the four of us make our way to the main exit, where another teacher formally escorts us out, the immense weight of loss and shock hanging over us like a sombre, invisible shroud.

As we step out of the school, the normal afternoon air is filled with the jarring buzz of my friends' conversation. They eagerly share their thoughts on what happened, their voices a mixture of shock and morbid excitement. I find myself lost in my silent world, the external chatter fading to a dull hum. My thoughts are consumed by the impossible sight of a winged being stepping out of a shimmering doorway. *Was it an angel? From heaven? Does that mean everything Cat told me is true?*

And if so, what does that mean for me? For my parents? I never noticed anything remotely paranormal about them, beyond Mum's constant warmth. My mind snags on why the being, the reaper, looked so ethereal, like a ghost. Then it hits me with chilling clarity. *Cat said as the medication wore off, I'd get 'the sight.' Is that why he looked like a ghost? Because the drugs are still in my system, partially obscuring my true vision?*

"Dev? Are you in there?" Clare asks, her voice edged with concern. Her worry seems contagious, as the others fall silent, turning their full attention to me. She waves a hand in front of my face. Liz positions herself directly in front of me, and I bump into her sharply.

"Oh! Sorry, guys," I stammer, pulled violently back to reality. "I was just in my own little world."

Liz steps aside, a strange, unreadable expression on her face, and we resume walking. We're nearing the end of the playground, close to my house.

"It's okay, Dev. We're just really worried about you," Clare says softly. "Do you want us to stay with you until your mother gets home?"

"No, it's fine, honestly," I say, trying to reassure them. "She'll be here any minute. You guys should head home before your parents start to worry. But thank you for walking with me."

Clare and Tom still look worried, but Liz's expression has shifted. She keeps darting her gaze around nervously. "She'll be fine," she insists, her voice surprisingly steady, almost uncaring, as she avoids looking at me. "We really need to go." Her abrupt tone sends an unexpected chill through me.

After a few awkward moments, Clare and Tom offer strained smiles and bid their goodbyes. I watch them walk away, their figures receding down the road, and turn towards my empty house.

My mother arrives about half an hour after I do. She finds me curled up on my bed, attempting to read, though the words are a meaningless blur. Relief sweeps across her face as she sits on the edge of the bed and gently strokes my arm. I put my book down and she envelops me in a strong, warm embrace.

Even though I feel so betrayed by her, so hurt by the secrets, I can't help it. I become completely overcome, sobbing uncontrollably into her shoulder, great, shuddering gasps racking my body. It's not just Mr. Harding. It's the thought of starting at a new school, the fear of worse bullying, and everything terrifying Cat told me, all of it crashing down at once.

"Your headmaster called me at work," she says softly when she finally pulls away, her own eyes suspiciously bright. "He told me how brave you were, Devika, how you took control of the situation. I am so, so very proud of you, darling."

Fresh tears well up at her unexpected praise. For a fleeting, dangerous moment, I almost confess everything. But the memory of their clinical discussion about me, the cold apprehension, holds me back. It is in this precise moment, feeling her warmth yet knowing her deceit, that I decide. *I am going to have to play a part. I will be a daughter in disguise.*

Thinking she understands my silent grief, she hugs me again. "Do you need anything, my love?"

I shake my head. "No, Mum. I'm just happy to read my book for now."

"Why don't you put some music on and try to relax? I'll go make your absolute favourite for dinner," she suggests, her smile gentle.

This time, I find my voice. I manage a small, watery smile. "Chicken Carbonara?"

"That's still your favourite, isn't it?" she asks, her smile widening, genuine and loving.

I nod. She beams, kisses my forehead—her lips still so hot—and then heads out, closing the door softly.

I lie there, cocooned in my duvet, my thoughts a suffocating chaos. The image of the winged reaper is etched in my memory. He was so different from the skeletal figures in books—he was majestic, beautiful, and terrifying, like a mythical hero. If I was cursed enough to see him so clearly, did anyone else? I strain to remember, but find only the general panic of the classroom.

Cat was right. The evidence is undeniable. *I must be paranormal.* I silently plead with her, wherever she is, to sense my terror and provide answers. But there is only a deafening, terrifying void where her comforting presence once resided.

I must have drifted off, because I surface from a hazy dream to the familiar sound of my father's voice.

"Devika, honey, it's time to wake up. Dinner is ready."

My fuzzy mind homes in on one word. "Chicken Carbonara?!" I bolt upright in bed.

My father chuckles, a mischievous glint in his eye. "If you don't hurry up, I'll eat it all myself!" He saunters out of the room, his laughter trailing behind him.

A flustered panic at the thought of missing out sends a surge of adrenaline through me. I tumble out of bed, my reflexes surprisingly sharp, landing silently on my feet. I dart towards the door, grabbing the frame for leverage, and propel myself down the stairs, using the bannister to swing down the entire flight in two swift, fluid movements.

I land lightly just as my father moves from the hallway to the kitchen. Emboldened, I leap playfully onto his back, genuine laughter bubbling up inside me. His surprised yelp of surprise then sends him into a brief, animated sprint towards the dining room, his breathless laughter echoing through the house.

As he enters the dining room, I plant my feet and cling to him, using all my strength to halt his progress, a silly game from my childhood. To my amazement, and his evident surprise, I completely stop him in his tracks. The playful gleam in his eyes shifts to a quickly concealed frown.

The realisation strikes me like a physical blow. I just displayed my unnatural strength, first at school, and now directly to him.

My mind racing, I quickly release my grip, feigning innocence. I dash around him and slip into my chair with a triumphant, slightly forced flourish. "I'm the winner!" I declare, my voice ringing with manufactured thrill. His laughter returns, but it's more subdued, and I can't shake the feeling that there's a new hint of calculation in his eyes.

My mother brings over our plates. "Did you fall out of bed, Devika? It certainly sounded like it."

"Kind of," I reply casually. "My legs got tangled, but I still beat Dad down here."

An almost imperceptible look passes between my parents, making me uneasy. As we eat, I feel my father's gaze on me, thoughtful and constant. I start to get seriously worried. *Is it too late? Has the damage been done?* I desperately hope he doesn't watch me take the medication again tonight.

The conversation is deliberately light. When my mother asks about PE, I keep my answers brief and straightforward, my guard firmly up. Then my father changes the subject.

"Your mother told me you were very brave today, Devika."

I shrug, picking at my food. "I just did what I could."

"You have always been very smart for your age," he says. "I'm incredibly proud that you tried to help." The words are kind, but something inside me, a cold knot of suspicion, feels a subtext I'm missing.

I glance up at him. For a split second, my vision goes funny. A strange, dark grey, foggy glow seems to swirl faintly around his head and shoulders. I quickly drop my gaze back to my plate, my heart hammering. *An aura? His soul? Like Cat said?*

"I need to ask you something important, poppet," he says, his tone carefully friendly, but with an undercurrent like an order. "And I need you to be completely honest with me."

I take a deep breath. I see the deep, irreparable cracks forming in what I thought was my normal, happy family.

"When your teacher got ill… did you see anything… strange? Anything at all out of the ordinary?"

My blood runs cold. I understand his real question. I force myself to meet his searching eyes, my voice deliberately innocent and bewildered. "What do you mean, Dad? I saw he was in distress, so I took action. What else was I supposed to see? Did I... did I do something wrong?" I add a carefully crafted tremor to my voice, hoping it's convincing.

He tilts his head up slightly. I see subtle, rapid movements on the side of his nose, as if he's just sniffed the air deeply. It's an intense, focused action. *Is he smelling me? My fear? My lie?*

After our tense dinner, I make my way back to my room. My parents exchange significant glances over my head as I decline to watch a film with them. As I start up the stairs, my father calls out, "Don't forget your three tablets now, Devika."

I hesitate, dreading he'll watch me again. After getting a glass of water from the kitchen, I head up, praying he doesn't follow. I go through my nightly routine, the familiar scent of my moisturiser a small comfort in a world losing all familiarity. As I leave the bathroom, I pause, catching the sound of hushed, urgent voices from downstairs.

Curiosity piqued, I remember Cat's method. Back in my room, I close the door, take a breath, and whisper, '*I must be silent.*'

I cautiously open the door. Miraculously, there's no sound. I creep out onto the landing and lower myself to the floor, listening. It's instantly, chillingly clear their conversation is anything but amicable.

"Sarah, I'm telling you, I am almost certain she lied," my father says, his voice harsh with contained aggression. "I could swear I briefly sensed the deception from her, that specific scent, but then it vanished."

"John, please," my mother's voice is pleading, desperate. "We have no idea about her full abilities. We can't assume her scent is the same as everyone else's. Have you forgotten we often can't tell when angels, or even highly skilled sphynxes, are lying? Until we know what type of witch she is, we simply don't know. Maybe she just didn't want to dwell on what happened today."

A tense pause. "Okay, Sarah, I'll let it go, for now," my father says, his voice cold. "But you saw her strength in the hallway. She is getting stronger. The current medication isn't working properly. I might have to bring this to Sean's attention tomorrow and seriously consider moving up the timetable for her integration."

"John, no!" my mother's voice cracks. "If you do that, it's all over! He will insist we bring her in early. He won't take the risk. And… and I'm not ready for that yet, John. I'm really not."

"You're getting far too attached to the girl, you always do!" he snaps. "You knew this would happen! We are doing this for the cause, for the good of our people. Just think: after her eighteenth, after the integration, we won't have to worry about anyone poking their noses into our business. We will finally be in charge of our own futures! Our pack will be the strongest in this entire country. Nothing will stop us if she works!"

His voice is filled with a chilling, fanatical fervour. My heart starts to shatter into a million irreparable pieces.

I don't wait to hear more. I scramble back to my room, a sob building in my chest, and manage to silently close the door before the tears come—huge, silent, and agonising. With trembling hands, I hide the three new tablets under my mattress. *He isn't my father. Not John.* My mind whirls. *What do they want with me? Why would I make their 'pack' stronger? And… did he just say I was a witch?* The word hangs in my mind, alien and terrifying.

Catherine M. Clark

Chapter 10:
Soul-Fire

The first weak light of dawn seeps through the gap in my curtains. I stir from a restless night, a bone-deep reluctance settling over me like a physical weight. I lie there, cocooned tightly in my duvet, wrapping it around myself like a shield. It's a flimsy barrier against the chilling uncertainty that now looms within the very walls of this house, but in this fragile moment, it feels like my only refuge.

The events of last night are a throbbing ache behind my eyes. I cling to the fading hope that it was all a nightmare, a cruel figment of my imagination. But as I lie here, swaddled like a helpless infant, I realise with a fresh pang of despair that I can't even recall my dreams; they remain frustratingly out of reach. A long, weary sigh escapes my lips. I recall the circular room where I first met Cat—a place of unnerving beauty and disquieting revelations. The thought of being involuntarily transported back there sends a shiver down my spine. For a brief moment, I feel a wave of profound relief knowing that for one night, at least, I stayed firmly here.

But a persistent, nagging voice of truth reminds me that I can't linger in this cocoon forever. Change, immense and terrifying, is on the horizon, promising to rewrite the very chapters of my existence. With a shuddering breath, I reluctantly prepare to face the day.

A sharp, decisive knock on my door makes my heart pound. My mother's concerned voice calls my name. Before I can answer, she lets herself in, her gaze homing in on the discernible lump that is me.

"Devika, are you still in bed?" she asks, her voice attempting a lightness that doesn't mask the underlying strain.

Grumpily, my voice muffled, I mumble, "No." I'm not nearly strong enough to face the day, to face *her*.

She chuckles softly, a sound that feels hollow to my ears. "Come on, kiddo, rise and shine! You don't want to be late again." Her tone is laced with something else—pity? Guilt?

"Fine," I sigh, the word heavy with resignation. "I'll drag myself out of bed, but don't expect my brain to cooperate."

"That's the spirit, dear," she says, the forced cheer in her voice a discordant note. "Your friends will be thrilled to see you."

After she leaves, I drag my leaden limbs to the bathroom and stare at my reflection, desperately searching for some small, comforting resemblance to the people I've called Mum and Dad.

I pull the scrunchy from my hair, letting the thick mass fall to my shoulders. I lean closer, pulling out a distinct silver section. How can my hair be this strange combination of coppery red and shimmering silver? John has plain brown hair. Sarah is a 'bottle blonde.' As I look at my own unnervingly silver eyes, I see how perfectly they match the streaks in my hair. They told me it was my 'genetic disorder.' But it looks far more like an inherited family trait.

I scan the rest of my face. My nose is straighter than theirs, my mouth fuller, my chin more pointed. There is no denying the cold, hard truth staring back at me from the glass. The painful, shattering realisation that they are not my biological parents hits me with the force of a physical blow, stealing my breath. The familiar sting of tears threatens, but I fight it back fiercely. If I start, I won't be able to stop.

As I hurry to school, my backpack feeling heavier than usual, I find myself alone. I don't mind the solitude at first. But as I walk along the road that borders Bloodwood, the creeping, prickling sensation of being watched returns, stronger than before. The fine hairs on my neck stand on end. I glance around furtively, my heart pounding, but see no one. When I force myself to look into the dense, shadowy depths of the woods, an overwhelming sense of a hidden presence grips me, cold and terrifying.

I quicken my pace, almost breaking into a run. Seeing a gap in the traffic, I impulsively dart across the road, putting as much distance between myself and the menacing woods as possible.

I reach my form class just as the final bell rings. As I step, breathless, into the room, my gaze is drawn like a magnet to the spot where Mr. Harding passed away. An icy chill runs down my spine. I make my way to my desk, my friends watching me with a mixture of relief and concern.

"I overslept," I explain, my voice still a little breathless.

"That's alright, Devvy. We were getting really worried," Tom says, his expression an intense, longing look that I find puzzling. "It's such a shame you're not allowed a phone. We could have sent you a text."

His words jog my memory. Liz is chatting on the other side of the room, so I'll have to ask her later.

"Hey, does anyone have an old phone?" I ask, trying to sound casual. "One where the vibration can be turned off, so it's totally silent?"

Tom immediately perks up. "I do! I do!" he exclaims, a little too loudly. "My old Nokia, the brick one. I can bring it in for you tomorrow!"

"Wow, thanks, Tom. If your parents have an issue, I can try and buy it from you," I say, a sinking feeling hitting me as I remember I have no money.

"No, it's fine, honestly. It's not worth anything. You can just have it," he says, beaming.

"Why do you suddenly want a phone now, Dev?" Clare asks, her head tilted with suspicion.

"I just want to be able to message you guys," I say, trying to keep the frustration from my voice. I feel a surge of anger. It seems increasingly likely that my parents are deliberately isolating me for some sinister reason.

The school day drags on. My mind circles obsessively around the conversation I overheard. *Sean. Scent Deception. Angels. Sphinx. Witch.* The words are a terrifying kind of proof. It makes me wonder, with a mixture of terror and forbidden excitement, if such creatures truly exist all around us, hidden in plain sight. I resolve to find a way to learn more about what I am.

The final bell rings. The thought of going 'home' makes my stomach churn. I find myself wishing Cat had visited last night. Her strange, ethereal presence would be a comfort now. Has the increased medication blocked her out completely?

I stroll home with my friends. As we approach the ominous stretch of Bloodwood, the unsettling sense of being watched returns. Having my friends beside me lessens the fear, but I stick close to the road, my gaze darting nervously towards the trees. They notice my renewed unease and ask if Mr. Harding's passing is still affecting me. I just nod. Telling them about unseen watchers and terrifying revelations wouldn't do me any favours.

As my friends are about to leave me at the park gate, another of those strange, intense waves washes over me, this one stronger than before. It feels like something is trying to forcibly break free from between my shoulder blades, causing me to arch backwards with a sharp hiss of pain.

A choked whimper escapes my lips. Clare catches me before I can collapse. Tom, his face a mask of alarm, immediately reaches for his phone. I manage to grab his hand. "No… I'm… okay," I gasp.

The sensation shifts, moving with alarming speed to my mouth. It feels as though my teeth are physically elongating. I can feel two incredibly sharp points, their tips like razors against my tongue. My vision blurs. Just like before with my father, I see a swirling, milky-white mist enveloping Clare and Tom. But Liz… Liz's aura is a murky, shifting grey, shot through with an aggressive orange. It's unsettling.

Then, as suddenly as it started, the sensation dissipates. The searing pain vanishes. My vision snaps back to normal.

"Dev! What's wrong with you?" Clare asks, her voice tight with panic.

"We need to get you help, Devika! This isn't normal!" Tom begs, his eyes wide with fear.

Liz, however, just looks at me, a strange, calculating expression on her face. It's a look that says she plans to get me alone later and demand answers. She's the only one of my friends with a vast collection of paranormal books. *Maybe she's read something… recognised something in me.* I sincerely hope not.

"Guys, I'm okay now, promise," I say, my voice shaky. "I think I just have a trapped nerve. That's why I was late, the pain flared up." I quickly shut up as I feel myself starting to babble.

Liz eyes me suspiciously but says nothing. Tom is not convinced. "Devvy, I really think you should see a doctor. Please talk to your parents tonight," he pleads.

An idea springs to mind. "Actually," I say casually, "my parents mentioned I might be having bad growing pains. They said they'd take me to the doctor this weekend if I still have issues." This seems to placate Tom and Clare. But out of the corner of my eye, I'm almost certain I see Liz shake her head, a tiny, almost imperceptible movement. *She's definitely going to be an issue.*

I say my goodbyes and make my way across the empty park. I pause at the end of my path and study my home. I was happy here, I think. Or at least, I thought I was. Now, I feel completely lost. *Was I adopted? Was I… kidnapped?*

I shake the thoughts away and head inside. My mother is coming down the stairs with a laundry basket, her usual bright smile absent. I tell her I'm tired and heading to my room for homework.

I toss my bag on the bed and start changing out of my restrictive uniform. As I pull a soft top over my head, the distressing sensation washes over me again, with even greater intensity. I don't want to alarm my mother. I swiftly turn on my stereo, cranking the volume high enough to drown out any sound I might make. I hurry to my bed and bury my face in a pillow, bracing myself.

I am just in time. The pain is excruciating, far more intense than anything I've ever felt. It's like something incredibly sharp is being forcibly, brutally ripped out from between my shoulder blades. My T-shirt feels painfully tight, constricting my breathing. I curl into a tight ball, a silent scream building in my throat as I bite down on the pillow. It feels like giant, invisible claws are tearing and pulling at my back. I try to look over my shoulder and realise my duvet is wrapped tightly around me, a result of my violent, involuntary writhing. The duvet is visibly bulging and trembling behind me, as if something large and alive is trapped there.

Just as I cry out again, another muffled scream into the pillow, the horrific tearing sensation mercifully disappears. The strange bulge vanishes. Almost immediately, a new wave of intense pain shoots through my gums. I tentatively probe my upper jaw with my tongue and am horrified to find my canines are noticeably longer and terrifyingly sharp.

Panic, cold and absolute, engulfs me. I struggle out of bed, my body feeble and shaky, using the corner of the bed for support. I peer, terrified, into the mirror. I am astounded to see two of my teeth, those newly elongated canines, gradually, visibly shrinking back into my gums. For a terrifying moment, they looked exactly like vampire fangs.

A powerful, electric surge of raw energy courses through me, leaving me dizzy and strangely exhilarated. I watch, utterly transfixed, as swirling, vibrant black-and-white colours begin to envelop me. At first, it's a thick, roiling fog, but as I move closer to the mirror, I realise it's more complex. It's like... like intertwined flames of pure, contrasting light and shadow, exuding an elegant, captivating, and profoundly alien beauty. *Soul-fire.*

As the intense burst of energy slowly subsides, I am left feeling bewildered, drained, and hopelessly frightened. I rush back to my bed, scrambling under the covers, pulling them tightly over my head as hot, uncontrollable tears stream down my face. I tremble violently. *What in God's name is happening to me? Am I turning into something monstrous?*

I cry myself into an exhausted, fitful sleep, consumed entirely by a desolate fear and a soul-crushing uncertainty about my future, about my very identity.

Catherine M. Clark

Chapter 11:
Bloodlines

I stir from a fitful, shallow sleep, my name echoing strangely in the dim room. My mother's voice, calling from somewhere outside my door, pulls me reluctantly from the murky depths. Groggy and disoriented, my body aching with a weariness that sleep hasn't touched, I blink at my surroundings. The familiar patterns on my wallpaper seem alien and threatening in the pre-dawn gloom.

"Devika, it's time to get out of bed, sleepyhead," she calls again, her footsteps soft on the stairs. "Dinner will be ready soon, love."

Dinner? Have I slept through the entire day? No, she must mean breakfast. My thoughts are a confused jumble.

With a groan that seems to emanate from my very bones, I try to push myself up, only to be met with an overwhelming wave of dizziness that sends the room tilting. I feel profoundly unwell, my head spinning. The haunting memory of Mr. Harding's gentle spirit and the terrifying transformation I witnessed in my mirror—the fangs, the swirling soul-fire—leaves me shaken to the core.

I hesitate, a cold sense of dread settling like lead in my stomach. The thought of revealing these monstrous experiences to John and Sarah fills me with a paralysing fear. What if they don't believe me? Or worse, what if they are somehow involved?

Her footsteps grow ominously louder in the hallway. My heart races, a frantic, trapped bird against my ribs. She knocks softly. "Devika? Are you okay?"

Her voice is deceptively gentle. I clutch the duvet tighter, a flimsy shield against the world. Peeking out from under the covers, I manage a barely audible, "I... I don't feel well, Mum. Can I please just stay in bed today?"

Her expression transforms instantly into one of deep, maternal concern. "Oh, darling, what's wrong? When did you start feeling ill?" she presses, her soft worry tugging at some deeply ingrained part of me.

I am utterly at a loss for words. After a long, suffocating pause, I decide to mention Mr. Harding, hoping to link my distress to an understandable trauma. "Well... I've been feeling... off... ever since... since Mr. Harding," I stammer, the lie feeling clumsy and inadequate.

The air grows thick with unspoken emotion. She takes a deep, steadying breath. "Oh, Devika. My poor love. I'm so sorry you had to go through that. Of course, you can stay in bed, sweetheart. I'll bring your dinner up on a tray later. Try to eat if you feel up to it, but don't worry if you can't."

Her soothing words wrap around me like a warm blanket, a tiny island of solace in a raging sea of fear.

I lie in the heavy stillness of the house, clutching the duvet, hoping to drift back into the oblivion of sleep. Time stretches on. What feels like an eternity later, the door creaks open. A shadowy figure, my mother, silently places a plate of food on the small table near my bed. She doesn't utter a single word before disappearing again.

Frustration, sharp and bitter, wells up inside me. I angrily turn onto my right side, a restless, agitated anticipation coursing through me. *What now?*

Then it hits me. A peculiar, intense pressure builds around my heart before shooting like molten lava through my entire body. My right hand is trapped beneath me, so I instinctively grab the duvet with my left and bite down on it, hard, to stifle the raw, primal scream of agony that tears through me.

A searing, tearing sensation rips through my back again, even more intense than before. I let out another anguished, muffled scream. Whatever is happening to me, whatever monstrous transformation is underway, is unfolding at an alarmingly rapid rate. In mere moments, the unseen force emerging from my back is strong enough to physically yank the duvet almost out of my desperate grasp, causing it to billow upward like a grotesque, trembling tent.

I brace myself for the pressure on my back, but it never fully comes. I dare to look over my shoulder and feel a sudden, disconcerting shift. The duvet begins to slowly descend, and I feel a strange, alien movement from inside my back, triggering a fresh surge of debilitating panic. When I finally manage a terrified glimpse, all I see is the duvet settling back onto the bed.

Almost immediately, a sharp, stabbing pain grips my gums. I recognise this terrifying sensation. I can feel the unnatural growth of two teeth and then, with a sickening scrape, their razor-sharp tips graze against my lower lip.

The visceral fear is overwhelming. I feel utterly, hopelessly alone. My most basic instincts urge me to scream for my mother, to seek refuge with her. Yet, the thought of trusting her after what I've heard is a horror all its own.

I can't resist the morbid urge to run my tongue over my teeth again. The two elongated, needle-sharp fangs feel even larger and more pronounced than before. My trembling fingertips trace their lethally sharp edges, a wave of nausea washing over me.

The sudden, distinct sound of the stairs creaking makes my blood run cold. Someone is coming. Fear turns to pure, undiluted panic. My heart thuds so violently I feel it might actually burst through my ribcage. A hysterical giggle escapes my lips as an image from the movie *Alien* flashes through my mind.

With fumbling desperation, I try to push one of the protruding fangs back up into my gum, but it refuses to budge. Just then, my bedroom door slowly, ominously creaks open. I try to feign sleep, but my breathing is loud and ragged in the sudden silence.

I sense her presence. Her voice, filled with a soft, maternal concern that now feels like a cruel mockery, cuts through the tension. "Devika? Are you okay, love? You still sound rather upset. Do you need anything? Perhaps… a hug?"

The idea of her staying, of her seeing me like this, is the absolute last thing I want. I take a risk, my voice muffled by the duvet I've pulled to my chin. "I'm fine, Mum. Just… tired."

"Are you… sucking your thumb, Devika?" she asks, concern still lacing her words. "I thought you stopped doing that a long time ago."

I am profoundly embarrassed, but strangely, her completely off-base comment helps to calm me fractionally. As I ponder how to respond, I feel an immense, shuddering wave of relief as the fangs begin to retract, sliding smoothly, almost painlessly, back into my gums. The terrifying black and white soul-fire begins to flicker and swirl around the only part of my body I can see, my hands. "No, Mum, I wasn't sucking my thumb. My mouth was just pressed against my pillow."

"Alright, darling. Well, I can stick around if you'd like," she offers.

"It's okay, Mum. I think I just want to try and go back to sleep now… and forget about Mr. Harding," I reply, my tone deliberately weary.

"Well, if you're certain. Why don't you at least try to eat something first?"

"Maybe later, Mum. The thought of eating just makes my stomach feel queasy."

"Okay, love. If you need anything at all, don't hesitate to let me know."

"I will. Thanks, Mum," I say softly, feeling a tiny, treacherous flicker of comfort.

I lie perfectly still, straining my ears. I hold my breath, waiting for the familiar creak of the stairs that will signal her departure. The silence stretches on, taut and unnerving. I can't shake the feeling that she is lingering just outside my door, listening.

Finally, after what feels like an eternity, the distinct creak of the top stair breaks the hush. I release the breath I hadn't realised I was holding in a long, shaky sigh.

I dare to peek out from under my duvet, my eyes darting nervously around the dimly lit room. The oppressive feeling of being watched still lingers. As I turn my head slowly to the left, a small gasp escapes my lips.

Cat is sitting there, perched elegantly on my small vanity chair. Her legs are crossed neatly at the ankles, her hands resting calmly in her lap. The chair has been silently moved to face my bed, and the quiet stealth of it sends a fresh shiver down my spine. Overwhelmed with a confusing mix of shock, relief, and burning curiosity, I blurt out, "How... how did you get in here? What are you? And where have you been?"

Her voice is calm and melodic. "I opened a plane door directly into your room once I detected your mother had finally left. My apologies for my absence, Devika, but I have had other pressing matters to attend to."

Stunned by the casual mention of a 'plane door,' all I can manage is a bewildered, "Okay."

My mind burns with the one question that matters most. *What am I?* I look to Cat, my eyes pleading for an answer. Her initial hesitation worries me, her beautiful expression shifting to one of profound sorrow. I know, with a sinking heart, I am not going to like what she is about to tell me.

"Devika," her voice is gentle but grave. "I'm not sure it's wise for you to know the full truth just yet. It could bring you a great deal of additional stress. I understand that you're strong, but everyone has their

limits." She senses my impatience and subtly motions with her hand for me to listen. "But, based on what I can sense and what you've overheard, I can surmise what your supposed parents are, and what your true parents might be. I perceive two distinct, powerful sides to your emergent nature."

My heart pounds, a frantic drumbeat against the silence.

"Okay," she begins, her expression grim. "One of your biological parents, most likely your true mother, is either a reaper or an angel of significant power."

"WHAT?!" The word bursts from me, far too loudly. I glance nervously at the door.

"Don't worry. I warded the room against both sound and scent as soon as I arrived, especially considering their own... heightened senses."

"What do you mean by that?" I ask, confused.

"We'll get to that," she replies dismissively. "First, your parentage. Based on your recent manifestations, the fangs specifically, it's rather evident what your true father must be." She takes a deep, steadying breath. "Your biological father, Devika, must be a born Vampire."

I can't believe what I'm hearing. "How? If I were part vampire, wouldn't I crave blood? And be... soulless, like in the stories?"

A soft chuckle escapes her, and for a fleeting moment, I feel a surge of irritation. It ceases abruptly when she senses my distress. Before I can gather my thoughts, she speaks again, her tone serious.

"We will need to keep a very close watch on your development. We have no precedent for how the vampire side of your heritage might interact with the reaper or angel side. It could nullify certain aspects or amplify others. Tell me, have you noticed any other changes, beyond the fangs and the back pain?"

I hesitate, but conclude I have no one else to trust. She is the only one who isn't lying to me.

Seeing my conflict, she offers reassurance. "Devika, remember, we are family, however distantly. Your safety is now my utmost concern. When I first learned of your existence, I realised you might be in considerable danger from those raising you. Please, you must try to trust me."

"Wait... WHAT?" I blurt out again. The fact that we are related, combined with the fantastical identities of my real parents, raises a terrifying new question.

"What on earth does that make you?"

She looks at me with a subtle, enigmatic smile forming on her lips. She taps her cheek thoughtfully with a long, slender finger. After a charged moment, her voice becomes very soft, very serious.

"Can you promise me not to panic, Devika, when I tell you something of profound significance?"

"Of course," I reply without hesitation. "Nothing can be more terrifying than what I'm dealing with right now."

She nods slowly, and with a quiet gravity that chills me to the bone, she reveals the final, staggering piece of information. I am so utterly poleaxed by her words that I almost tumble off the bed as I instinctively recoil.

"I, Devika, am the goddess Hecate. And I am one of the current, and some say eternal, rulers of the Underworld."

As she finishes speaking, a look of profound, almost weary sadness creeps across her beautiful face. She drops her head slightly, as if burdened by her own awesome, terrible identity.

"You're... you're a demon?" I stammer, my voice trembling with fresh fear. "Are you... Lucifer? Or... Satan?"

Hecate shakes her head slowly, a soft, pitying *tut* escaping her lips. "I am not a demon, child. Nor am I Lucifer, though I know him well. He can be a rather cocky and annoying bastard at times. And I am most certainly not 'Satan,' as there is no singular entity embodying that simplistic concept, although my associate Lucy has used that term to scare someone deserving. We are generally on the side of what you might call '*good*,' or at least, cosmic balance. I am known as a Daemon Goddess. And as far as I am aware, I am the very last of my kind. Just because I rule the Underworld, it does not mean I am '*evil*.' I rule it, with the often-reluctant help of Lucifer, primarily to keep the true demons firmly in check."

Chapter 12:
Goddess Unveiled

Hecate

I observe the girl, Devika. She trembles with fear, perched precariously on the edge of her bed, yet an underlying strength allows her to maintain her balance. As I watch, she begins to relax fractionally, her breathing evening out before she cautiously readjusts her position. She settles in a way that suggests, quite prudently, that she could still make a quick escape. I cannot help but feel a twinge of disappointment that she is not reacting as trustingly as she had promised. Perhaps I have revealed too much, too soon. This child carries burdens far heavier than she knows.

"I… I don't understand," Devika stammers, her silver eyes wide as she scrutinises my face, perhaps searching for horns or a tail. "You said you're not a demon, but now you're claiming to be a demon goddess?"

A small chuckle escapes me at her entirely predictable, human-centric question. The millennia of misconceptions weigh heavily.

"No, Devika, I am not a demon! A god, one of the first, named his original creations according to their essence. In the beginning, there were four primordial gods of balance; two of light and life, and two, known as the Daemon gods, embodying death and darkness. The word is not spelt the same. It is d-a-e-m-o-n."

She presses on, her brow furrowed. "Then... why are you the ruler of the Underworld? Isn't that... Hell?"

I sigh internally. A weary resignation. There is no time for a comprehensive history lesson, but she needs context if she is ever to trust me. Her trust is paramount.

"We don't truly have time for this, Devika."

"Oh." She drops her head, her shoulders slumping. She looks utterly exhausted and fragile. I relent.

"In the beginning, when the first gods shaped your world, there existed a delicate equilibrium. However, over uncounted millennia, the two primary factions began to question their purpose. This escalated into a catastrophic war, resulting in the death of most of the original gods. With the old order gone, the few survivors, like myself, redefined our roles. Some who wielded death and darkness, like me, consciously embraced maintaining balance—what you might call 'good.' Conversely, some aligned with light, tragically turned towards corruption and tyranny—what you would call *'evil.'* Ultimately, it was, and always is, a matter of conscious choice."

I pause, observing her. She looks utterly captivated, her fear momentarily forgotten. I hold my breath, waiting.

"So... what power do you have, exactly?" she asks. Her directness is an encouraging surprise.

To earn her trust, I must be honest. "I hold dominion over death and darkness, Devika," I state plainly. "I also possess a minor ability to heal, though typically only certain creatures linked to my domain. *And,*" I add, revealing a more volatile aspect, "I am the last remaining deity with the innate ability to wield hellfire."

Devika's eyes are wide. Her next response takes me by surprise.

"I grow the teeth of a vampire," she says, the words raw with fear, yet tinged with a strange defiance.

A small, reassuring smile touches my lips. I lean forward slightly. "And that's perfectly okay, Devika. Remember, it's what you do with your abilities that truly matters. Part of your soul resonates with a born vampire, yes, but you still have a choice. Always remember that. Now, why don't you explain everything you've been experiencing?"

She hesitates only briefly, then squares her shoulders. "Okay," she says, her voice steadier. "I keep feeling this… wave wash over me. It always starts with this awful pain in my back, between my shoulder blades. It feels like something is trying to rip right out. Then the vampire teeth grow, but they don't stay for long. And the last part is my vision. I started seeing what I thought was fog around my friends, swirling. But when I looked in the mirror… it looked more like a kind of fire, black and white flames dancing all around me."

She takes a deep, shuddering breath. She looks lighter, as if a great weight has been lifted. I wish I had managed to reach her sooner. I carefully consider her words before I reply.

"Based on what you've described, the black and white fire is almost certainly your own soul's aura, your life force made visible to your awakening sight. Soon, you should be able to perceive the auras of others clearly. Generally, the darker the aura, the more inclined the individual is towards malice. This confirms my suspicion that your biological mother was likely a reaper. Angels, for some inexplicable reason, cannot typically perceive the souls of other angels."

"What you are likely thinking is correct. Reapers are technically a type of lesser angel, but they can see the souls of almost everything. The intense pain in your back… that almost certainly indicates that you possess wings, Devika. It hurts so excruciatingly because your body, suppressed for so long, is fighting their emergence."

"WHAT!!!" Devika shouts aloud. If I hadn't warded the room, her so-called parents would have heard that.

"Are you telling me I have wings? Real wings? How am I possibly going to hide those? And what will John and Sarah do if they see them?" she asks, her voice spiralling into panic.

I take a calculated risk. I rise from the conjured chair and move smoothly to the bed, sitting on the edge next to her. I expect her to scramble away. She doesn't. She just stares, frozen. Then, she flings herself at me, wrapping her thin arms tightly around my waist and burying her head against my chest. She begins to cry—deep, heartbroken, terrified sobs that shake her petite frame.

I hesitate for only a fraction of a second, surprised, then gently return the hug, pulling her trembling shoulders close.

"Devika, listen to me. You can control it," I tell her softly. "Normally, someone with your heritage would have been taught how to consciously control these shifts by now. The medication they are giving you is suppressing not just your abilities but your physical maturation into your true form."

As I talk, she stops crying. She tilts her head back, her tear-streaked face filled with a dawning, horrified understanding. "They... they have been drugging me every day since I was twelve," she says, her voice wobbly. "It started right after I got dizzy spells. They took me to a doctor I'd never seen before."

"I believe they set it up so you would take it willingly, without suspicion. I am so deeply sorry you're going through this, little one."

She speaks again, her voice laced with a new bitterness. "I overheard them talking to someone named Sean. After I stopped taking the pills properly, the changes started becoming more frequent and more painful."

"Resisting the changes only makes it more painful," I explain. "You have to try to let it happen. Once you manage one complete, voluntary shift, you will gain significantly more control. You might only struggle then when you're extremely scared or angry."

I cannot believe they are using chemical suppressants on her. If they continue, it could be fatal. They may not fully understand what she is, focusing solely on a witch aspect. I've heard unsettling rumours about the wolf packs attempting to reintroduce potent magic into their bloodlines. If they succeed, especially with a being of Devika's potential, it could pose a significant threat to the fragile balance of this world. I wish I could intervene now, but there are far more urgent, world-threatening matters demanding my attention.

"I understand that you believe you are in danger, Devika. But why drug you simply to prevent the transformation? What do they gain?" I ask, probing gently.

"I… I don't really know," she replies, sounding small and lost. "All I know is that this Sean person is in charge. They're worried about me. Sean told them to increase the dosage. And if that doesn't work… they'll have to carry out their plan early. They mentioned me turning eighteen, and an 'integration'."

"It's clear they don't want you to realise the full extent of your powers," I surmise, thinking aloud. "I suspect they don't know you can physically shift forms. They probably think you only possess latent magical abilities because of the witch element. They are doing this to ensure you remain docile. And then, most likely, they will introduce you to a carefully selected mate when you turn eighteen, someone from their own pack, hoping to bind your power to theirs." The disgusted expression on her face tells me I perhaps should not have mentioned that last part.

"Are you serious?" she asks, her voice filled with revulsion. "You think they want me to… to sleep with someone?"

"They do, Devika. It is the most logical conclusion, I confirm gently. They likely just think you're a dormant witch and want to forcibly introduce your bloodline into their pack. They don't seem to realise that your inherent abilities, part vampire and part reaper or angel, probably won't help them in the ways they imagine. Trying to introduce another shifter lineage, like lycanthropy, into such a mix will likely make everything more volatile."

"I… I think you're right," she says suddenly, her eyes widening. "I heard them mention wondering what type of witch I might be. Oh god. What can I do? Can you… can you please just take me away from here? Now?" she asks, her voice small and pleading.

"I can't watch over you constantly myself, Devika. My own duties are too demanding," I explain regretfully. "But I will speak to a trusted friend, someone powerful and discreet, to see if he might be able to extract you safely when the time is right." I look into the saddest, most desperate eyes I have seen in a very long time.

"But why can't I go with you? Now?" she begs, clutching at my arm.

"Honey, I simply can't. It would raise too many alarms. Everyone here believes these people are your parents, not just pretending to be your parents. I need to speak to my friend first, to find a way to get you out cleanly, without leaving a trail." I watch as her face falls, raw sorrow washing over her. It nearly breaks my own ancient, weary heart.

Her voice croaks as she finally asks the question hanging between us. "Who... who are the people downstairs, Cat? What are they?"

I have to tell her the truth now, for her own safety. "You need to promise me again, Devika, that you will continue to act normally around them. If they even suspect you know the truth, it will put you in infinitely more danger."

"I promise. I'll try. I already know they can't be my real parents," she says, a surprising, determined strength in her voice. I feel a surge of pride for her.

"Devika... about the people downstairs... John and Sarah... they are..."

I am cut off mid-sentence as Devika suddenly jerks away, her eyes wide with fear, staring past me towards her bedroom door. I instantly ready myself for an attack, but quickly realise it isn't necessary. I finally register the sound—someone is coming up the stairs, their footsteps heavy and deliberate. I failed to sense them, my focus too intent on Devika.

I quickly open a shimmering plane door in the corner of the

room. "shit," Devika mutters, scrambling frantically back under her covers. As I walk towards the portal, I realise with a pang of concern that she is not yet truly able to accept her new reality. The lingering terror in her eyes as she tries to hide worries me deeply.

Before stepping through, I turn back one last time. "Practice shifting, Devika. Focus on embracing the changes, not fighting them. It will help you gain control." She nods mutely, huddled under her covers, looking smaller and more stressed than ever.

Just as the plane door closes silently behind me, I subtly alter the ward on her room, instructing it to gradually dissipate over the next few hours so my departure will not be sensed. I breathe a silent sigh of profound relief as I close the portal completely, just as I sense the girl's bedroom door opening on the other side. My presence here, if detected by the wolves, could put this unique, endangered girl in even greater danger.

Catherine M. Clark

Chapter 13:
Secret Plans and Fashion

Hecate

After returning to the opulent solitude of my palace, I pace my private chambers for a good ten minutes, a cold, divine anger simmering within me. My first, visceral instinct is to simply ask Lucifer to deploy a legion to swiftly and decisively eliminate those disgusting, power-hungry wolves from the face of the Earth for what they are doing to a member of my own ancient bloodline. However, I know, with a frustration that chafes, that doing so would blatantly violate the precarious rules of non-interference set thousands of years ago. Then again, perhaps it is time to reconsider those archaic rules.

Once I manage to wrestle my anger back under control, I summon a trusted shade and send it with swift instructions to locate Nathaniel. He is to come see me as soon as possible. *Urgently.*

I feel a growing unease, a certainty that trouble is brewing on a grand scale. Persistent, troubling rumours speak of the clandestine construction of a formidable army somewhere on Earth. A particularly gifted, if frail, seer delivered a chilling prediction: the world, she claimed, was rapidly approaching a period of profound, global mourning, powered by a force 'beyond her mortal imagination.' Since receiving that dire prophecy, I have been quietly making contingency plans. I refuse to leave the survival of this world to chance.

While I sit contemplating these heavy burdens, a shimmering plane door ripples open, and my oldest friend, Nate, walks through 45 minutes later from the hidden entrance to my secret council chamber, a heavily warded space designed for complete privacy. I take every precaution to ensure no one knows precisely who works for me on certain… delicate matters.

As he approaches, I silently curse him not to do it. If he does, I swear by the Styx, I am finally going to clip those magnificent wings.

Yep, he's going to do it again, I can feel it!

He approaches, his expression serious, and drops fluidly onto one knee, bowing his head deeply.

"Goddess Hecate, you summoned me." His voice is formal, devoid of the easy familiarity we share in private.

"Nathaniel," I say, my voice tight with annoyance. "What have I told you, countless times, about calling me that and about kneeling before me?"

"It is the rule, my goddess. Expected protocol," he replies, his head still bowed. I feel a mischievous urge to make him stay like that until he complains of boredom, but I cannot be bothered with the pointless theatre right now.

"Nathaniel, you may rise," I say, finally giving in. "Now, come and sit down. I have something important I need your help with."

He rises gracefully and sits on the couch, pointedly leaving a chasm between us large enough that Devika could have sat between us if she were here. I tut audibly.

"Nate, you are my friend. How many more centuries must I tell you? You can just call me Cat when it's just us."

"Always, goddess," he replies stubbornly, his gaze fixed somewhere past my shoulder. "If I start breaking the rules in private, I may inadvertently break them in public. Then you will be forced, by ancient law, to cut off my wings. I will always follow the established rules." He finally meets my eyes, a flicker of warmth in their depths. "But it is an honour that you still see me as a friend."

"Yes, well, you will always be my friend, Nate. You know that. And I swear to you, I will never hurt you, no matter what protocols dictate."

"Thank you, goddess." The corner of his mouth twitches, like he's trying not to smile—the infuriating creature.

"You're messing with me, aren't you?"

"No, goddess, I would never," he says, the very picture of angelic innocence, as his mouth twitches again.

"Whatever," I sigh, rolling my eyes heavenward. "You're getting more like Lucifer every year. Do you have any actual news for me regarding your primary task? The Harper witch?"

Nate pretends to clutch his heart dramatically. "That is the biggest insult you have ever laid upon me, Cat! Comparing me to *him*! I am so much better looking, wiser, and generally more pleasant than Lucy could ever hope to be."

I roll my eyes at his predictable performance.

"Regarding the assignment," Nate continues, his demeanour shifting back to professional seriousness, "I have made significant efforts to connect with various supernatural groups. As usual, some have mentioned vague rumours about a faction gathering strength, but their sources remain conveniently anonymous." His expression mirrors my own bewilderment. *Why is this proving so difficult?*

"However," he goes on, his tone becoming more animated, "in relation to Elspeth Harper herself, our strategy appears to be producing promising results. I have managed to 'coincidentally' encounter her in town several times, particularly at her favourite coffee shop. Initially, she appeared extremely wary. I suspect she can feel the latent power within me."

"Yes, allowing her to sense you was a necessary, calculated risk," I explain. Elspeth, as one of my very distant blood relatives, possesses just enough power to make my contingency plan feasible.

Her unwavering moral compass is also a significant advantage. We had considered binding Nate's powers so she wouldn't be able to tell he has power, but decided against it; any deception would almost certainly shatter her trust later.

"So, have you made any tangible progress?" I ask, a hopeful urgency in my tone.

Nate leans back, a mixture of boyish excitement and slight apprehension on his timeless features. "Well, the first few attempts were… underwhelming. But today… today I took a more… proactive approach."

"Wait," I interject, holding up a hand. "Nate, we agreed—no using your specific abilities around her."

"Relax, Cat," he replies with a confident grin. "I only subtly influenced the general foot traffic around the coffee shop. I merely… orchestrated things slightly so it would be bustling when she arrived." He pauses, his eyes lighting up. "I was already at a small table. When she got her coffee and started looking for a seat, she looked distinctly disappointed. So, I just… asked if she wanted to join me. She hesitated, but then… she accepted."

A broad, radiant smile spreads across his face. It is undeniably clear, even to my ancient eyes, that he is utterly smitten. I cannot help but feel a small, unexpected swell of pride—Elspeth is of my bloodline, after all. This romantic development only makes my plans seem more promising. Now, I just hope he will still go along with what I ultimately have planned, even with these burgeoning feelings involved.

"That's fantastic news, Nate," I encourage him. "So, what is she like? Up close? Have I made the right choice?"

His smile widens even further, if that's possible. I have never seen him look this genuinely happy. He is, after all, one of the primary celestial guardians of the plane doors between the human world and the Underworld, a role that keeps him from much interaction with mortals.

"She's… she's truly an amazing woman, Cat," Nate finally exclaims, his voice filled with an almost boyish wonder. "I never knew humans could be so... engaging, so intelligent, so... vibrant."

I smile genuinely now. I was initially worried that asking him to cultivate a relationship for strategic purposes was akin to making him act as some kind of celestial prostitute, a role utterly beneath his dignity. However, if he genuinely cares for her, then maybe, just maybe, he might have finally found the companion he has been subconsciously searching for all his long, lonely life.

"So, how did you leave things with her?" I ask.

Nate actually looks like he is physically blushing, a faint rosy hue spreading across his high cheekbones. I have never seen an archangel blush before. Oh, this is definitely going to be fun.

After a brief, false start, he finds his voice. "Well... I, ah... I asked her if she might like to join me for dinner sometime? And... she agreed. Tonight, in fact. Unless... you have something else, something urgent, for me to do?" His face falls slightly at the thought.

I decide not to let him suffer. "No, Nate. You absolutely can, and should, go on your... date." I deliberately emphasise the word and watch with amusement as he blushes again, fidgeting like a nervous schoolboy. Yes, this is definitely going to be fun.

His face returns to beaming, his relief palpable. "Oh, good! So, what did you need me for so urgently then, Cat?"

My amusement fades. "When I was physically scanning for a candidate, I came across Devika first. I initially ruled her out because she was just a child. But something about her signature felt... off. When I looked more closely, I discovered, to my horror, that she was in potentially great danger."

I proceed to tell him everything—about the wolf pack, the medication, the overheard conversations, her frightening transformations, her mixed heritage, and my brief, interrupted visit with her earlier.

When I finish, Nate looks as disgusted as I feel. "I still cannot believe that the Lycans descended from the same primordial gods as we did," he says, his voice tight with anger, his own power flaring close to the surface. "They are an utter disgrace to their ancient, noble heritage."

"I know, Nate," I soothe, placing a calming hand mentally on his simmering rage. "But right now, we need to find her a safe way out."

"Perhaps I could just go and quietly… wipe out the wolves involved?" he suggests, his eyes glittering with cold, angelic fury.

"As tempting as that is—and believe me, I considered sending Lucy to handle it—we cannot risk that kind of exposure. Not with whatever else is brewing. And even you probably couldn't take on a whole wolf pack alone without revealing your true nature. We need to get her out cleanly."

"Yes… you're right, of course, goddess," Nate concedes, though his jaw remains tight. "Although I must admit, it would have been rather satisfying watching Lucifer deal with them," he adds, a flicker of an almost evil grin touching his lips. I never knew he secretly enjoyed Lucifer's particular brand of R-rated problem-solving.

After Nate leaves to prepare for his date—following a comical panic attack about what constitutes appropriate human attire—I reflect on his choices. In all my millennia, I never thought I'd witness an archangel in the throes of a full-blown fashion crisis. Before he departed, I quickly conjured a suitable, modern outfit for him: dark jeans, a well-fitting shirt, a stylish leather jacket. One must keep up with human trends, after all. It simply wouldn't do to stick out like… well, like an archangel in archaic battle dress.

I leave my secret chamber and head towards my master bedroom suite. As I approach, I see my two favourite hellhounds waiting patiently, Jax and Thunder, their massive forms almost blending into the dimly lit corridor. They are remarkably intelligent creatures; they understand perfectly why they must wait here, and not outside the hidden chamber.

I give them both a deep scratch behind their large, pointed ears, eliciting low rumbles of pleasure, before letting them pad silently into the room. After changing into my comfortable, flowing robes, I settle down to attend to the endless administration of the Underworld. Yet, my thoughts inevitably return to Devika.

An interim solution comes to mind. I summon another shade, one I know to be particularly subtle and observant. I explain the delicate issue, outlining exactly what I want them to do. Then, I send it carefully through a small, temporary portal, instructing it to watch over Devika, to be my unseen eyes and ears.

I make sure I pick the right shade for this task. I need one that won't take undue advantage of the situation. I pick one that was borderline, almost saved before her untimely demise. She was a relatively nice girl when she was human, but made poor choices. When I discovered her soul being tormented by a particularly vicious demon, I intervened and offered her the chance to drink my blood, binding her loyalty to me in return for her service. She will do nicely. She will watch over Devika.

Catherine M. Clark

Chapter 14:
I Think I'm a Monster

Devika

My father steps quietly into my dimly lit room, the soft creak of the door breaking the heavy silence. I remain curled tightly under my duvet, a makeshift fortress against a world that has become hostile and terrifying. My untouched dinner sits forlornly on the desk, its aroma fading into the stale air.

"Stay home from school tomorrow, Devika," he suggests softly, his voice a surprisingly gentle balm against the chaos raging inside me. "Spend the day doing something you love. You know, drawing always helps you process things." His words barely penetrate the thick wall of heartbreak surrounding me. He can't possibly understand.

I manage a slow nod, hidden beneath the covers. My voice is thick with unshed tears as I whisper, "Okay. Thank you." I feel a flicker of misplaced gratitude for this small reprieve. I don't know how I can possibly face school, face anyone, with the crushing weight of what I now know. He leaves without another word.

After a long pause, I peel back the heavy layers of the duvet. A foolish twinge of hope flutters in my chest at the thought of Cat returning, but the room remains empty, silent, still. A tight, cold knot of anxiety twists in my stomach. Terrifying questions about my true identity, about the dark secrets buried in my past, and about the nature of the people controlling my fractured world swirl ceaselessly in my mind.

I cannot shake the world-altering feeling of Cat's revelation. The calm, matter-of-fact pronouncement that I am part reaper or angel, and part vampire, shakes me to my core. It makes me feel utterly alien, grotesque... a monster. My limited knowledge of vampires, gleaned from forbidden horror stories, paints them exclusively as soulless predators. As for reapers, all I know is the chilling folklore that they collect the souls of the dead.

A sudden, jarring realisation hits me. I exclaim aloud into the empty room, my voice a harsh whisper, "Oh my God! I completely forgot to tell Cat that I saw a reaper yesterday! In the classroom!"

The thought of possibly having to collect souls myself someday fills me with a profound, soul-deep fear. I feel utterly lost. I still don't truly understand why I couldn't have just gone with her last night. Being a goddess, couldn't she use some powerful magic to make people forget me? But my logical mind reluctantly kicks in. Too many people would need their memories erased: my teachers, my friends, Dr. Evans, neighbours...

Cat mentioned a 'pack,' a term my father also used. The word, according to the paranormal books I've devoured, usually refers to a large group of shapeshifters, most commonly wolves. The terrifying thought that John and Sarah might be wolves makes my skin crawl.

My mind is drowning. One question circles back: why is Hecate, this ancient, powerful goddess, even helping me? She said I was 'of her blood.' Does that mean I'm part god, too? No, that seems impossible, too fantastical even for my new reality. I've heard myths about the goddess Hecate, but most consider her a legend. Yet... she is undeniably real. The implications are staggering.

I lie rigidly on my bed, feeling like I am losing my sanity. After a long while, my tears finally stop, leaving my eyes dry and burning. I stare blankly at the ceiling when my mother enters again, carrying a glass of water. I see the inky darkness outside my window and realise with a jolt how incredibly parched I am.

She switches on the main light, its sudden brightness stinging my sensitive eyes. She places the water on my bedside table.

"You haven't eaten anything. Would you like a sandwich?" she inquires gently.

"No, thank you, Mum. I really don't have an appetite."

"Are you certain? Well, I brought you water. You must be thirsty. And please, Devika, don't forget your medication. Remember, you need to take three now, sweetie," she reminds me, her tone casual, yet somehow pointed.

I dread her watching me. "I promise I won't forget, Mum," I assure her, hoping my track record will satisfy her.

To my immense relief, she simply picks up the uneaten, now unappetising, plate of food and walks out, saying a quiet, "Goodnight, sleep well."

Once she's gone, I quickly open my bedside drawer and grab the medication. The bottle is plain white, with no pharmacy label, no doctor's name, no dosage instructions. How many other obvious clues have I missed? I tip a small bunch of the white pills into my palm, returning the extras to the bottle. I study the three small tablets. They look so innocuous.

I briefly debate taking them, clinging to a desperate hope they might stop all this, let me go back to my normal life. But remembering Cat's warnings, remembering my parents' cold conversation, I clench my fist and shove the pills deep into the pocket of my jogging bottoms. I'll flush them later. I want to see what I really look like after the change. I need to know. I want to see if wings will truly grow from my back. A strange, unexpected part of me hopes for beautiful, majestic white wings, like the reaper I saw yesterday. His wings were pristine. If I have wings like his... then maybe, just maybe, being a monster might be worth it.

I have a rough, fragmented night, plagued by nightmares of losing control, of the vampire side of me becoming dominant, needing blood. I wake up gasping, my pyjamas drenched in cold sweat, to the sun streaming weakly through my curtains. Feeling utterly drained, I head straight for a long, hot shower. As I step onto the landing, I hear my parents moving about downstairs. I had hoped they would have left by the time I woke, no such luck.

After my shower, I stand before the steamy mirror. The condensation obscures my features, but I can still see the exhaustion etched deeply around my eyes. Taking a deep breath, I steel myself for the performance ahead.

As I enter the hallway, the woman portraying my mother is waiting at the top of the stairs. An intense awkwardness washes over me; it feels like I'm in some strange stage play, completely uncertain of my role. She, however, seems perfectly at ease, the very embodiment of a practised actress.

"Good morning, darling! How are you feeling today?" Her voice is deliberately cheerful, full of a cloying concern that makes the knot in my stomach tighten.

"I had a rough night. Lots of bad nightmares," I reply, opting for partial honesty.

She steps closer and wraps her arms around me in a maternal hug. My body instinctively tenses, resisting the closeness that now feels like a lie. She must sense my discomfort, for she pulls away after only a second, her gaze searching mine. "Is everything alright, Devika?"

"As I said, I didn't sleep well."

I notice her take a slight, almost imperceptible sniff, an instinctive, animalistic action. Her expression softens. "I understand, darling. Well, try to get some proper sleep today. I've already called your school and informed them you won't be returning until Monday at the earliest."

"Thank you, Mum," is all I can manage, feeling a confusing mix of gratitude for the time off and guilt for the opportunity it provides me to search the house.

After she offers to make breakfast—which I decline—she gives me another quick, perfunctory hug and heads downstairs. I get dressed and decide to draw for a while, waiting patiently for them to leave. By the time the front door finally closes, I'm just putting the finishing touches on a drawing I've been working on since my birthday, which came to me in one of my strange, trance-like states. It's a scene of unicorns in a sun-drenched field. By a lake sits a house, and by the lake are four girls. Three I don't recognise, but the fourth, I realise with a jolt, is an older, happier version of myself. I have never drawn myself before.

I notice other peculiar details I don't remember adding: a huge black dog-like creature covered in flickering flames; a tiny, shimmering fairy on one girl's shoulder. A sharp, painful pang of longing hits me. I wish, with all my battered heart, that what I have drawn could be real.

After waiting for what feels like an eternity, my gnawing curiosity gets the better of me. I make myself some toast and then, with a shaky sense of determination, I begin my systematic search of the house. The kitchen and living room yield nothing. Next, I turn to the dining room and a single, dark wood sideboard. Inside, I discover a jumble of old files and dusty boxes.

After an hour of sifting through old bills and warranties, just as I'm about to give up, my eye catches a few thick, leather-bound photo albums tucked in the bottom corner. With cautious curiosity, I lift one out. The first page is a formal wedding photo of John and Sarah. She radiates a timeless beauty in a flowing white gown from the 1940s or 50s; he stands stiffly beside her in a dark suit. They look blissfully happy, but what sends a chill down my spine is the undeniably outdated style of their attire, their hair, the very quality of the photograph itself.

Page after page is filled with foreign faces in dated clothing. I scan the faded black-and-white and sepia images, but find no one I recognise. A sickening lurch in my stomach—despite their youthful appearance now, these images suggest a past far older than I had ever conceived.

I stumble upon a large photograph of a formal group gathering. At the centre stands a stern, imposing man I don't recognise, flanked by a shockingly young John and Sarah. Engrossed, I initially overlook the faded, handwritten inscription scrawled beneath the photo. When I finally notice it, my heart begins to race. It reads, quite clearly: *'Sean and the Lorcan Pack, Gathering of 1938.'*

The name Sean sends a ripple of cold recognition through me. The word 'pack' makes my skin crawl. The date feels like an entire lifetime ago, yet my parents look ageless, vibrant. If this were taken in 1938, they would be well over sixty, probably much older. It seems impossible… unless they are shifters, who perhaps age differently.

With trembling hands, I carefully place the photo album back exactly as I had found it. I spend the next two hours searching the rest of the house but find nothing else. Drained and defeated, I make myself some lunch and turn on the Tv, seeking mindless distraction. There's nothing on, so I reach for one of the few videotapes my parents allowed me to buy: 'The Craft,' a film about teenage witches. Knowing what I suspect now, they must have deliberately allowed it because they think I am one. The thought sends another chill through me.

Just as I'm getting engrossed in the film, the house phone rings. It's my mother, calling on her lunch break.

"Devika? It's Mum. How are you feeling now, love?"

"I'm okay, Mum. Just… distracting myself," I respond, trying to sound normal.

"Oh, good! What have you been up to?"

Her question is vague, unlike her. *Is she testing me?* "Well, I finished that unicorn drawing. And I made lunch. Now I'm just watching one of my favourite films."

Her voice softens with clear relief. "Oh, I'm so glad you've eaten! I was starting to get worried. And let me guess—the film wouldn't happen to be that one about the witches again, would it?"

"Maybe... maybe not," I reply with a playful, evasive shrug in my voice.

She chuckles. "Honestly, Devika, I don't know how you watch that over and over. Listen, if you're feeling up for it, perhaps we could order a takeaway for dinner?"

A genuine flicker of excitement sparks within me. "Ooh! Chinese! Can we have Chinese?"

"Haha! How did I know? Yes, darling, of course."

"Great!" I exclaim, my voice full of the most uncomplicated enthusiasm I have felt in days. After we hang up, I find myself mentally scolding my excitement. I worry my enthusiastic response might make them suspicious, might make them think I was simply feigning my illness to avoid school—even though there is now a significant sliver of truth in that notion.

As the film approaches its climax, an unsettling, prickling sensation creeps over me. Then it hits me with full force. Panic surges through my veins. I leap frantically off the sofa, sprinting towards the stairs. In my blind hurry, I stumble on the rug, nearly stumbling headfirst.

Reaching the top of the stairs, breathless, the peculiar, intense feeling envelops me. I race against time, against my own body, determined to reach the larger bathroom mirror. I need to see this time.

Just before I cross the threshold, I yank my top off over my head, leaving my bra on. I have to witness whatever terrifying transformation might be unfolding. A dizzying, paradoxical blend of intense excitement and paralysing fear grips me.

I barely make it, positioning myself in front of the large mirror just as a sharp, tearing pain shoots violently through my back. Following Cat's advice, I fight the urge to resist. I take deep, ragged breaths, trying to remain calm. To my profound surprise, as I relax, the pain actually lessens, becoming manageable. I grip the cold edges of the sink, bracing myself. A powerful tension builds in my back. It jerks violently, making me gasp, and then a grotesque popping sensation reverberates through my bones.

My legs tremble as I watch my wide-eyed reflection. The movement in my back intensifies. Then, without warning, everything seems to freeze. An incredible, almost violent release surges through me. A loud *whoosh* of displaced air echoes in the small room, followed by a sharp *snap*, like a heavy sheet billowing in the wind. The sound is exactly as if a massive bird has burst into the room, its powerful wings flapping wildly just behind me.

Startled beyond measure, I leap back, crashing into the shower screen. I can't see anything directly behind me; whatever emerged blocks out almost all the light as I spin clumsily in the cramped space, shampoo bottles clatter, my hairbrush skitters across the floor, the soap dish shatters.

I shut my eyes tightly, then force myself to turn slowly back to the mirror. As I catch the first proper glimpse of the enormous appendages unfurled behind me, my eyes fly wide in shocked astonishment. Instead of the beautiful, ethereal white wings I had foolishly expected, I am confronted with massive, undeniably real, slate-grey wings extending majestically from my back. They don't shimmer with celestial light, but in contradiction, I find I can see everything in the room with preternatural clarity, even in the near darkness they create.

I trace the sleek, powerful edges with my eyes, from the densely packed, smaller feathers to the larger, broader ones further down. At a prominent joint partway along the wing, I discover small, wickedly sharp black claws protruding menacingly. This is completely unlike the reaper's wings. As I instinctively flex my cramped fingers, I see the claws in the mirror flex and unflex in perfect, eerie sync with my hand movements.

My initial, overwhelming reaction is one of crushing disappointment. But as I continue to observe them, the slate-grey colour, with its subtle variations and intricate patterns, is actually quite beautiful in its own way—powerful, almost regal. The one detail that still sends a shiver of revulsion through me is the presence of those sharp, predatory claws.

Before I can dwell on it, a familiar ache begins in my gums. I watch, transfixed with a mixture of horror and morbid fascination, as my fangs slowly, smoothly descend again. Just as I'm focused on this unsettling transformation, my vision shifts, it looks exactly like the hollow quills of my wing feathers are suddenly ignited, catching fire. I spin around frantically, causing even more destruction.

Standing before the mirror again, I realise with immense relief that I am not, in fact, engulfed in actual flames. The enigmatic black-and-white fog swirls rapidly around me, a hypnotic dance of pure light and shadow. Leaning in, I see the fog transform into that ethereal, impossible fire that licks harmlessly at the trailing edges of my magnificent grey wings, casting a mesmerising, iridescent shimmer. The soul-fire highlights the unique, complex texture of my wings, making them look even more stunning, more majestic, than the stark white wings of the reaper.

Yet, even as I marvel at this terrifyingly beautiful sight, an insidious thought gnaws at me. Will others ever see me as I see myself now—powerful, strange, perhaps even beautiful? Or am I destined to be viewed only as a monster? The question hangs heavily, a despairing echo in my chaotic thoughts as I try to reconcile the dazzling image before me with the unsettling doubts whispering the same dreadful conclusion over and over. *I think… I think I'm a monster.*

Catherine M. Clark

Chapter 15:
Wings of Revelation

I cannot stop looking. Despite the chilling fear coiling in my gut, the sight of my wings reflected in the bathroom mirror holds me utterly captive. I spend maybe fifteen minutes just trying to consciously move them. I manage small twitches, a ripple of feathers, a slight extension of the joints. The control, however minimal, sends an unexpected, exhilarating thrill through me... until my gaze catches my reflection, and the memory of the fangs reminds me of the monster lurking within.

Cat mentioned I would be able to see people's souls. I assume the sight of my wings glowing with that black and white fire was my own soul-fire, my life force, running visibly through them. She also said if I just let the change happen, it wouldn't hurt as much. She was right. My every instinct was to fight it. If I had just embraced the change all those years ago... could I have been free from the chronic, debilitating pain? Instead, John and Sarah chose to drug me, suppress me, making me feel like I was physically falling apart. It's still so hard to comprehend how people who claim to love you can be so deliberately cruel.

The thought of it all, the sheer magnitude of the betrayals, makes me lose track of time. A glance at the clock on the landing tells me hours have passed. With a surge of panic, I focus, willing the wings to vanish. After a few tense moments, feeling a strange internal shifting, they retract, leaving my back feeling strangely bare, though still aching dully. I quickly tidy the mess I made, throwing away the broken soap dish fragments and wiping up spilt shampoo.

Just as I'm about to put my T-shirt back on, I notice something in the mirror. I turn carefully, angling my body. Faint, intricate markings stretch across my skin where the wings had emerged. I gasp. A delicate, detailed outline covers my entire back, from shoulder to shoulder, down towards my waist. It is unmistakably the image of folded wings, like a subtle tattoo etched just beneath my skin. It is impossible to hide. A monster, permanently marked.

After tearing myself away from this new problem, I hurry downstairs. I wash my lunch plate, put away the VHS tape, and make sure everything looks untouched. I desperately hope they won't notice anything amiss. Then I go back to my room and grab a book—one of the few fantasy novels they, ironically, allowed me to have. Now I understand why they forbade most books about paranormal creatures. They didn't want me to pick up any clues and figure things out. Well, they failed.

I settle on my bed, angled facing the door, propped up on pillows. I flip the book open to a random page, hoping I look convincingly absorbed. Within minutes, I hear the front door click shut. My mother is home, earlier than usual. A sure sign she's going to check on me. I hear her soft footsteps on the stairs, the telltale creak of the fifth step echoing ominously through the quiet house.

A sharp knock, and the door creaks open before I can respond. She is clearly determined to see if I am up to anything. I take a deep breath, trying to shield my chaotic thoughts, and look up from my book with a carefully crafted expression of casualness.

"Hey, Mum. How was work?" I ask, my voice light and steady.

She enters slowly, her gaze sweeping methodically over the room, over me. It feels like she's searching for hidden clues. "Oh, just another day, darling," she replies, her tone bland, but her eyes watchful.

"My thoughts kept drifting back to you. How are you feeling now? Any better?"

I lower my novel slowly. "Just… trying to distract my mind," I say, feigning a teenage nonchalance. "Decided to read for a bit, after the film."

She nods, but I can practically see the wheels turning in her sharp mind. "I know that witnessing someone's death can be incredibly traumatic," she says, her voice laced with a practised compassion that now feels utterly false. "And he was your favourite teacher, wasn't he?" She pauses, her gaze a confusing mix of what might be a warped form of love and undeniable worry. "I actually got another call from Mr. Davies today."

My stomach drops. "He just wanted to make sure you were doing okay," she continues. "He also mentioned that three other students from your class stayed home today. The main reason for his call was to let parents know the school has arranged for a counsellor to come in on Monday for anyone who needs to talk."

I understand immediately. She is concerned I might actually talk to this counsellor, that I might reveal the 'genetic disorder,' the isolating restrictions, the forbidden books, the lack of a phone. She absolutely does not want me discussing any of this with an outsider. Ironically, despite my growing desire to talk to someone, I agree with her. It would achieve nothing and might put me in more danger. I decide to actively reassure her.

"Honestly, Mum, by Monday I'm sure I'll be mostly over it. The last thing I want is to dwell on it all with a stranger," I tell her, injecting a note of weary finality into my voice.

I see her shoulders relax. She looks visibly relieved, though still a little tense. As I watch her, I see it again—the same thing John did twice. Her nostrils flare for a fraction of a second as she takes a deep, seemingly unconscious sniff of the air. After she does this, she finally seems to relax fully. I have clearly said the right thing.

"You've always been such a strong girl, Devika," she says,

her voice laced with that cloying mix of pride and concern.

Without thinking, the words tumble out, a strange, defiant sort of dark humour. "Well, maybe I am Supergirl."

Her expression shifts, a fleeting frown at my flippancy, but it melts quickly into a warm, indulgent smile. "Yes, darling," she replies, her eyes sparkling. "Maybe you are."

I cringe internally. My mind flashes to the countless times I've been told to avoid books about the paranormal, any discussion of superpowers. It feels incredibly patronising now, understanding why. It's as if they were clumsily trying to ease me into accepting my witch heritage while controlling the narrative. My recent anger at being forbidden from watching 'Buffy the Vampire Slayer' with my friends now burns hotter, the injustice of it all sharp and clear.

Her next words catch me completely off guard, pulling me from my resentful thoughts. I thought I had been so careful. But I must have missed something.

"So, what else have you been up to today, besides reading and watching your film? Why were you looking through the cupboards in the dining room earlier?" she asks, her tone deceptively casual, her eyes sharp.

My mind goes blank. Panicked, I blurt out, "How… how did you know?"

She smirks, a knowing, smug glint in her eyes. It's the look she always wears when she thinks she has me cornered. She delivers her trademark, infuriating line with a condescending, sing-song tone, "A mother always knows!"

I roll my eyes internally. It's a tiresome, patronising ritual that always accompanies my rare attempts at even the most harmless mischief. It happened for years when they tried to curb my enthusiasm for drawing my fantasy creatures, always finding my hidden sketchbooks and trotting out that same infuriating phrase. Eventually, they stopped trying to halt my creations and instead took to meticulously scrutinising each piece, asking endless, pointed questions before keeping them for a few days 'to admire them properly'. Why? What are they looking for?

Now, facing her question, my mind races frantically. "I... I just got bored, Mum," I mutter, the only half-believable explanation I can find. "Really bored. And I just... looked around for something different to do. Sorry." I sigh theatrically, trying to look genuinely regretful.

"Well, I understand that, darling," she begins, her expression softening. "It's no wonder you've grown bored with that witch movie. Aren't you getting tired of it by now?"

I just shrug, hoping she'll drop it.

"Yeah, well, after 'The Craft' finished, I looked around downstairs for an old book or a magazine, just something different. My mind felt too chaotic to draw again. I found nothing, so I came up here to read instead," I reply, keeping my tone even.

There is a slight, almost imperceptible catch in her breath as I mention looking for other books. Her responsive smile falters into a fleeting, quickly suppressed frown. *What was that?* It feels as if she can see straight through my deception.

"Well, your father will be picking up the Chinese takeaway soon. Would you mind if I took a look at the picture you finished today?" she asks, her tone a familiar blend of polite curiosity and unwavering expectation.

It's as predictable as the ticking of the clock downstairs. "It's just over there, on my desk," I state flatly.

She walks over, her fingers delicately lifting the large drawing pad. After a long moment that feels stretched thin with tension, she returns to the bed, the picture held almost reverently. Her next question follows the same, well-trodden path.

"Who are all the people in this picture, Devika?"

"No idea," I answer automatically, trying to sound bored. "Just random faces I made up."

"And the setting? The house, the lake?" she presses, leaning slightly closer.

"Nope. Just a completely made-up place." I am getting increasingly frustrated with their repetitive questions about my drawings. Their constant probing has actually made me draw less often, though the compulsion is still there, like an addiction. I realise now that's probably why they bought me all those expensive new supplies for my birthday—to subtly encourage me to draw more. But why?

"Okay, darling," she says finally, her smile returning, though it doesn't quite reach her eyes. "Well, I'm going to take this downstairs, scan it carefully like I always do, and then put it safely with the rest of your collection. In the meantime, while we wait, fancy a game of chess?"

I really don't want to. All I want is to be left alone. But I have to maintain the disguise. They are already suspicious. I have no real choice.

"Sure, Mum. Just let me finish this page first."

"Lovely. See you downstairs when you're done," she says, her gaze briefly, pointedly dropping to the book in my hands—*Nineteen Eighty-Four*—before she turns and leaves, taking my drawing with her.

Chapter 16:
The Missing Girl

Over the weekend, everything unfolded with a tense, suffocating predictability. The weight of constant vigilance hangs heavily over me. I cannot shake the ever-present fear that my parents—John and Sarah—might catch a glimpse of the intricate, tattoo-like markings on my back, or worse, sense the powerful wings that seem to hover just beneath my skin, yearning to break free. Ever since I embraced the transformation on Friday, I've been fortunate enough to avoid further involuntary complications. The only tangible change is a persistent, almost electric thrumming across my shoulder blades—a restless, longing warmth.

Despite these unsettling feelings, I manage to navigate the long weekend with a convincing semblance of normalcy. I participate mechanically in our usual family activities—shared meals, television, polite conversation. But my heightened awareness makes me painfully conscious of their subtle, assessing glances whenever they believe I am distracted.

As Monday morning finally rolls around, the familiar routine feels heavier than ever. I make my way downstairs, each step echoing with nervous anticipation. The warm aroma of coffee and toast does little to ease the anxious coiling in my stomach. They are already at the table, their eyes fixing on me the moment I walk in.

"Morning, darling," my mother's voice cuts through the charged atmosphere, deliberately cheerful. "How are you feeling this morning? Are you absolutely sure you're feeling up for school today?"

I know exactly why she is asking. She is worried I might have changed my mind, that I might want to talk to the counsellor.

"Yeah, Mum, I'm good," I reply, forcing brightness into my voice. "I told you I'd be fine. I still feel sad about Mr. Harding, obviously, but I think I can deal with it now."

I study their faces. This time, it's John who does it—a tiny, almost imperceptible sniff as his nostrils flare for a fraction of a second. I have firmly decided now to only call them by their names, at least in the privacy of my own head. John's face is a carefully neutral mask. I have no idea if they believe my performance.

"Well, that's good to hear, darling, very brave," John says smoothly. "But remember, if you find it hard being back at school today, just tell the headmaster you need to come home. I've already spoken to him again this morning."

They really are pulling out all the stops to make sure I don't talk to anyone official, aren't they? But, I concede internally, it is somewhat nice to know that if I have other issues—like uncontrollable wing-sprouting—I have a pre-approved excuse to come straight home.

"Thank you, *Dad*," I correct myself quickly in my head. "I'm confident I'll be okay." I take a final gulp of orange juice, eager to leave, but he stops me.

"Why aren't you eating breakfast, Devika?" he remarks, his tone light, his eyes sharp.

"I'm not really that hungry," I reply with a small shrug. "Just a little nervous. I promise I'll have a big lunch later."

"Well, see that you do," Sarah insists, her voice firmer. "We certainly don't want you fainting at school from lack of food and having the teachers think we don't feed you properly." *Causing any kind of official scrutiny is highly undesirable for them.*

"Honestly, I will be fine," I reassure them. His slight nod seems to indicate my attempt was successful.

With a final promise to call if I have any issues, I quickly wash my glass and grab my school bag. After closing the heavy front door firmly behind me, I pause on the top step. The sensation is strangely, intensely akin to escaping from some kind of invisible confinement, leaving me to ponder, with a fresh wave of dread, just how much longer I can endure this life built on lies.

Lost in a tangled mess of thoughts—wings, fangs, vampires, reapers, lies—I wander distractedly through the quiet morning park. The world fades into a hazy blur. My mind is completely consumed by an endless, terrifying loop of worries. It isn't until a firm, sudden grip on my arm jolts me violently back to reality that makes my heart leap into my throat.

As I whirl around, a profound wave of relief washes over me, so potent it almost makes my knees buckle. It's Clare. Her familiar smile is edged with concern, but her presence instantly calms the frantic panic inside me.

"Dev! Are you okay? I was calling out your name!" she exclaims, her voice a soothing melody amidst the chaos raging in my head.

"Oh! Clare! Sorry… I was just… daydreaming," I reply, the words tumbling out. Without thinking, overcome by a desperate need for comfort, I fling myself at her, wrapping my arms tightly around her in a fierce, clinging embrace. In that single, unguarded moment, the carefully constructed dam within me finally bursts. Hot, unstoppable tears stream down my cheeks as I cling to her like a lifeline in a drowning sea. I sob uncontrollably against her shoulder as if the very fabric of my fragile existence is unravelling.

"Hey, hey, Dev! Shhh. What's wrong?" Clare's gentle voice breaks through my ragged cries, full of the unwavering understanding that only a true best friend can offer.

My voice is swallowed by sobs. Just as I hear our names being called in the distance—Tom and Liz must be approaching—I muster the strength to pull away. I wipe furiously at my tear-streaked face with the sleeve of my blazer. "Clare… please… please just keep this to yourself. Don't tell the others I was crying like this."

"Sure, Dev. Of course," she urges gently, her eyes filled with a deep concern that makes my heart ache with guilt. "But I really hope we can have a proper private chat later? So you can explain what's really going on?"

"I will," I promise, resolutely deciding I have to share at least some of the truth with her. I need an ally. But Cat's stark warning makes me tremble.

Just as I regain some semblance of composure, Tom appears, jogging lightly toward us. "Hey Dev! Missed you over the weekend! Are you okay?" he calls out, his cheerful, caring warmth making my heart give an unexpected, confusing flutter.

Clare glances sideways at me with a quick, knowing look. We have often speculated that Tom might have a crush on me.

"Hey Tom," I respond, my tone relatively steady. "I'm fine now, thanks. I missed you, too."

His face visibly lights up. "Good! Oh, hey, I remembered the phone for you!" he says brightly, pulling out his old, reassuringly solid Nokia 3210 and its chunky charger.

I am so touched that he remembered. I act impulsively again, leaning forward and giving him a quick, spontaneous kiss on the cheek, followed by a brief, awkward hug. I fight back a fresh wave of tears. When I step back, his face is absolutely beaming. I immediately worry I've just made things infinitely more complicated. Clare catches my eye and gives me a subtle, warning look.

Shortly after, we see Liz approaching, talking intently on her own phone, her expression unusually grim. The way she glances up and briefly meets my gaze sends an inexplicable chill down my spine.

Taking a deep breath, I decide to take a risk, to test my new ability. I concentrate hard, trying to perceive Liz's soul, her aura. Just as I am about to give up, I close my eyes for a second, take another deep breath, and feel a subtle, almost imperceptible shift occur within them.

When I reopen my eyes and refocus on Liz, I see it. I see a definite aura surrounding her, but it's startlingly different from the bright white mist I saw around Clare and Tom yesterday. Liz's aura is predominantly a murky, sludge-like grey, shot through with streaks of a vibrant, aggressive orange. It's a deeply unsettling, repellent combination. The visual confirmation raises alarming questions about what she might have done to so drastically alter her soul's aura at such a young age. This new insight makes me deeply wary of her.

As my enhanced vision starts to fade, I quickly glance towards Clare and Tom, sighing internally with relief when I see their auras are indeed that pure, bright white light. Before Liz reaches us, she pockets her phone and offers a bright, slightly forced smile. I quickly shove the old Nokia deep into my school bag. I lean closer to my other friends and whisper urgently, "Don't mention the phone to Liz, please. Not yet." They give me puzzled looks but nod in silent agreement just as Liz joins us.

"Hey girl! Hope you're okay today," Liz greets me, her tone perfectly friendly. But now, my trust in her is irrevocably gone.

"Yeah, I'm glad to be back too," I reply, forcing a smile that feels brittle and false.

"Well, we're glad you're back; it's definitely not the same without you," Clare says sincerely.

"Yeah, we all feel the same," Liz agrees readily, though her smile still doesn't seem genuine. "But we'd better get moving, guys, or we'll be in detention!"

She is right. We set off together towards the school gates. As we walk along the path next to Bloodwood, I initially feel safer, flanked by my friends. Until we reach the halfway point. Then, inevitably, I get that same creepy, prickling feeling, as if we are being silently watched from the dense trees. I keep my gaze fixed firmly forward, resisting the powerful temptation to look.

As we come around the final bend, we see a very different issue unfolding ahead. All the disturbing feelings about Mr. Harding's death come flooding back. Clustered near the main entrance are several police cars, their blue lights off but their presence imposing. Even more alarmingly, a local news reporter is standing there with a cameraman, filming a piece right outside the school.

"Whoa. What's happening now?" Tom voices the question on all our minds.

"I have no idea," Clare responds, her voice hushed with worry. "It wouldn't have anything to do with Mr. Harding, would it?"

"I doubt it," I say, even as a cold premonition washes over me. "They wouldn't usually call the police days after the event."

We slow our pace, carefully crossing the road towards a group of kids from our year. Tom wastes no time. "Alright, Chris? What's going on?"

Chris, a tall, quiet boy, turns to face us. "It's Katie. Katie Armstrong. She didn't return home from school on Friday. No one has seen or heard from her since."

"What? Katie's missing?" I reply, shocked, my friends echoing my concern. "Seriously? No one has seen her since Friday?"

"Nope, no one," he confirms grimly, then turns back to watch the reporter.

The only coherent thought in my head is that I absolutely must avoid appearing on the news. I know John and Sarah would immediately lock me up at home if they saw my face associated with a missing student investigation. I turn abruptly to my friends. "Right, I'm going straight inside. I really don't want to be late for registration."

"What? You don't want to stay out here, see if we can get on Tv?" Tom asks, typical teenage excitement overriding his concern.

"No thanks, Tom. Definitely not."

"I'll go in with you, Dev," Liz says immediately, falling into step beside me. I am not surprised she also seems keen to avoid being filmed.

Tom and Clare hesitate for only a second before deciding to join us. They catch up just as we pass through the imposing wrought-iron school gates, leaving the morbid spectacle behind us.

Catherine M. Clark

Chapter 17:
A Tangled Web

When we finally enter the main school building, it's like stepping into a ghost town. The usually bustling corridors are unnervingly deserted. Everyone, it seems, is still outside, chasing their potential fifteen minutes of fame during the news report or just morbidly fascinated by the police presence. We silently make our way through the echoing quiet to our form room.

My mind immediately splinters, torn between the heavy weight of my own hidden issues and this new, chilling worry about Katie. *Could her disappearance somehow be connected to me? To the supernatural world I'm unwillingly becoming a part of?* I didn't know her well, so I struggle to see why she would be a target, unless it was random, or unless she, too, held secrets.

"What do you honestly think happened to Katie?" Tom asks eventually, his voice low, breaking the heavy silence.

"No idea," Clare suggests tentatively. "Maybe… she just ran away from home?"

"Maybe," Tom replies, his voice tinged with a genuine sadness that touches me. "But I've never heard her say anything bad about her parents, have you?"

If only he knew. I would be lying if I said I hadn't considered running away myself over these past few terrifying days. For now, I cling to the hope that Cat—the goddess Hecate—will somehow help me.

"I've heard nothing negative either," Clare muses. "Unless

she's just been hiding it really well."

As Clare speaks those words, 'hiding it well,' I notice Liz, who has been unusually quiet, casting furtive, almost calculating glances in my direction. *What could those looks possibly mean? Does she know more than I realised?* After seeing the strange, unsettling colour of her aura, a cold suspicion coils in my stomach. I start to seriously question if our initial meeting years ago, our shared interest in the paranormal, was somehow orchestrated. The paranoid thoughts race through my mind, my breath quickening, my head suddenly light and dizzy.

The conversation fades into a meaningless hum. An overwhelming panic starts to build, threatening to crest, to swallow me whole. I press my trembling hands hard against my face, burying my forehead onto the cool wood of the desk, my breathing becoming rapid and shallow.

I jump violently when someone touches my shoulder.

"Hey, Dev, are you okay?"

My head spins as I look up, Clare is leaning over me, her face a mask of deep concern. Tom is crouching solicitously beside me, his expression mirroring hers. But Liz... Liz remains pointedly in her seat, her concern appearing mild, almost detached. For now, I can't focus on her; I am on the precarious brink of a full-blown, humiliating panic attack.

I shift uncomfortably, leaning over to tuck my head between my knees, my heart racing a painful tattoo against my ribs. The sheer intensity is unlike anything I've ever experienced. Even when I first learned about my supposed 'genetic disorder,' I felt only a brief flicker of manageable distress, nothing close to the suffocating dread that envelops me now, stealing my breath.

Clare wraps an arm around my shoulders in a comforting side hug, her touch grounding me slightly. "Hey girl, shhh, everything's okay," she says softly, her voice a calming balm.

"Devvy, what's happening?" Tom chimes in anxiously.

I want desperately to respond, to explain the terrifying whirlwind of emotions, but the words are physically stuck in my throat.

"Sor..ry," I manage to gasp, trying to take deep breaths between short, fast gasps for air.

"Thin..gs…"

"Have…"

"Just…"

"Hit me…" I finally say, sounding completely breathless.

"Oh, Dev. Is this about Mr. Harding? About being back in this room?" Clare asks gently.

I manage a silent, jerky nod. Clare knows me so well; even now, she can see through my crumbling façade. At this moment, I wish with all my heart I could share everything with her, but Cat's warning echoes too loudly.

"Hey, Dev," Clare continues softly, "the headmaster mentioned there's a school counsellor available this week, if you ever feel like… talking about it?"

My eyes are drawn unwillingly towards Liz, who watches us now with a more focused intensity. I see the visible concern etched on her face—her brow knitted, her lips pressed tightly—and I feel a sudden, illogical urge to ease her specific worry, perhaps because she has the same tense expression Sarah did yesterday. "I… I will be fine," I manage to say, aiming for a confidence I absolutely do not feel. "Honestly, the last thing I need is to talk to a stranger; it'll just bring everything horribly back. I promise you all, I'll be okay."

Clare's gaze remains steady, a heartbreaking mixture of deep empathy and sadness. "Well, okay, Dev. But I'm always here for you, you know that."

"Thanks, Clare; you're a true friend," I reply, my voice thick with gratitude. I slide my own arm around her waist, pulling her closer for a fleeting moment, while my eyes train back on Liz. I am not surprised to see her frown deepen slightly at my pointed comment about friendship, but she also looks somewhat relieved that I've declined the counsellor option. A sharp pang of guilt twists in my stomach. Am I being unfair?

As I release Clare, our other classmates begin to filter noisily into the room, breaking the tense intimacy of the moment. Tom hesitates before reluctantly reclaiming his seat, his eyes still shadowed with a lingering worry. I sit in silence as the classroom fills, unable to concentrate. Clare and Tom continue to give me frequent, concerned looks. But Liz... Liz doesn't seem bothered at all now. She is chatting animatedly with the girl next to her, seemingly having forgotten my panic attack. She is giving me intensely bad vibes. I need to be much more careful around her.

Just as the last straggler enters, the headmaster, Mr. Davies, walks in, his face grim, followed by a woman I have never seen before. The classroom falls silent.

"Good morning, everyone," Mr. Davies begins, his voice heavy. "We have a few important matters to deal with." He indicates the woman beside him. "This is Mrs Flowers. She is going to be your substitute maths teacher and your form tutor for the foreseeable future." He pauses, letting the sad implication sink in. "As you may also know, we have a counsellor available in the school this week. If any of you feel you need to talk, please go to the main reception desk."

His expression darkens further. "Now, onto a more urgent matter. As you may have noticed, the police are here. This is because one of your classmates, Katie Armstrong, did not return home after school on Friday. After Mrs Flowers has taken the registration, a police detective will come in to talk to you all. Please, I urge you, help them in any way you can."

He leaves, looking profoundly sad and burdened. I feel genuinely bad for him. After Mrs Flowers takes the register, two smartly dressed people, a man and a woman, knock briefly on the door and walk to the front of the class.

The man appears to be in his late forties or early fifties, with neatly cropped dark hair just beginning to grey at the temples and a slightly crooked nose. His thin lips are pursed in a contemplative manner. The woman beside him exudes an immediate, profound air of sharp authority. She wears a perfectly tailored pantsuit in a severe navy blue, her mousy brown hair pulled back into an unforgivingly tight bun. Her expression is stern, sharp, and utterly unyielding. I instinctively shrink back in my seat. Her piercing eyes seem capable of seeing right through my carefully constructed façade, right into my terrified core.

"Good morning, everyone," the male detective begins, his voice calm and professional. "I am Detective Casey. We need your assistance. Our primary goal is to track Katie Armstrong's movements on Friday. We are interested in absolutely everything you might remember—any peculiar comments she might have made, any unusual interactions, or strange occurrences. If you have any recollections, no matter how insignificant, we strongly encourage you to come forward."

He gestures towards the door. "We have been allocated an interview room. Please let your form tutor, Mrs Flowers, know if you wish to speak with us. She will compile a list, and we will reach out to you. If you feel more comfortable having a parent or teacher accompany you, please inform Mrs Flowers. Additionally, we may need to reach out to a few of you who did not explicitly request to speak with us. In such cases, your parents will be contacted beforehand for their consent."

The female detective steps forward slightly. "And I am Detective McKenzie," she states, her voice clipped, efficient. "Those of you we may call upon have nothing to be worried about. We may simply need clarification on a specific part of the day. Also, for procedural clarity, I will primarily be the one talking to the girls, and Detective Casey will be talking to the boys."

As soon as she says that, I start to silently, desperately beg in my head, my hands clenched tightly under the desk. *Please don't call upon me, please don't call upon me, please, please, please don't call upon me.*

The two detectives leave as quietly as they entered. A heavy silence falls, then the classroom erupts in an anxious buzz. Mrs Flowers allows it for about five minutes before clapping her hands sharply for quiet.

"Right," she begins. "This week will be different. For the remainder of this morning's double period, you are to go quietly to your usual Art classroom and continue with your ongoing project work. Before you go, if you have any information for the police, please come and see me quietly now. And please, be respectful to others as you move around the school today. Remember that some students may be struggling significantly."

As she says that last part, both Clare and Tom immediately glance towards me with renewed concern in their eyes.

Chapter 18:
Whispers and Shadows

The day unfolds as a tangled, oppressive web of muted emotions and hushed conversations. Having missed school on Friday, the day Katie went missing, leaves me feeling like an outsider peering in through thick glass. Everyone seems to be abuzz about her, whispering theories, their faces etched with varying degrees of shock and morbid curiosity. I feel adrift, sifting through disconnected fragments of information. Throughout the long, tense day, classmates intermittently approach Mrs Flowers, their voices low, presumably to add their names to the list for the detectives. Girls periodically dash out of our classroom and others nearby, suddenly become overcome with tears.

Oddly, perhaps mercifully, my usual bullies are unnervingly quiet today. Yet, even in this strange reprieve, I am almost certain I hear Penny murmur darkly to her friend as I walk past their table in Art, '*I wish it were Devika who went missing instead.*' The venomous sting of those whispered words linger, a cold poison seeping into my already fractured self. But I force myself to push it aside; far more pressing concerns are currently gnawing at me.

Clare and Tom hover near me almost constantly, their eyes filled with deep, unwavering concern. They repeatedly ask if I am okay, but words feel cumbersome, inadequate, dangerous. I mostly retreat into the solace of my own troubled thoughts, offering only vague reassurances.

During History class, I turn numbly to my essay on the Tudor monarchy, but even that usually welcome distraction offers little respite. The dense text feels disjointed, incomprehensible, as if my mind is actively rebelling against the crushing weight of the unspoken, supernatural crisis unfolding within me.

Lunchtime brings no relief. The usually boisterous cafeteria buzzes with nervous whispers. My friends and I huddle together, our faces drawn and anxious. Clare and Tom exchange theories about Katie—did she run away? Was she taken?—their low voices wrapped in a palpable fear that only amplifies the dread coiling in my own stomach. Liz remains mostly silent, picking at her food. The usual easy laughter feels distant, alien today, replaced by an oppressive silence that hangs over our table like a storm cloud.

After lunch, the tension continues throughout the school. Students are quietly called out of lessons, summoned via discreet notes delivered by prefects to room 5C, where Detectives Casey and McKenzie wait. The stark reality of the police investigation casts long, ominous shadows over our afternoon. I spent the morning unsuccessfully trying to immerse myself in my Art project, but inspiration continues to elude me completely, even during history.

Yet, the strange, unsettling day isn't entirely without its own peculiar oddities. In the afternoon, during double French, a sudden, intense prickling sensation crawls up my spine—that now horribly familiar feeling of unseen eyes fixed on me. I subtly glance out the window, pretending to watch a bird, but the school grounds seem somehow distorted, subtly out of focus. As I quickly turn away, unnerved, a distinct shadow flickers at the very edge of my vision—a fleeting, yet unmistakable human silhouette where no actual person could be. It seems to skitter rapidly across the far corner of the classroom before dissolving seamlessly into the normal shadows. It leaves a residue of cold fear that clings to me like a second skin. *What was that? A ghost? Or am I truly losing my mind?*

I cannot escape the school fast enough when the final bell rings. The sight of uniformed police officers still standing guard at the main gates is deeply unsettling. The reporters are gone, at least for now, a small comfort. My thoughts drift to my parents—how will they handle this? A cynical part of me suspects they might use Katie's disappearance as yet another excuse to keep me isolated at home under their watchful eyes.

As we walk home, the unnerving sensation of being watched resurfaces the moment we pass the shadowy edge of Bloodwood. Unable to shake it, I find myself asking aloud, "Do you guys think they'll search the woods again? For Katie?"

"They already did, Dev. All weekend," Liz replies immediately, her tone clipped, factual, and uncharacteristically cold. She doesn't look at me as she speaks.

"Oh. Right," I murmur, more to myself. "I'm surprised my parents didn't mention it." Why would they keep that from me?

"Maybe they just didn't want to worry you," Tom suggests thoughtfully, ever the optimist.

"Maybe," I echo faintly, though the doubt gnaws at me. Liz's sharp gaze lingers on me again, scrutinising. Disturbing questions spiral in my mind. *Is she hiding something? Could she be connected to John and Sarah? To their pack?* The thought makes me feel slightly nauseous.

Thankfully, Liz is the first to part ways, branching off down her street with only a cursory wave. Once she is safely out of earshot, Clare immediately voices the thought I've been uncomfortably contemplating. "Okay, am I imagining things, or has Liz been acting really... strange today?"

"Yeah, I definitely noticed," I admit without hesitation, relieved.

"Has she? How so? She seemed okay to me," Tom asks, genuinely confused.

"Honestly, boys never pick up on these kinds of things," Clare chuckles, nudging him playfully. I manage a small, weak smile.

"Seriously? I'm not that oblivious!" Tom huffs, feigning offence.

"Whatever her reasons are, she's still our friend," Clare continues, her expression turning earnest. "I just hope she'll open up to us eventually."

"She could be, I suppose," I concede noncommittally.

A beat of silence passes before Tom speaks up again. "Do you… think maybe I should catch up to her? Offer to walk her the rest of the way home?"

Clare and I exchange a quick glance. "Nah, it might be best to just leave her be for now, Tom," I suggest carefully.

As we approach the park gate near my house, Clare envelops me in another warm, comforting hug. "I'm really glad you came back to school today. We really missed you."

"I missed you guys too," I reply honestly. Just then, Tom flings himself forward, wrapping his long arms around both of us in a spontaneous, slightly awkward, squishing bear hug.

"I missed you, too, Devvy! And I'd miss you too if you were off, Clare!" he declares, beaming with a goofy grin. Clare and I chuckle, the shared laughter lifting some of the heavy weight I'd been carrying. Yet, almost immediately, the daunting thought of re-entering the lion's den looms over me again.

Clare detangles herself. "Right, I'd better head off. My parents have given me strict instructions not to hang around. See you both in the morning."

"Have a good evening!" I call after her. "Hey, I might send you a message later on the phone, if I can get away with it!"

Clare turns back, her face lighting up. "Oh yeah! I completely forgot Tom gave you his old mobile! Cool! I'll look out for it!"

Tom turns back to me. "Oh, yeah, we forgot to tell Liz. Don't worry, I'll text her later to let her know."

Panic, sharp and immediate, jolts through me. "NO!" I exclaim, far too loudly. Clare pauses mid-step, turning back with a frown. Tom practically jumps out of his skin.

I quickly call out to Clare, trying to sound calmer. "Clare! Please... don't let Liz know I've got the phone yet, okay? I'll try and explain later." She gives a hesitant, uncertain nod before continuing on her way.

"Why not, Dev?" Tom asks, confused.

My mind races. "I'm... just trying to avoid trouble, Tom. I found out recently my parents know Liz's parents quite well. If Liz accidentally mentioned the phone to them, her parents might innocently mention it to mine. You know?" I desperately hope the hasty, convoluted lie holds. "Please, just... keep it between us three for now?"

His eyes light up at the idea of a shared secret. "Oh! Right, yeah, okay. Sure, Devvy. Our secret."

"Thank you," I add truthfully. "I've just got this really bad feeling about things lately." As expected, Tom follows me onto the path. "I guess you're walking me home then?" I say with a sigh.

"Of course," he replies earnestly. "If someone did take Katie, I'm definitely going to walk you home every day until we find out what happened."

"Thank you, Tom. You're being very... generous," I say, forcing a delicate smile.

He looks at me with that familiar, intense warmth. "It's my pleasure, Devvy. Can't let anything bad happen to my favourite girl, can I?"

I cringe inwardly. Tom is incredibly sweet, but I know, with a certainty that makes me feel even worse, that he harbours deep feelings for me that I simply do not, cannot, share.

The walk across the road is blessedly short. Before he leaves, I ask, "Hey, Tom, did you definitely turn off all the sounds and the vibrations on the phone?"

"Yeah, totally silent mode. Don't worry," he assures me. "I still don't get why your folks are so strict about phones, though."

"I don't either," I lie smoothly. "Maybe they think it'll distract me from my studies."

"Yeah, I guess," he concedes, looking slightly downcast. "Well, I'd better head off."

"Be careful walking home, Tom."

"I will, Devvy, promise." He brightens at my concern. "Bye then. See you in the morning."

I watch him go before finally turning towards my own front gate. Key clutched in my hand, I stand frozen on the doorstep as an overwhelming, suffocating wave of fear washes over me. My legs tremble. The primal urge to turn and run, to never look back, roots me to the spot.

Under my breath, a desperate, broken whisper escapes my lips. *"Please, Cat... Hecate... please, get me out of here soon. I don't think I can take much more of this."*

A dark shadow flickers in my peripheral vision, making me jump violently. I spin around, but the space is empty. The deep, chilling unease settles even deeper into my bones. I take several deep breaths, trying to calm my racing heart, and turn back to face my front door.

It swings open suddenly, silently, just as I lift my key to the lock. I jump again, my heart feeling like it's going to burst from my chest.

"Devika? I thought I heard someone. What on earth are you doing, just standing there?" Sarah asks, her eyes scanning the area around me.

I place a hand over my frantically racing heart. "Sorry... S.. *Mum*," I stammer, catching the slip just in time. "A... cat or something just darted out from the bushes and made me jump. And then you startled me. Honestly, I feel like I'm going to have a heart attack myself." I wave my key vaguely at her. *See? I was just about to let myself in.*

For reasons beyond my comprehension, she chuckles softly. "Oh, Devika. You can be so dramatic. Come on in, tell me all about your day." She turns and heads down the hallway, expecting me to follow.

I hesitate, reluctant to enter that prison. But I follow her anyway. I have no other choice.

Catherine M. Clark

Chapter 19:
A Desperate Gamble

Last night's dinner was awkward as hell. I try, with every ounce of my being, to act normal, to engage in their mundane conversation, but it is really, really hard. This whole impossible situation, the crushing weight of these secrets, is undeniably taking its toll. I am beginning to realise, with terrifying clarity, that it might be too much for me to handle alone. I'm only sixteen. I'm not equipped to deal with ancient goddesses, kidnappers posing as parents, wolves, soul-seeing, fangs, or wings.

We ate in the formal dining room again, and the whole experience felt like being trapped on a brightly lit stage, each of us playing our designated role in some twisted family drama. John and Sarah seemed engrossed in their steaks, seemingly oblivious to the violent storm brewing just beneath my surface. Their voices sounded muffled, distant, as if I were listening from underwater, with only the sharp, grating clinking of their cutlery against the porcelain plates cutting through the fog. I push my own well-done steak around my plate, my appetite having vanished again, as I watch them eat their rare meat, the red juices pooling around it, practically swimming in blood. The sight makes my stomach churn.

As I sat there, a thought, sudden and sharp, crashes into my mind. *Maybe... maybe I should just follow in Katie Armstrong's footsteps. Maybe I should run away.* It must be safer out there, somewhere, than staying here, passively waiting for someone else to fix my very big, very real, potentially deadly 'kidnappy' problem. Once the thought takes root, I cannot shove it back down. A frantic part of my mind immediately begins contemplating it—when would be the best time? What would I need to take? How would I get out without them noticing?

I still don't know what else to call these people. Technically, legally, they are my parents. But I just wish, with an aching intensity, that I knew what really happened to my real parents—the reaper, the vampire, are they still even alive, if they are, where are they! Right now, I feel so profoundly betrayed by them. The biggest, most immediate betrayal, the one that stings most acutely because it feels so personal, has to be Liz. I still hold a tiny, flickering hope that maybe there's some other explanation for her strange aura, her odd behaviour. But for now, I know I have to keep treating her like my friend.

Also, during dinner last night, John questioned me about Katie's disappearance. I knew I had to be honest to a degree, but also incredibly careful. I am now positive about two things. One: they possess some uncanny ability, likely scent-based, to tell when I'm lying. And two: I am increasingly certain they have a secret mole at my school, someone tasked specifically to keep an eye on me. That mole, I am almost entirely sure, is Liz.

I reached a pivotal, terrifying moment during that tense dinner where I felt an overwhelming need to validate the insistent whispers of doubt, to test my horrifying beliefs. As I sat there, pretending to eat, an exhilarating, terrifying mix of raw nerves and paralysing fear coursed through me. I forced myself to concentrate, trying deliberately to see if I could somehow shift my perspective again, to glimpse the hidden auras concealed just beneath their carefully maintained human exteriors. *I want to see their souls. Let me see their souls,* I chant relentlessly in my thoughts, clinging to the fragile hope that sheer intention would open the floodgates of perception once again.

A suffocating silence enveloped me for several long minutes, during which I battled a bitter sense of despair. Just when I teetered on the very edge of defeat, my eyelids fluttered uncontrollably, as if they had a mind of their own. Out of this peculiar moment, my vision sharpened dramatically, revealing an astonishing, horrifying sight. Tangible streams of ethereal, coloured smoke dance and spiral vividly around both John and Sarah. My heart feels like it physically drops into the pit of my stomach, cold and heavy as lead. Keeping a composed exterior felt utterly laughable and impossible as my worst fears crystallised right before my eyes. Their souls, their auras, are indeed enshrouded in colours sickeningly reminiscent of Liz's.

To my profound, gut-wrenching dismay, the first dominant hue swirling around them both is that same, aggressive, vibrant orange. The second, an ominous, murky dark grey, clings thickly to them like a menacing storm cloud. A chill of pure, unadulterated dread coursed through my veins, more paralysing than anything I had ever experienced. The overwhelming urge to flee last night was intense, to bolt from the room surged powerfully within me. I was consumed by a singular, haunting question that screamed silently in my mind: *How?* How could these creatures with such dark, corrupted souls have ever been the fun, jovial, seemingly loving parents I remembered? I am left reeling, struggling to reconcile this horrifying revelation with the cherished, now potentially fabricated, memories of my childhood, wondering sickly if their very souls had somehow darkened gradually over the years while I was held captive in this twisted, counterfeit reality.

I didn't sleep well again last night. I had foolishly hoped Hecate would pay me another visit in my dreams, offer some guidance. *No such luck.* The immense weight of my terrifying situation is rapidly becoming far too much for me to bear alone.

Fear, sharp and urgent, pushed me to take another risk. After John and Sarah went to bed, I retrieved the old Nokia. Heart pounding, I sent a single, crucial text to Clare, asking if she could meet me earlier than usual this morning, at the northwest corner of the park near Bloodwood. It's the furthest point from my house within the park, hopefully beyond the range of any casual prying eyes. She agreed immediately.

I warned her I might not be able to leave early, but I concocted an excuse: Clare wanted help with history before school, and with the Katie situation, the school itself would be too much of a circus to concentrate. To cover myself further, I had Clare send me a specific text: *'Hey girl, don't forget we agreed yesterday we'd meet a bit earlier tomorrow morning so you can check over my History work for me before school. Need your brain! See ya!'* This way, what I planned to tell John and Sarah would be partly true, hopefully reducing the risk of them scenting a complete fabrication.

I got dressed extra early and headed downstairs just before eight. As I entered the kitchen, John and Sarah were already at the table. I felt their eyes track me, sharp and assessing.

"You're up and dressed very early this morning, Devika. Did you have another bad night's sleep?" Sarah asks, her tone deceptively casual.

Okay. Game on. "Oh! No, not really. Um, did I forget to mention it? Clare wanted to meet up a little earlier today. She wants me to quickly check over her History project, as she's feeling the pressure a bit with our upcoming exams," I reply, deliberately babbling slightly.

"No, darling, you definitely didn't mention it," Sarah says slowly, her eyes narrowing.

John lowers his newspaper. Like clockwork, his nostrils flare slightly as he frowns. "I really don't think it's fair for Clare to put this kind of burden on you, Devika, especially not now. Shouldn't she be asking her parents for help?" His voice is as cold and emotionless as a dead fish.

"Dad! She's my best friend!" I respond, a little too sharply, injecting genuine feeling into my voice. "I would do absolutely anything to help her out. It makes me happy that I can." My heart pounds painfully. I didn't think he'd understand the concept of friendship, not with a soul as dark as his.

"Why couldn't you discuss her project at school?" Sarah asks, her eyes still scrutinising me.

"Mum, it's just too distracting at school right now. Clare wanted to go through it with me somewhere quiet. And we're not having our usual classes this week, remember? These projects are worth thirty percent of our final grade."

John clenches his jaw, unconvinced. I think he's going to forbid me from leaving. But then he surprises me. "Fine," he says curtly. "Go and help your friend. You don't have that much time left together at this school anyway." It feels like a veiled threat.

A suffocating fear courses through me. I quickly make a single piece of toast and eat it standing by the counter. I wash my plate, grab my bag, and call out a cheerful goodbye, trying to mask my overwhelming anxiety.

Once outside, I close the door and immediately bend over, hands on my knees, fighting a panic attack. It's relatively minor, and I manage to regain my composure fairly quickly. *Right. Focus. Clare.*

I walk to our designated meeting spot at a much faster pace than usual. As I get closer to the secluded corner of the park, I see Clare already waiting, her expression full of worry.

"Hey Dev! You made it! What's going on?" she says immediately.

I sit down beside her. "Before I start, Clare, please just get out your history coursework folder."

She frowns, her concern deepening, but pulls out a thick, bulging folder. I take it and let the pages fan out across my lap. I take another deep breath, glancing around to ensure we are completely alone.

"Clare," I begin, my voice low and urgent, "I see you as my absolute best friend. Probably the only person left in the world I feel I can truly confide in right now. But I can't explain everything. It's too much. Too dangerous."

She tilts her head, her voice calm but curious. "Okay, Dev. But what about Tom? And Liz?"

"I believe Tom is a good friend," I admit slowly. "But not for this. As for Liz..." I hesitate, the weight of the accusation pressing down on me. "Things have come to light, Clare. Things I've seen, things I've heard, that lead me to believe I absolutely cannot trust her anymore. And I honestly think you shouldn't either."

Clare opens her mouth to interject, but I raise a hand. "Clare, listen. I set this up as a test. If Liz suddenly shows up, it'll just confirm everything. Please, promise me you won't share anything I tell you today with anyone else. Especially not Liz or Tom. If you do, I genuinely believe I will be taken away somewhere, and you may never see me again."

Her eyes widen dramatically in shock. "Dev! Are you being serious? Taken away?"

"Yes, Clare. Deadly serious. I know Liz has been secretly spying on me, probably for years, reporting back to the people I thought were my parents. And Clare... I have this terrible, horrifying feeling... I think I might have been kidnapped as a baby by them. And somehow... I think Liz is involved."

Clare gasps, her hand flying to her mouth. I just nod again, slowly, miserably.

"But how? Why?" she presses, her shock rapidly shifting into fierce, protective determination.

"A woman approached me," I explain, my voice a shaky whisper. "She claimed to be a very distant blood relative. She's trying to find a way to help me escape."

"Can't you just go to the police?"

"She told me explicitly not to," I reply urgently. "She said they have powerful allies and are extremely well-protected. She told me to act as normally as possible, which is becoming impossibly difficult. But now, Clare, everything is beginning to make a horrible kind of sense."

"What do you mean?" she inquires, leaning closer.

"All the rules! The strict curfews, never having friends over, never being allowed out. They've deliberately kept me isolated, always claiming it was for my 'fragile health.' It was all just a facade, Clare! The so-called 'genetic disorder' they used to control me, to drug me… it's all just a lie! A massive, elaborate lie!" The words spill out of me in a torrent.

Clare shakes her head, denial warring with horror on her face. When she finally looks up, her eyes glisten with unshed tears.

"Hey, hey, none of that now," I say softly, touching her arm. "Listen, if I'm right about Liz, she'll probably show up here very soon. She can't see you crying like this."

"Okay… okay," she replies, her voice thick and croaky. Without warning, she throws herself at me, hugging me tightly, her history coursework tumbling onto the damp grass. I gently push her back. "Clare, seriously, if Liz sees you like this, she'll ask questions."

"You're right. I'm sorry," Clare says, her face a mixture of frustration and simmering anger. "But Dev… I really, really hope you're wrong about her. It's just… God, I didn't even know Liz properly until I met you, and now…" Her voice trails off as a flicker of realisation crosses her face.

"What is it?" I prompt gently.

"I just remembered something," she continues slowly, her eyes widening. "Liz actually started at our school the week before you did. And during that first week, she kept to herself, acted really standoffish. I heard her say once, 'I'm not interested in making friends; I'm only here for one specific person.' Then, on your very first day, she practically bumped right into you, almost deliberately, and then suddenly wanted to be your best friend. Why didn't I see how weird that was? And thinking back… Liz looked so annoyed when you started talking to me too."

"Clare, we were only seven," I reply quickly, hoping to ease her sudden guilt. "But… you're right. I remember that day too. She definitely wasn't happy about you joining our group."

As I lean down to pick up the scattered pages, a sudden flicker of movement catches my eye. I turn my head, my heart leaping into my throat. For a terrifying split second, I think I see Liz's shadow sneaking through the trees, but it dissipates into thin air.

"What's up, Dev? What did you see?" Clare asks, her voice sharp with concern.

"Nothing's wrong. I just… thought I saw something move over there. Must have been mistaken," I say with a shaky laugh.

Clare scans the area, her brow furrowing. Then she sighs. "Well," she says flatly, "it looks like you were actually right the first time, Dev."

"What do you mean?" I ask, my stomach plummeting.

"Liz is here," Clare confirms grimly. "She just saw us, over by the main path. And she's making her way over here now." Her expression morphs into a volatile mixture of protective anger and palpable fear.

"Okay. Okay. I'm sorry, Clare," I implore urgently, placing a hand on her arm. "Just… act normal now. Please."

Taking a deep, visible breath, Clare composes her features. I quickly pick up the course work that fell to the ground and begun flipping through her coursework, pretending to read, trying to focus on anything other than the approaching footsteps of our supposed friend.

"Hey guys! You're both out much earlier than usual this morning," Liz says brightly as she finally approaches, though the forced cheer barely masks the irritation simmering just beneath the surface.

"Hi Liz. Funny, you're out pretty early too," Clare replies casually, effortlessly deflecting.

Liz's face tightens almost imperceptibly. "Yeah, well, after all the chaos yesterday, I decided to leave a bit earlier today. I see you both thought the same thing."

"Actually, Clare asked me yesterday if I could meet her here before school to go over her history work," I jump in, sticking to our cover story. "She's getting worried about it, aren't you, Clare?" Clare nods emphatically. "But honestly," I continue, turning back to Liz with feigned enthusiasm, "it looks really solid. Probably even better than mine, if I'm honest. So, I'm not jealous at all, promise!"

I carefully shuffle the pages and hand the folder back to Clare.

"Thanks, Dev. You're seriously the best," Clare says, managing an awkward smile.

"Hey, just doing my part, helping out a true friend," I reply, adding emphasis, hoping the subtle dig lands.

"So," Clare says, changing the subject, "should we head to school now, or wait for Tom?"

"Might as well head to school now," Liz responds instantly.

"Actually, let's wait for Tom," I chime in, deliberately contradicting her.

There's a brief, tense pause. "Sure," Liz concedes, her tone cooler. "Let's wait for Tom then."

"Okay, well, we'd better head over towards our usual meeting spot," I suggest reasonably.

Clare shoots up from the bench, her movements jerky. A fresh wave of protective concern floods me. *Am I putting her in terrible danger just by telling her this much?*

"You okay there, Clare?" Liz asks, her voice sharp with suspicion.

"Yeah! Yeah, I'm fine," Clare replies quickly. "Just... had a rough night. The situation with Katie has me really on edge." Her response is perfectly crafted.

Smart move, Clare. We rise together, the tension hanging between us as we start walking towards the park gate, waiting for Tom, and wondering what fresh hell today will bring.

Catherine M. Clark

Chapter 20:
The Weight of Knowing

We only had to wait ten minutes for Tom to show up, but those ten minutes stretched endlessly, each second laden with an awkwardness that hangs in the air like a thick fog. Liz shoots us a series of sideways glances, her brows knitting together in a way that makes my nerves fray even more. My paranoia begins to bubble up again, a familiar sensation that coils tightly in my stomach. As we pass the woods, they seem to pulse with life, but I can't shake the feeling that something—or someone—is watching us from between the trees again, adding to my tension and worry.

As soon as Tom arrives, he and Clare animatedly start to discuss the latest episode of *Buffy* like we usually would, their laughter ringing through the air. I struggle to concentrate. Normally, I would be engrossed in their retelling, hanging on to every quirky detail they mixed into the plot. But today, a cloud of distraction weighs on me, pulling my thoughts from the vibrant conversation to the shadows lurking in the woods.

With every passing moment, the intensity of that sensation grows. My heart races, and I feel the fine hairs on the back of my neck prickle like electric tendrils. A shiver cascades down my spine, forcing me to glance back into the thicket. It feels as if an unseen presence is inching closer, creeping up behind me, making me feel like I am in danger.

"We'd better get to school. I'm sure it will be a circus again like yesterday," Clare suggests, her soft voice breaking through my thoughts as she places a hand on my arm. The unexpected touch jolts me, and I nearly jump out of my skin. All three of them stare at me quizzically, their expressions a mix of concern and confusion. I feel a flush heat my cheeks, the spotlight of their attention making me self-conscious.

Desperate to escape their questioning looks, I start walking towards school, my pace quickening. Tom and Clare instinctively fall into step beside me, their chatter continuing, but I feel miles away, trapped by an invisible weight that presses down with every stride.

The reporter is back, giving updates that no sign of Katie Armstrong had been found. As we pass, I hear her say they plan to search the woods again today. Like yesterday, we went around the gathering crowd and head to our form classroom. When we enter, Clare takes the seat next to me instead of the one in front.

Liz stares at Clare as if she'd lost her mind. "Erm, that's my seat, Clare," she states, raising her eyebrows.

"Sorry, Liz. If we're allowed to work on our projects again, Dev and I are going to work on our history projects together, so it's logical for us to sit together," Clare replies smoothly. Liz frowns at us, then sits next to Tom, who also looks perplexed.

The rest of our class turns up quicker today, and Mrs Flowers arrives not long after. Once everyone is seated, she takes registration and addresses the class. "As you may be aware, Katie still hasn't been found, so the interviews will continue today. I will go around in a moment and hand out post-its to those of you scheduled for today. After your interview, you will be allowed to go for a break, but you are asked not to leave the school grounds. Two of your classes will go ahead as usual this afternoon: geography and PE. This morning, you can work on whatever coursework you want again."

I'm relieved to learn that some classes have returned to normal, but as I pull out my history coursework, an overwhelming sense of dread washes over me. The thought of having to attend PE fills me with anxiety. How can I possibly face my classmates with those

I Think I'm A Monster

tattoo-like wings adorning my back? The mere idea of Liz seeing them sends chills down my spine; she would undoubtedly rush to tell my so-called parents what she'd seen.

PE had completely slipped my mind until this moment. My thoughts are a tangled mess, and I desperately need a moment with Clare to brainstorm some kind of plan.

The morning drags on painfully. Two hours before lunch, I decide to slip away to the girls' bathroom, hoping Clare might take the cue and follow me while silently praying that Liz won't tag along.

As I enter the bathroom and approach the mirror, I stare at my reflection. The shimmering silver strands of my hair cascade down, a sharp contrast against the deeper red hue. It strikes me as peculiar how my hair differs from everyone else's; what would be considered ginger on most is transformed into a vibrant red on me. My silver eyes sparkle in the fluorescent light, glinting as if they contain actual silver.

Turning on the cold water tap, I splash my face, feeling the sharp chill awaken my senses. As I study my reflection, my lips form the desperate words, "How the hell am I going to get out of PE later?"

Just as I finish the question, a flicker of movement catches my eye. I spin around, heart racing, and track a shadow darting through the dim corners of the room. "What are you? Why are you following me?" I call out, my voice wavering. The shadow halts, and two ominous red eyes materialise within its dark form. Terror surges through me, and I instinctively back up, the edge of the sink digging into my lower back.

"What are you?" I repeat, my voice shaking.

"Who are you talking to?" A voice pierces the tension, startling me. I nearly jump out of my skin, but then I realise it's Clare, walking toward me with a look of concern.

Relief floods over me. "Oh, it's just me talking to myself," I say, managing a weak smile. "I hoped you would follow me." I turn quickly to check where the shadow had been, but it has vanished. A shiver runs down my spine.

Is this what has been watching me from the woods?

"Well, I wanted to check if you were okay," Clare says, narrowing her eyes. "You've been distracted all morning, and it's not like we can—"

I interrupt her, placing a finger over her lips. "Shhh," I whisper urgently, glancing around. "You need to be careful what you say. She might be spying on us."

Clare's eyebrows shoot up, but she quickly mimes zipping her lips shut, then leans in. "So, what's up?" she whispers.

Taking a deep breath, I try to gather my thoughts. "I need to get out of PE. There's something I can't let..." I hesitate, then whisper, "Liz, see."

"What is it?" Clare asks, her eyes widening.

"You wouldn't believe it if I told you," I admit. "I just need a good excuse that won't let *you-know-who* go blabbing to, well, *you-know-who*."

Clare chuckles softly. "Will you tell me everything else when you can?" she probes gently.

"I will, Clare. It's just hard to find the right time when I'm sure we aren't being spied on," I reply. "My biggest worry is that you won't believe me or be able to see what I want to show you."

"Dev," she says firmly, her eyes locking onto mine with unwavering sincerity, "When you're ready, I will believe anything you tell me. I promise." She envelops me in a warm hug, and for the first time today, I feel a glimmer of hope.

"With regard to PE," she continues, "the only thing I can think of that won't cause issues is to pretend you're upset about Mr. Harding. They might suggest seeing the counsellor, but you don't have to. Just say you need a moment."

I nod. It's risky, but I'm relieved to have a plan. "Thanks, Clare. That's perfect. If I leave near the end of geography class, will you cover for me?"

"Sure, no problem. Just make sure to try and get upset," Clare replies.

"It's not an issue. I have enough to work with right now," I say, realising just how true it is.

Clare gives me a serious look. "Yeah, you do. I really hope this woman can help you out, and if there is anything I can do, I will."

Again, I remind her to watch what she says out loud by placing a finger over my lips.

"I believe you, Clare. I couldn't wish for a better friend," I say, feeling both lucky and like the unluckiest girl in the world.

She mouths, "Sorry," then gives me another hug. When she pulls away, she looks like she's about to cry. I grab some tissue and dab her eyes.

"Come on, I need you to be strong if I am to get through this," I say, trying not to start crying myself. "We better get back before they send a search party for us, too." Before we leave, I reach into the pocket of my skirt and pull out all the tablets I've been hiding. I flush them down the nearest toilet and then follow Clare out. She frowns, looking confused, but I just shake my head. Just before I walk out, I do a quick scan of the room for the shadow; there's no sign of it, but I know it's still there.

The day drags on monotonously. Near the end of geography, I let the wall around my emotions crumble; within an instant, I start to cry. I allow everyone to see it, then shoot up from my desk and hurry out of the classroom.

I make my way to the familiar bathroom, locking myself inside a cubicle. It isn't long before I hear the door swing open, followed by the clicking of high heels.

"Miss Lorcan, are you here?" a voice calls out, smooth yet laced with concern. It's Miss Patterson, the deputy headmistress.

"Yes, Miss Patterson," I manage, my voice strained. I so want to burst out of the cubicle and beg for her help. "I'll be okay, really. It's just that I had a relapse regarding Mr. Harding—everything with Katie has stirred up so many feelings."

"That's completely understandable," she replies gently.

"Remember, a counsellor is available. Otherwise, you can head to room 2F for a while. It's available today. Would you like someone to accompany you, or can I call your mother?"

The thought of her calling my mother jolts me alert. "I appreciate the offer, but I think I'll be fine on my own," I say quickly. "If it's not too much trouble, though, it would be nice if Clare Swanson could come check on me later."

"That's perfectly okay," Miss Patterson assures me. "I'll go let her know."

"Thank you, Miss," I call after her, relieved my plan hasn't gone sideways.

While I sit there, my mind drifts back to the shadow. I need answers, so I take a chance. "Are you here still watching me?" I say out loud. A shadow slides across the inside of the cubicle door. When it stops, the red eyes reappear.

"Can you talk to me?" I ask. It looks like it shakes its head.

"Did you have anything to do with the disappearance of Katie Armstrong?" I ask, needing to know if it's a friend or foe.

The shadow vigorously shakes its head, and I sigh in relief. Then, it points. I stand on the toilet seat and look over the cubicle, following its direction. My vision zeroes in on the woods outside the window—the same woods that always make me feel like I'm being watched. My heart pounds.

Is there someone else out there watching me? Are they the ones who took Katie?

Just as I'm about to ask my next question, the bathroom door opens. When I look back, the shadow has vanished.

"Dev, you still in here?" Clare calls out.

"Yep," I reply.

"This is becoming a thing. Miss Patterson came to see me, and I don't have to attend PE either. Thanks, bestie."

"It's my pleasure, bestie," I say, stepping out. The bell rings as I walk to the sink and splash water on my face. My eyes are puffy;

even though I have been fake crying, real emotions fuel them.

"Let's head to the classroom I was told I could use," I say to Clare.

"Sure." I then lead the way out of the bathroom and head towards the classroom 2F.

"By the way, Liz is not happy at all. She tried to tell Miss Patterson that she should be with you as well, but she told her you can only have one friend for support."

"This day is going to bite me in the arse," I say, dreading what might happen when I get home.

The dimly lit room feels both comforting and eerie. I slump into a chair, exhaustion weighing me down. Clare sits next to me, her eyes full of concern.

"Dev, I know you've got a lot on your plate, but you're not alone. We'll figure this out together."

I nod, grateful. "I just hope I can get through this without things getting worse."

With that, we settle into the quiet room, the weight of my secrets hanging heavy in the air. Whatever comes next, I know I have a true friend by my side.

Catherine M. Clark

Chapter 21:
Kracis

As Clare and I sit in the quiet solitude of Room 2F, a sour pang of guilt churns in my stomach. I've never skipped a class in my entire life. It feels alien, a deep, unsettling crack in the foundation of the good, rule-following girl I'm supposed to be. In hushed tones, we agree to use the time productively, to work on our nearly finished history projects. The room is engulfed in a thick, almost companionable silence that stretches for twenty minutes, punctuated only by the soft, rhythmic scratch of Clare's pen and the rustle of paper as I pretend to review my notes.

Eventually, Clare breaks the silence. Her voice is soft, but it cuts through the quiet with unnerving precision. "So, Dev," she begins, setting her pen down with deliberate care. "Are you going to explain the cloak-and-dagger routine? The secrets? The panic?" Her tone is inquisitive, but a tremor of the worry she's been holding back since the park this morning shimmers beneath the surface.

I let the folder of notes rest on my lap, taking a moment to corral my chaotic thoughts. This needs to be delicate. I have to test the waters before I throw her into the deep end of my impossible new reality. "Clare," I start, my voice low and serious. "I need you to be completely, brutally honest with me right now. Can you do that?"

I watch her closely. Her brow furrows as she processes the strange formality of my request. Without missing a beat, she meets my gaze. "Always, Dev. You know that. What's up?"

The unwavering sincerity in her eyes gives me the courage I so desperately need.

"Okay… Clare, do you… do you really, truly believe in the paranormal? In all the things we read about?" My heart starts to hammer against my ribs, a frantic drumbeat of hope and fear. I need her answer to make sense, to give me some sort of anchor.

This time, she hesitates, her expression shifting as she weighs her thoughts. "Yes, Dev. I… I really do," she says finally, her voice steady and thoughtful. "I mean, think about it. All the stories, the legends, from so many different cultures, for so long… surely some of them have to be based on truth, right?" Her gaze holds mine, silently urging me to open up. "Why… why are you asking?"

I take another deep, shaky breath, steeling myself to pull back the curtain. But there's one more thing I have to know. "Clare… in your books… can shifters, like wolves, tell if you lie to them?"

The question clearly catches her off guard. A frown of confusion creases her forehead, but she answers readily enough. "Uh, yeah, Dev. According to most of the lore, anyway. Predator shifters—wolves, big cats—they have insane senses. The books say you give off a scent, a change in pheromones or something, when you lie. They can pick up on it instantly." Her eyes narrow. "Again, Dev, why are you asking this?"

Her eyes suddenly fly wide open, the gears in her mind visibly spinning. "Wait… oh my god, Dev! Are you… are you trying to tell me that you think *you're* a shifter?"

"No!" The word bursts out of me, far too quickly. I squeeze my eyes shut and shake my head, the absurdity of it all crashing down on me again. Taking this next step could destroy what little normalcy I have left. But the loneliness is a physical weight, threatening to crush me. I need one person. One ally. Or I'm going to shatter into a million pieces.

Here we go.

"Clare…" I begin again, my voice a raw whisper. "I… I think

the people who raised me, John and Sarah... I think they're shifters. Wolves, maybe. And... and Liz, too." I force myself to meet her gaze. "And Clare... they are bad people. Truly bad. Their souls... are dark."

Clare just stares, her mouth slightly agape. She does this weird, disbelieving grimace-smile thing, shifts uncomfortably, and lets out a short, nervous laugh.

I don't move. I don't blink. I just stare back, my expression as dead, as devoid of humour, as I can possibly make it.

Her awkward laughter dies in her throat. "Wait... you're not winding me up, are you? You're serious?" The smile is gone, replaced by dawning confusion. "You really believe they're shifters? Why? What proof could you possibly have?"

"The woman who's helping me, Cat... she's paranormal. She confirmed it. And... Clare, this is going to sound crazy, but... this shadow thing... it's been following me. And it has glowing red eyes."

"WHAT!!!"

The word explodes from her, echoing off the bare walls. Her eyes dart frantically around the room, searching the shadowy corners as if expecting something to leap out. Raw, escalating fear transforms her face, and for a heart-stopping moment, I regret everything.

"Is... is it here? Now?" she whispers, her voice trembling, her eyes huge.

"I... I don't know," I lie, trying to sound more confident than I feel. "But look, I don't think it wants to hurt me. If it did, it's had plenty of chances. I'm actually starting to wonder if Cat sent it to... to protect me?"

Her brows knit together. "Okay, but who *is* this Cat person, Dev?" The last traces of her earlier nonchalance have evaporated, replaced by a deep-seated worry. She looks at me as if she's finally considering the possibility that I've completely lost my mind.

I take another breath, remembering Cat's request for discretion. "I can't tell you that. It's her secret. But she said... she only found me because I'm part of her ancient bloodline." The words hang in the air between us, heavy and unbelievable.

Clare's eyes widen even further. "Okay... wow. So... what does that make you?"

I hesitate, the words feeling like sand in my mouth. "She... she described me as a hybrid. Of two different paranormal types." I let the bombshell drop. "It's why I couldn't do PE, Clare. Because everyone would see what's on my back." I quickly add, "Though, I don't actually know if anyone human can even perceive it." A familiar knot of fear tightens in my stomach.

"Then there's only one way to find out, isn't there?" Clare's voice is suddenly firm, laced with a quiet determination I've never seen in her before. It's a flicker of bravery that momentarily pushes back her fear. "Show me, Dev. Show me your back."

Can I trust her with this? *Really* trust her?

I have to.

With trembling hands, I turn slightly in my chair and lift the back of my shirt, just enough to expose the lower part of my back where the markings begin. I hold my breath, waiting for what feels like an eternity. The silence stretches on. Finally, I turn back to face her. My heart sinks. She's tilting her head, her expression a mixture of intense concentration and frustration.

"So?" I ask quietly, already dreading the answer.

"Dev... I honestly can't see anything. Just your back. What was I supposed to be seeing?" she asks, looking genuinely frustrated, and maybe a little disappointed.

"There should be... what looks like a huge tattoo. An outline of wings, covering my whole back," I explain, the hope draining out of me. "It feels... raised. To me, anyway."

Clare immediately reaches out, placing her hand flat against my back. I jump at the contact; her skin is ice-cold against mine.

"Hey! Warn a girl!" I exclaim, trying to inject a little levity into the suffocating tension.

She grins slightly, though her eyes are still serious. "Sorry!

But Dev, you might want to choose your words more carefully. That last bit sounded a tad suggestive." She pulls her hand away, her expression turning sympathetic. "Okay, I definitely felt something. It's very faint, like a slight ridge under the skin, but I absolutely cannot see anything. Sorry." She shrugs. "But hey, I'm not surprised. The books all say normal humans can't see most paranormal stuff unless the being wants them to, or there's powerful magic involved. I guess... maybe I'm just one hundred percent, boringly human."

"Crap!" The word escapes me as I slouch back in my chair, the weight of my isolation pressing down with renewed force. "Clare, I really, really need you to believe me. I honestly don't think I can go through this alone," I confess, my voice thick with desperation.

She shuffles her chair closer, wrapping her arms around me in a tight, reassuring hug. "Dev, listen to me. I *do* believe you. Honestly." She pulls back just enough to look me in the eye. "Besides, you've given me a couple of pretty big signs yourself recently."

My heart gives a cautious flutter. "What? What signs?"

Her expression turns serious again. "Well, think about it! PE the other day? You were so incredibly fast and strong. That tug-of-war... it was like you were powered by something else entirely. It definitely made me think, even then, that you might be more than just human."

Her words spark an unexpected flicker of pride, momentarily pushing back the fear. "Oh yeah... that was something else, wasn't it?" My mood lifts a fraction. "So... you do really believe me? About everything?"

"I do, Dev. I just... I wish I could see some concrete evidence for myself, you know? Something undeniable."

An idea, reckless and brilliant, sparks in my mind. *The entity... it came when I called it in the bathroom. Maybe...*

"Wait a sec, Clare," I say, a nervous excitement bubbling inside me.

"Okayyy," she replies cautiously, eyebrows raised in

anticipation.

I turn away from her, my gaze sweeping the dimly lit classroom. My heart begins to pound as I focus my will. The familiar tendrils of anxiety wrap around my chest, but I push them back. "Please... please come out," I call softly into the heavy silence. "I really need your help. Please." I hold my breath, hoping with every fibre of my being that it will hear my plea.

Instantly, a deep shadow bleeds out from the darkest corner of the room, detaching itself from the gloom cast by a towering bookcase. The dim light seems to bend around it, refusing to penetrate its unnatural darkness as it glides silently along the wall. It stops abruptly, directly in front of us, encroaching on the weak pool of light surrounding our desks.

My finger shoots out, my hand shaking. "There! Clare! Look! The shadow!"

Just as I speak, two gleaming, malevolent red eyes ignite within the heart of the shadow, piercing the darkness like molten embers. My gaze flickers back to Clare, desperate for confirmation.

She squints, her brows knitting together as she strains to see into the gloom. Her lips press into a thin, worried line.

"You... you can't see it, can you?" I ask, the brief exhilaration slipping away, replaced by crushing disappointment.

"Nope. Sorry, Dev. Nothing," she whispers, her gaze dropping, mirroring my own growing hopelessness.

I turn back desperately towards the shadow. "Please!" I plead aloud, my voice cracking. "Is there any way you can let my friend see you? Just for a moment?" The shadow seems to shake its indistinct head from side to side. "Please!" I sob, hot, frustrated tears finally spilling over and streaming down my cheeks. "I need someone! I can't do this alone!"

My heart feels heavy enough to sink through the floor. I am completely, utterly lost, trapped in a turbulent sea of terror. Clare shuffles her chair closer again, her arms wrapping around me in a comforting, grounding embrace. For a brief, precious moment, I find solace in her steadfast presence.

Then, the shadow's red eyes flash with a startling intensity, a pulse of dark energy that sends a fresh spike of fear through me. The light fades back to its normal, haunting crimson.

"OH MY GOD!!!"

Clare's shout is pure, unadulterated terror. She shoves herself away from me, her chair screeching across the floor. My head whips towards the door, expecting to see Liz spying on us. Nothing. I look back. Clare isn't looking at the door. She's staring, wide-eyed with horror, at the wall where the shadow hovers. I spin my head back, looking at Clare again and see it—dawning, terrified recognition in her dilated eyes.

She slowly lifts a trembling arm, her finger pointing directly at the shadow.

"Clare?" I ask tentatively, hardly daring to breathe. "Do you... see it now?"

She doesn't answer, just keeps pointing, her entire body shaking.

"Clare? Are you okay?" I ask, more urgently.

Still no response. I wave a hand in front of her face. Nothing. I gently take her face between my hands, turning her towards me. Her eyes remain locked on the shadow, but then, with a visible effort, they snap back to mine.

"There's... a shadow... with glowing red eyes... right over there," she whispers, her voice a ragged rasp.

"I know, Clare. I told you. I... I called it, remember?" I say quietly, trying to keep my own voice steady.

"Are... are we in danger?" she whispers, her terrified eyes darting from the ominous shadow back to me, searching for reassurance.

"No. No, I really don't think so," I reply, projecting a calm I absolutely do not feel. "I would never, ever intentionally put you in danger. You know that."

"Thanks," she says, her voice still shaky but laced with a faint trace of relief.

I manage a weak chuckle. "Are you going to be okay? Please tell me you're okay."

"I... I think I will be," she says, though her hands are still clenched tightly in her lap. "It's just... a lot. Seeing... that."

I turn my own attention back to the shadow. I lock my gaze with its unsettling red eyes and take a deep breath. "Did Cat—Hecate—send you to watch over me?"

The shadow doesn't hesitate. In the flickering light, I clearly perceive a nod. A simple, silent affirmation. *So Cat is looking out for me.*

"Okay. Is... is there any way for us to talk properly?" I press on, my heart pounding with a mixture of curiosity and apprehension.

Again, it nods.

"How?" I whisper.

The shadow begins to advance, its form undulating like thick smoke as it detaches completely from the wall. Clare's chair squeaks loudly as she clearly has moved away as the shadow advances, but I barely register it. My mind is laser-focused on the approaching shadow, a terrifying presence that seems to defy the very laws of reality.

It stops within arm's reach, coalescing into a more defined, three-dimensional shape. An icy chill runs down my spine as it slowly extends a shadowy arm. Its finger, cold and ephemeral, grazes my right forearm.

I frown, confused. "I... I don't understand."

"What? What does it want?" Clare asks, her voice tight with fear.

"I don't know!"

This time, the shadow presses its finger harder against my arm. The touch is impossibly cold, yet my skin itself doesn't feel it. It's bizarre.

"Do I need to do something? Or do *you* need to do something?" I say desperately, looking at the creature. "I don't understand! Please, just… do whatever you need to do so we can talk!"

"Devika! What are you doing? Stop! It could hurt you!" Clare's voice is sharp with rising panic.

"It's okay, Clare! If Cat sent it, then it won't hurt me," I reply, secretly crossing the fingers of my left hand in my lap, praying I'm right.

"Dev, I really don't like this," she says, her voice shaking.

Before I can answer, the shadow's finger sharpens, the tip morphing into a long, wicked-looking claw. It presses down. I gasp as a sharp, white-hot sting pierces my skin. A small bead of bright red blood wells up around the tiny wound. The shadow figure lowers itself, its red eyes fixed on the blood. I flinch, trying to pull my arm back, but its other shadowy hand clamps down on my wrist, holding me fast.

Panic, stark and overwhelming, surges through me. I fight against its grip, but it's like pulling against iron. It's impossibly, unnaturally strong. Clare, seeing my struggle, grabs my other arm and pulls, adding her strength to mine.

"Devika! Get away from it! Now!" she begs.

"I can't! Clare, I can't!" I cry out, my voice now laced with panic.

Clare puts her entire weight into it, and I feel myself start to slide backwards in my chair. But the grip on my right arm remains firm, sending a sharp, aching pain into my shoulder joint. Then, suddenly, another shadowy arm wraps around my waist from behind, pulling me forcefully back into the chair.

My heart hammers against my ribs so violently I feel it in my throat. An intense pressure builds rapidly in my back, in my jaw. *Oh god, no.* I'm losing control. I'm going to shift. Right here, in front of Clare. They'll all know. John, Sarah, Liz… they'll know the medication isn't working. The government will hunt me. I'll be a freak in a cage.

'Sorry if I scared you, but you did give me permission.'

The voice isn't a sound. It's a thought, echoing inside my skull—genderless, emotionless, accentless.

'I have to feed on your blood, just a little, to establish a direct mental connection. Only my master, Hecate, can hear my thoughts without me first feeding, I'm called Kracis.'

The explanation is so bizarre, so matter-of-fact, that my panic recedes. I feel one last, gentle draw on the cut, and then the shadow abruptly releases me and moves back.

"Dev? Are you okay?" Clare asks, her voice still shaky as she looks me over.

I glance down at my forearm. The cut isn't bleeding. It's a clean, thin line, almost healed already. "It… okay now, Clare. It… Kracis… it just needed some of my blood to talk to me."

"What?! Can you hear it talk? In your head?" Clare's eyes are wide with a mixture of fear and fascination.

"Yeah. It's… like a weird, flat echo in my mind."

"Wow. Okay. That's… fascinatingly creepy," Clare says, attempting a shaky grin. "Must be because you have no brain, I suppose. But, you know, Dev, the whole blood-drinking thing? Still seriously unsettling."

"Ha ha, very funny," I reply dryly. "You think you're so clever." An idea strikes me. I turn back to the shadow. "Kracis? Could you do the same with Clare? Could she hear you then, too?"

'Yes. It is possible,' the voice echoes in my head. *'But I would likely need significantly more blood from her. Yours is… inherently powerful. Is that what you command of me, Mistress?'*

"Whoa! Hang on a minute!" Clare says quickly, folding her arms. "I did not agree to this!"

I show her the tiny mark on my arm. "Look, it's not that bad. Then you could talk to it, too. But… it said it would need more of your blood, since mine is apparently… powerful, or something."

"Erm… yeah, I think I'm good for now, thanks," Clare says

firmly, shaking her head.

"Are you sure?"

"Yeah, Dev. Pretty sure. I think I need some time before I voluntarily take on any more weirdness, especially blood-drinking shadows."

I sigh. "Okay. Fair enough." I turn back to Kracis. "Clare doesn't want to. So... do you have a proper name? Besides Kracis?"

'Kracis is the designation given to me by my creator,' the name resonates in the empty chamber of my thoughts.

"Kracis. Okay then," I murmur. "So, Kracis... did Cat say anything else? About why she sent you? Or if she plans to help me escape from them?" My heart begins to race again with a desperate, fragile hope.

'My goddess, Hecate, instructed me primarily to keep watch over you, Mistress. And to protect you, should the wolves decide to harm you before she is able to arrange your extraction.'

"So they *are* wolf shifters? Is that all you know?" I press, desperate for any scrap of information.

'Yes.'

The simple answer is a fresh wave of disappointment.

"Wait, they are definitely wolf shifters?" Clare asks, her interest piqued despite her fear.

"Looks like it," I confirm grimly.

"Oh. That's... not good," she says immediately, looking worried again.

"Why? What's wrong with wolf shifters?"

"Well, Dev, in practically all my books, wolf shifters are the bad guys! Like, seriously aggressive, territorial, pack-mentality villains!" She starts looking around the room again nervously.

'The girl is largely correct,' Kracis adds unexpectedly. *'Wolf shifters are usually predatory and dangerous, particularly to outsiders. But... not all of them choose the path of darkness.'*

An uncomfortable thought flickers in my mind. "Um...

Kracis? Do you… watch me all the time? Like, when I'm… in the shower?"

'I always watch you, Mistress.'

The response is instant, without a hint of hesitation. An involuntary shiver runs down my spine. It's a peculiar, unsettling mix of feeling strangely protected and completely violated.

"Oh. That's… just fantastic," I say dryly.

I can see the gears turning in Clare's head as she processes my side of the conversation. "Okay, I'm definitely getting the sense that Kracis is a bit of a creepy pervert," she chimes in, raising a knowing eyebrow.

"Yeah, seems that way," I reply, feeling the heat rise in my cheeks. I turn back to the shadow, trying to sound authoritative. "Kracis. When I am in the bathroom, showering or changing, you are *not* allowed to watch me. Stay out."

'I will comply, Mistress,' the voice assures me, still eerily calm.

Curiosity gets the better of Clare. She leans closer to the shadow. "Hey, Kracis, are you a boy or a girl?"

'I am neither, now,' Kracis answers in my head after a slight pause. *'Though I believe… I was once designated female when I lived a mortal life. But that was an eternity ago. I do not remember much of that life.'* For the first time, there's a faint, almost undetectable note of melancholy in its mental voice.

"Oh," I say quietly, turning to Clare. "It says it doesn't really have a gender anymore, but it thinks it was a girl, a long time ago."

Clare nods slowly. "Okay. Well, that's definitely better than the creepy male alternative, I suppose."

"See?" I tease her. "If you'd just let it do its little blood-drinking thing, you could've heard for yourself."

"Erm… no thanks. Still good," she says, an involuntary shiver running over her. "You can be the official 'shadow whisperer' for now."

"Chicken," I mutter.

"Whatever," she retorts, sticking her tongue out.

'Shifter is coming!'

The warning cuts urgently across my mind.

"What?!" I exclaim aloud. "Kracis just said a shifter is coming!"

"What?! Where? Here?" Clare says, scrambling her chair back towards the table, her eyes darting to the door.

"I don't know!"

As I speak, the shadow that is Kracis sinks silently, straight down into the floor, vanishing completely. The exact moment it disappears, the classroom door opens.

Liz stands there, her hand on the doorknob.

She walks coolly into the room, then freezes just inside the doorway. Her head tilts slightly before she continues towards us. She stops dead again, halfway across the room. With a chilling certainty, I see her nostrils flare distinctly, just like John and Sarah do. What is she smelling? Our fear? Kracis's lingering presence? A cold dread washes over me. I shouldn't have involved Clare. I've put her in terrible danger.

"Dev? Clare? What are you two doing hiding in here?" Liz asks, her voice attempting normalcy. She doesn't look concerned. She looks annoyed. Resentful. "How are you doing, Dev? Feeling okay now?"

"Yeah, Liz, I'm okay now, thanks," I reply quickly, forcing a smile. "I just… had a small relapse, thinking about last week. I'll be fine."

"Good," she says curtly. "Well, we missed you in PE. Our relay team totally lost without you two."

"Oh. Sorry about that," I say automatically, a pang of guilt hitting me, followed by a wave of relief that I avoided the changing rooms. "We promise we'll be there for the next practice."

I feel a dizzying sense of relief that, for once, I am telling the

absolute truth. I shouldn't have to hide my back anymore.
    Hopefully.

Chapter 22:
When Nightmares Bleed into Day

The next few days pass with a deceptive smoothness, a fragile veneer of normality stretched thin over the abyss of yesterday. Clare, bless her resilient heart, seems to be shouldering the weight of it all. Her laughter reaches me in fits and starts, tiny, fleeting bubbles of the ordinary, but they sound muted, like a melody played underwater.

It's a stark, painful contrast to Tom. He's become a shadow with a pulse, constantly hovering, his gaze so heavy with concern I feel like I'm wading through molasses. He watches me as if he expects my bones to turn to dust at any moment. It's not endearing; it's suffocating. Each anxious glance is another bar in a cage I can't see but can definitely feel. My nerves are stretched taut like overtightened guitar strings, and his relentless proximity gives me no room to breathe.

His self-appointed duty of accompanying me to the park gate has become a ritual I dread. The path, usually a comforting corridor of rustling leaves, now feels like a gauntlet. The whisper of the evening breeze does nothing to dispel the oppressive weight of his presence; it just stirs the unease, making the shadows dance with my anxiety.

This evening unfolds without dramatic implosion, but the nagging itch of uncertainty, a persistent thrum beneath my skin, refuses to settle. I'm still turning over what Liz might have told John and Sarah. *Did she paint the full, terrifying picture, or just sketch the outlines?* I'd already confessed my relapse—a confession that felt like laying a heavy stone at their feet. I suspect Liz has likely filled in the gruesome details, each word tightening their parental grip.

And then there's Kracis. A silent, unseen guardian, her presence a strange, dark comfort in the periphery of my senses. The knowledge soothes some of the frantic buzzing in my mind. I find myself yearning to connect with her, to dive into those deeper, shadowed conversations about the world I'm now part of. But John and Sarah are always there, their proximity a tangible barrier. I hesitate, caught between the desperate need for understanding and the paralysing fear of being discovered. So, I'm left to churn through my own thoughts, the weight of them a lonely vortex in my mind, making me feel even more isolated now that I technically have allies.

Today begins with the deceptive lullaby of routine. But as I step outside, the path across the park feels… different. An unsettling chill, colder than the morning air, seeps into my bones, raising gooseflesh on my arms. My dream from last night surfaces, unbidden and vivid. It was a horrifying echo of Mr Harding's fate, the same suffocating sense of impending doom. I could feel a consciousness hidden in some dark, desolate place—not malevolent, but terrified. Utterly, primordially scared. Then, the crushing pressure, the same invisible weight that heralded the reaper's appearance, returned, squeezing the air from my lungs before—*snap*—it vanished. When I had the dream, I ended up shooting bolt upright in bed, drenched in a cold sweat, my heart hammering against my ribs like a trapped bird.

Now, as the woods lining the far edge of the park come into view, I freeze. My breath catches. A cold, hard knot forms in the pit of my stomach. The scene ahead is wrong.

"Hey, Dev," a voice calls, startling me so badly I nearly jump out of my skin.

I spin around, my pulse leaping. It's Liz, walking towards me, her expression unreadable.

"Morning, Liz. Do you… do you know what's happening?" I

ask, gesturing vaguely towards the woods, where the subtle flashing of blue lights is now visible through the trees.

"No idea," she replies, her tone a little too casual. "But it can't be good, not with that many police cars."

"Reckon they're searching for Katie again?" I ask, but the words feel hollow. A cold certainty settles in my bones. This is something new. Something worse.

"Maybe we should take the long way round," Liz suggests, her sharp, assessing eyes meeting mine. "Knew you wouldn't spot them until you were right on top of it. Figured I'd head you off."

"Thanks," I manage, the familiar tension coiling in my gut as my skin prickles.

"Come on, then," she urges, already turning.

As we make our way towards the midway exit, my heart thuds a nervous rhythm. Nearing the path, I spot Clare and Tom approaching, their faces etched with a mixture of morbid curiosity and genuine concern.

"Hey, guys!" I call out, relief washing over me. At least the scrutiny won't be solely Liz's.

"Have you heard?" Tom shouts, his voice strained, sending an icy shiver down my spine. His face is pale, worry carving deep lines across his forehead.

"Heard what?" Liz replies, a flicker of annoyance in her eyes.

"Another kid's gone missing," Tom says, his gaze darting between us. It lands on me, his eyes shimmering with fear. *Great. This crush isn't dying a quiet death. If only he knew, he'd run screaming.*

"Do you know who it is?" I ask, my own heart thrumming as we step out of the park, the sounds of the town suddenly louder.

"Not yet. We should get to school, find out what's going on," Clare says, her voice wavering, her lower lip caught between her teeth. She looks terrified. "God, I hope it's not someone we like."

The weight of her words hangs in the air. "I don't have to worry about that," I assert, the words out before I can stop them, sharper than I intend. "The only ones I truly care about are right here." I glance at my friends. "Obviously," I add quickly. "I wouldn't wish this on anyone else, of course not."

"You're too hard on yourself, Dev," Clare says gently, her voice soft with an empathy I don't deserve. "People like you. It's just the mean ones who are too stupid to see how brilliant you are." She offers a small, warm smile.

"Whatever," is all I can manage, my mood sinking further.

Their answering chuckles feel jarring. I shake my head, a small, exasperated sigh escaping me, before turning and starting the walk towards school.

The scene that unfolds is one of controlled chaos. The school is almost swallowed by law enforcement. Three news crews are entrenched near the gates, their cameras like unblinking eyes. The air is thick with hushed, urgent conversations and a palpable sense of dread. Tears stream down the faces of students clustered in anxious groups. The headmaster is in a tight huddle with three high-ranking police officers, their presence lending an even more unsettling gravity to the situation.

Curiosity battles with deep foreboding as we approach the nearest group of boys.

"Hey, guys," Tom says, his casual tone falling flat.

"Hi, Tom. Did you hear? It's Danny. Danny's gone missing," one of the boys replies, his voice flat. The name hangs in the air, cold and heavy.

"Really?" Tom echoes, his stare wide and disbelieving.

"Not a thing," another boy, Christopher, interjects. "Just like with Katie. All anyone's saying is that Danny didn't make it home yesterday. Seen leaving school, same as Katie was. Maybe… they've run off together?" He offers it as a weak possibility, but his eyes betray his doubt.

"Thanks, guys," Tom says, turning back to us, his face visibly paler.

"What in the world is going on around here?" Clare asks, a worried crease deepening between her eyebrows. "Now Danny's gone too... What if they've been kidnapped?"

We all shake our heads in unison. But my own worries are a tangled, darker knot. My mind snags on Kracis, on the way her unseen presence seemed to direct my attention to those woods. *If only I could find a moment to speak with her properly.* But using my emotional fragility as an excuse to sneak away for a chat with my demon familiar would land me in a world of trouble. John and Sarah would probably lock me in my room and throw away the key.

After registration, the two detectives enter our form room. They introduce a raft of new safety rules. The most significant is that we can only leave the school premises if a parent is physically waiting at the gates. Otherwise, we have to walk home in pre-approved groups, verified by a teacher with a register. It's a small comfort, knowing we'll be watching out for each other. Or, more accurately, that they'll be watching out for me, and I'll be pretending not to be the reason we might need it.

The rare burst of warmth from the sun inspires us to take our lunch outdoors, secretly hoping to catch any updates from the police search. Carrying my tray—pizza, chips, and a surprisingly crisp salad—I'm the first to step into the fresh air. I make my way to our usual table under the sprawling oak tree. For a moment, it's almost normal.

Then, just as I take my first bite, a faint whisper, like the brushing of silk against my mind, flickers through my thoughts.

'*Devika.*'

My breath hitches. "Kracis? I can barely hear you. What's wrong?"

'*I am losing the connection,*' her voice is thin, strained, like a distant radio signal. '*To maintain it, I must feed... a little... each day, until I have become accustomed to this plane. It fades quickly now.*'

Oh! A cold wave washes over me. *Feeding. Of course.*

'*May I? Or do you no longer require the connection?*' There's a faint, almost imperceptible note of vulnerability in her mental tone.

"No, it's... it's fine. Can you use the same cut? So people don't... notice."

'*Yes. That is possible. Thank you.*'

"Are you talking to yourself again?" Tom's voice cuts in, laced with that damnable concern.

Panic, cold and sharp, lances through me. I snatch my left arm down to my side. Almost instantly, I feel it—that familiar, icy touch gripping my forearm. I brace myself.

"I just had..." I begin, but as Kracis reopens the wound, a sharp, searing jolt of pain, far more intense than before, makes me suck in a breath through gritted teeth. My eyes water. As the faint sucking sensation begins, I manage to finish, my voice shaky, "...a song stuck in my head." I force a weak smile.

"Are you okay?" Tom presses, his brow furrowed. "You looked like you were in pain."

I fumble for a response, but Clare, thank god, has walked up behind him. "She cut her arm yesterday, remember?" she says smoothly, sliding onto the bench beside me and blocking Tom from doing the same. "Bet she just caught it again. Don't worry so much; she isn't going to keel over." She says it with a light chuckle, but her eyes, when they meet mine, are sharp with questions.

As Tom reluctantly moves to the other side, Clare leans in. "Everything okay, really?" she whispers.

"Yeah," I whisper back, my gaze flicking to my hidden arm. "It's just Kracis."

Her eyes dart around us. When her gaze drops, she sees the fresh slick of blood welling from the cut. Her breath catches. "Again?" she murmurs, dismay in her voice.

I Think I'm A Monster

"Yes," I whisper, acutely aware of Liz settling in next to Tom. "Need to keep up the connection."

"I don't like this, Dev."

"What don't you like?" Liz asks, her head tilting as her nostrils flare, just for a second, her brow tightening. *Can she actually smell my blood where Kracis has reopened the cut?*

"What's going on at this school?" Clare asks, quickly deflecting.

Kracis's grip on my arm suddenly releases. The cold spot begins to fade. '*Thank you,*' her voice says, clearer now, louder in my mind, resonating with a surprising sense of relief.

As we pick at our lunch, the conversation circles back to the disappearances. A knot of frustration tightens within me. I wish I could articulate the chilling certainty that's taken root in my soul.

Just as we're nearing the end of the break, an unsettling sound slices through the air. Sirens. Distant at first, then rapidly escalating. Then, a piercing scream echoes from the front of the school, sharp and raw with terror. It sends a jolt of ice through my veins.

Instinctively, we scramble to our feet and make our way towards the front gates. There's another scream, closer this time, more desperate. As we round the corner of the science block, I see a woman, her body contorted in grief, crouching over something on the pavement. An ambulance screeches to a halt. My heart hammers against my ribs.

Then the truth, cold and brutal, hits me. The woman is Mrs Armstrong, Katie's mum. She's cradling a small, still form in her arms, her face a mask of agony. It's Katie. Lifeless. Pale.

A choked gasp escapes my lips. My hand flies to my mouth. The synchronised screams of Clare and several other girls pierce the air. Police officers, their faces grim, begin to move towards the growing crowd, commanding us to retreat. In the sudden surge of bodies, panic washes over us. Teachers appear, trying to herd the frightened, jostling mass of students back.

The atmosphere is thick with cloying anxiety. Students are openly sobbing. Even Clare is visibly shaken, her eyes fixed on Katie's still form—so small, so pale, like a discarded porcelain doll on the unforgiving concrete. A knot of something cold and heavy twists in my stomach, unfurling like a dark, venomous flower. *My nightmare... it wasn't just a nightmare. I sensed her death. I felt her fear. Maybe... maybe if I hadn't dismissed it... could I have saved her?* The thought is a fresh stab of agony.

My gaze flicks to Liz. She stands at the edge of the frantic crowd, her expression unnervingly blank. She's just as outwardly unmoved as I am. If I feel like a monster for my lack of tears, for the cold dread coiling inside me, what does that make her?

While everyone is reeling, Liz chooses that exact moment to turn her unnervingly perceptive gaze on me. "Hey, Dev," she says, her voice cutting through the chaos with unnatural calm. "How did you cut yourself on your arm?"

My blood runs cold. "I... I don't know," I stammer. "Must have caught it on something. Why?"

"Just wondered," she replies, her eyes narrowed. "You've been acting... differently recently."

A chilling realisation settles over me: I am monumentally bad at this. At pretending. It's terrifyingly clear that John and Sarah have their doubts, and they've sicced their paranormal bloodhound on me to sniff out the truth. A desperate plan begins to form. I need to create distance, to pull away from Liz, and convince Clare, subtly, to follow my lead.

Later, we wait in a subdued, anxious silence in our form classroom. Miss Patterson enters, her face pale. "Everyone, please make your way to the main hall. Quietly."

We shuffle out, my friends and I instinctively lagging at the rear of the snaking procession—a defensive habit born of years of bullying, of being targeted for my silver-streaked red hair and unsettling eyes. My friends' quiet, unwavering solidarity, their choice to join me in my self-imposed exile at the back of the class, has always been a protective, albeit threadbare, cloak against the cold sting of isolation.

Once everyone is gathered in the oppressive silence of the main hall, the headmaster and the two detectives take the stage.

"As you are all now unfortunately aware," the female detective begins, her voice crisp, "we found Katie Armstrong while searching the woods for Danny Williams. Because of this, arrangements will be made for you to leave school via the rear entrance. We would prefer a parent to meet you. If not, you will be escorted home by a police officer."

She pauses, letting her words sink in. "Tomorrow," she continues, her voice hardening, "please adhere strictly to the safety plans. Do not travel to or from school alone. Not until we find this… this monster and ensure they can harm no one else."

At the word 'monster,' a cold, sharp dread pierces me. My breath catches. My heart hammers against my ribs. *They're hunting for me. I am the monster.* The room seems to tilt, the faces blurring.

"Dev, what's up?" Clare whispers urgently.

"What?" I manage, my voice a hoarse croak.

"You look terrified," she says, her eyes searching mine. "And you're biting your nails again, look."

I glance down. My thumbnail is trapped between my teeth. I snatch my hand away. Liz, sitting on Clare's other side, turns her head slowly, her unnervingly steady gaze landing on me. She doesn't say anything, but her cool, appraising eyes roam over my face, my trembling hands, like a scientist observing a particularly volatile test subject. She's looking for cracks in my façade, and I have the sickening feeling she's finding them.

Catherine M. Clark

Chapter 23:
The Nature of the Beast

After what feels like an eternity suspended in the grey, oppressive fog of the school assembly, I finally make it home. The journey is a strange tableau: me, Clare, Tom, and Liz, trailed by a uniformed police officer like a sombre, blue-clad shadow. The walk feels unnaturally long, each step heavy, the air thick with an awkward, unspoken tension. John and Sarah, with surprising ease, agreed to my walking back with my friends under escort. An odd mix of state-sanctioned comfort and profound unease settles over us.

Once inside, the click of the front door feels like a portcullis dropping. I head straight for my room, the familiar four walls a welcome shield. I quickly shuck off my school uniform, the fabric feeling tainted, and change into my favourite worn sweatpants and a soft, oversized T-shirt. My plan is simple: immerse myself in a book and stay there until Sarah gets back. However, as I perch on the edge of my bed, deciding to use the time to talk to Kracis, that familiar, unwelcome itch begins to prickle under my skin—the insistent, desperate surge of my creative urges—the need to draw.

It feels like an uncontrollable compulsion, a pressure building behind my eyes. I sigh, a ragged exhalation of defeat. I won't find a moment's peace until I honour the impulse. With resigned determination, I move to my desk, pull out my sketchbook and pencils, and inhale the grounding, earthy scent of paper and graphite.

Tucking my mobile deep into a drawer, a symbolic severing, I pause. Then, in a whisper that feels both pathetically hopeful and desperate, I call out, "Kracis? Are you here? If you are… can you keep me company?"

A subtle shift cools the air. Her ethereal shadow-form instantly materialises against the far wall, a shimmer of coalesced darkness that makes the very atmosphere crackle and hum.

'*Devika,*' her voice resonates in my mind, sharp with an urgency that strikes my core. '*I believe you are in far more danger than my master realises.*'

A cold knot tightens in my stomach. "I do too, Kracis, but there's not much I can do about what is going on."

'*We need to get you out of here, that's what we can do,*' Kracis says, almost sounding panicked.

"I can't leave till Cat says I can, she said it would raise too much concern with everyone, making it impossible for me to live a normal life with everyone looking for me," I say, resigned to the fact of my situation.

'*If I feel things are getting worse, I will go to her and beg for her to remove you from this place.*'

"Thank you," I breathe, my gaze locked on her swirling form. "Kracis… don't you ever get bored? Just… watching over me?"

Her shadowy head tilts. '*I find this realm… endlessly fascinating. The few fragmented memories I possess from my time here are starkly, violently different. This is the first occasion I have returned since my awakening in the underworld.*'

A shiver, cold and sharp, traces its way down my spine. "What… what exactly are you now?"

'*There are many names for what I have become. Most in your world, and mine, would refer to me as a Shade, or a Shadow Demon,*' she replies, her mental voice smooth, like polished obsidian.

I freeze. The pencil clatters from my numb fingers. Disbelief, cold and absolute, steals my breath. "Did you… did you say you're a demon?" The word tastes of ash and fear.

'*Yes. Why does this surprise you?*' Her tone is casual, as if commenting on the weather.

"I... I'm not sure," I stammer, my mind reeling. "I mean, aren't all demons inherently evil? I thought you were something Cat created."

'Not all demons are malevolent any longer. Not since Hecate and Lucifer took governance of the underworld. Things have... changed,' she explains, a subtle undercurrent of fierce loyalty in her tone.

"Wait, hold on." My head is spinning. "Are you seriously telling me that Lucifer... *the* Lucifer... is real? I thought Cat was joking about him."

'He is,' she affirms, seeming to lean closer.

"But... he's the Devil! The source of all evil!" I protest, my understanding of the universe crumbling.

'Lucifer is, in fact, a Daemon Archangel. One of the Firstborn,' she corrects me, her unseen gaze suddenly intense.

"Born?" My confusion deepens. "I thought a god created them."

'Created, born—it is all part of the same cycle. A cycle that, at its most fundamental level, often involves sex. Haven't you learned that fundamental truth of existence yet, child?' she presses, her mental voice tinged with something I can't decipher—amusement? Impatience?

"Yes! Of course, I've... been educated on that," I splutter, heat rising in my cheeks. "I just... I realise I know nothing about any of this." A swell of frustration and mortifying embarrassment washes over me.

'You will learn. In time,' she assures me. *'I can sense the power coursing through you, Devika. It hums like a captured star. It is clear why the wolves are drawn to you. But you are not what they anticipate. If they discovered what you truly are, they might perceive you as an unacceptable threat. One they would seek to eliminate. I have overheard their whispers; they intend to bring you into their pack*

before you turn eighteen. They believe taking you to their territory early will grant them full control.'

An icy dread sweeps through me. "Are you serious?" I whisper. "Control me?"

'I am sorry if my words have upset you,' she says, the crimson glow of her eyes seeming to soften.

"No, it's… okay," I exhale, trying to regain my composure. "I just… I hope Cat gets me out of here soon."

'I share that hope,' Kracis affirms. *'Especially since whatever… thing… that lurks in those woods is now killing children.'*

My heart hammers. "Is there… is there really a monster in there?" I ask, glancing towards the darkened trees visible from my window.

'I believe so,' she replies, her form becoming denser. *'And it appears to be a blood drinker. The unfortunate girl they discovered… she was completely drained. There was nothing left in her; she was utterly, horrifically bloodless.'*

I cross my arms tightly. "Great. Just what I need. Why can't Cat, or your Hecate, or even Lucifer just swoop in and handle this?"

She shakes her shadowy head. *'They are not permitted to interfere directly. The balance must be maintained. There are protectors here—shifters and witches who will step in. We also have Angelic Guardians. Until they arrive, you must be cautious.'*

"Can't you handle it?" I press. "Or are John and Sarah just letting children get killed?"

'I have my limitations, Devika. In direct confrontation, I am at a disadvantage. The wolf shifters here… they remain passive unless they perceive a direct threat to their pack. They do not truly care about humans, not beyond their potential use as… fodder.'

"Wonderful," I mutter. "Okay, one final question."

'Of course.'

"If you're a demon," I force the word out, "should I be letting you… drink my blood?"

'It is the only viable way for us to communicate. And I am certain you are far more powerful than I. A mere thimbleful of your blood can fully sustain me for an entire day. It is… remarkable.'

"Okay. Well, I'm glad you don't need much."

'As am I. To communicate with your friend, Clare, I would require significantly more.'

"Right. Well, let's not do that," I say quickly. "She isn't interested anyway."

'Let us not,' Kracis replies, followed by a strange, soundless, emotionless chuckle that makes a ghost of a smile touch my lips. Finding that small point of connection, I slip back into my drawing, the pencil gliding more smoothly across the paper.

I lose all track of time until the creak of my bedroom door jolts me back to reality. Adrenaline, sharp and cold, floods my system. It's Sarah, silhouetted in the doorway. My eyes dart around the room, but Kracis has vanished, leaving the air feeling oddly flat. I'm surprised by the pang of loss. I was actually starting to… enjoy her company.

Then, my gaze falls to the sketchbook. What I've drawn… it feels wrong.

"Hey, sweetheart. Are you okay?" Sarah asks, her warm hands settling on my shoulders. The touch, once comforting, now feels like the grip of a prison guard.

"Yeah. I'm fine," I reply, my voice too bright.

"I'm so sorry about that poor girl, Devika. I hope it didn't upset you too much."

"I didn't really know her," I admit. "Clare got a little upset, but I think she'll be okay."

"That's good," she says, her eyes sharp in the reflection of my window. "Oh, you've been drawing, haven't you?"

I hesitate, my heart sinking. "Um… yeah," I mutter, wishing I could snatch the book away.

"Who is that?" she inquires, leaning closer to study the

shadowy, tormented figures.

"Um... I think... I've drawn what it might feel like for Danny," I say quietly. "You know... scared, and trapped in the dark."

"Really? Why draw something so... dark?" she asks, her brow furrowed in a display of concern that feels manufactured. "It's very... intense. And who is that... thing... with him?"

"What?" I say, startled.

"There," she says, her finger tapping the page. "In the shadows, beside him."

I lean closer. It's not a person. It looks like the grotesque, elongated shadow of a monstrous snake, but one that has writhing, grasping arms. A cold dread trickles down my spine. I didn't consciously draw that. "I... I think I was trying to draw a snake," I improvise, my voice shaky, "but I mucked up the shading. I don't plan to keep this one."

"Well, I would still like to keep it and put it with the rest," Sarah says, her tone too saccharine. "However, I still don't understand why you would choose to draw something so profoundly dark."

I sigh, a deep, weary sound. "I guess I'm just... not exactly feeling all light and fluffy right now, am I?"

"Yes, I suppose not," she replies, a fleeting, unreadable expression on her face. "Have you finished it?"

I shake my head, the urge to rip the page from the book overwhelming. "Yeah, I guess," I hear myself say instead.

"That's good," she responds, a faint, almost predatory smile touching her lips. "I'll take it then, shall I? And scan it in."

"I'm really not bothered. You can throw it away."

"Don't be like that, Devika," she replies, a sharper note in her voice. "I will certainly not throw away one of your drawings."

I merely shrug, a leaden weight in my chest. Why did I draw that weird, armed snake? If I was going to unconsciously draw something monstrous, I would have thought it would have been a vampire, given what Kracis said about Katie.

As Sarah reaches over me to pick up the sketchbook, she asks, "Do you fancy burgers for dinner?"

"Yeah. Don't mind," I respond, my voice a little more animated.

"Hey, why are you biting your nails, Devika?" she asks suddenly, her voice sharp with disapproval.

I look down at my left hand and grimace. My nails are a wreck. "Sorry. I guess I'm just... anxious."

She nods, her expression softening into practised sympathy. "Try not to dwell on it, dear. It's terribly sad, but it's really the parents' responsibility, isn't it, to allow their child to walk alone like that? I just can't fathom going through something so utterly avoidable. But I have faith in you, Devika; you're wise enough never to put yourself in that kind of vulnerable position."

I stare at her, a silent gasp caught in my throat. Victim blaming, wrapped in a saccharine compliment. It's the nastiest, most callous thing I have ever heard her utter. "Yeah," is all I can manage, my voice a whisper, strangled by a surge of cold fury. I wish I had the courage to tell her exactly where to shove her condescending platitudes. *Maybe one day.* The thought is a small, bitter coal of anger glowing in my stomach.

"Good girl. I'll call you when I order the burgers," she says, her tone dripping with condescension. "And if you have homework, you'd better get started."

"I will," I reply through gritted teeth. With a final, dismissive pat on my shoulder that feels more like a shove, she strides out.

Left alone in the ringing silence, I begin to mechanically tidy my desk. The poisonous echoes of her words linger like a bad smell. With a sigh, I climb onto my bed and seek refuge in my book, having no desire to be around her suffocating negativity a moment longer than necessary.

Kracis

I remain cloaked in the deepest shadows, an unseen observer, as the shifter—Sarah—takes possession of Devika's drawing. A surge of incandescent fury, cold and sharp, courses through my ethereal form. The primal urge to manifest, to confront this deceiver, is almost overwhelming. Yet, a creeping doubt twists in my gut. Could I truly defeat this creature if it chose to shift?

The element of surprise is on my side. But the moment I reveal myself, it could strike back. The thought of it harming me is chilling, but the horrifying image of Devika in even greater peril because of my recklessness is worse. Perhaps the rational course is to return to the underworld, to plead for Hecate's intervention.

Yet, a deeper, more primal instinct holds me rooted here. I feel an inexplicable, burgeoning connection to this girl, this fragile, incandescent spark. It feels as if everything—the fate of worlds, perhaps—hangs in the delicate balance of her existence. Since tasting her blood, I have felt… different. Clearer. More focused. Her essence energises me in a way nothing else ever has. I haven't felt the gnawing hunger, the desperate need to kill, for days.

Is this… what feeling truly alive again is like? The thought is both terrifying and exhilarating.

Part of me, a newly hopeful part, wonders if Hecate intended for me to be Devika's permanent guardian. Hecate has always treated me with a certain detached warmth. But Devika… her unconscious kindness, her simple need for companionship, resonates deeply within me. I sense that she, beneath her fear, genuinely enjoys my otherworldly company. In many ways, we are kindred spirits, both ensnared by invisible chains.

For me, those chains began when I drew my last mortal breath uncounted centuries ago. Awakened in the underworld, I was brutally shackled to a demon of monstrous cruelty. It was Hecate who pulled

I Think I'm A Monster

me from that soul-crushing existence and offered me a new allegiance under her command. Yet, even this felt like another set of chains, gilded perhaps, but chains nonetheless.

Devika, my bright, unknowing Devika, also bears her own burdens, shackled by prophecies and deceptions she has only just begun to comprehend. I know with a grim certainty that awareness often comes with its own terrifying perils. My god, Hecate, is kind, in her own way, but she does not desire my company. Being around the raw, chaotic energies of demons in the underworld for so long nearly shattered my mind.

I am starting to feel a glimmer of hope, but I don't want to lose it. The only way that could happen is if I can convince my master to let me stay with Devika. I need to protect her. Perhaps... perhaps I can persuade her to run away. Then, just the two of us, we could stay together. Then, I could truly protect her from everyone. Even, if necessary, from Hecate herself. The thought, bold and treacherous, sends a thrill of defiant purpose through me.

I don't know how, but I am starting to feel again. Emotions, sharp and vivid, prick at my consciousness. That shouldn't be possible. I lost my soul to the darkness eons ago. *What... what in all the hells is happening to me?*

Devika

After I polish off the last of my burger, a heavy silence descends. John leans forward, his brow furrowed with that parental concern that sets my teeth on edge.

"Devika, I need to talk to you about your latest drawing," he says, his pale blue eyes eyeing me with apprehension.

"Why?" I retort, instantly wary. My stomach clenches.

"It... it worries me, sweetheart," he says. "I don't want you to get too caught up in what's happening. Why would you choose to illustrate something so dark?"

His words hang heavy and accusatory. "I... I don't know," I reply slowly. "They were just... on my mind. Sometimes I can't really control what comes out on the page."

John exchanges a quick, meaningful glance with Sarah. The look is freighted with unspoken concerns that exclude me entirely. I've stumbled into a conversational minefield.

"Can you tell me... did you feel that... that sensation again, before you created it?" John prods gently. "You remember? That strange feeling you tried to explain when you were little?"

His question blindsides me. I hoped they'd forgotten. The precursor to my more... unusual drawings. If they can see through my lies with such ease, how can I possibly explain the truth? The truth that sometimes I draw things in a trance, only to surface later and see, terrifyingly, what my hands have done?

"Well, Devika? Did you?" he presses, his tone hardening.

"As I mentioned," I begin, choosing my words with painstaking care, "they've both been occupying my thoughts. I had Danny on my mind, and where he might be. So I drew him cowering in the dark, looking scared, which could easily have snakes in it. The thought of being trapped in the dark with one of those things... that would definitely scare me, too." I offer a weak shrug.

His nostrils flare, just for a second. *He's trying to scent the lie.* A deep frown follows.

"All right, Devika," he finally replies, his voice neutral. A tiny wave of relief washes over me.

"Also," he continues, "I'll be picking up more of your medication tomorrow. You must be running quite low."

A tight, uncomfortable knot forms in my stomach. If this continues, they might discover I haven't been taking the damn things at all. Not all week.

"How have you been feeling, by the way, since your dosage was increased?" he asks, leaning in.

How am I supposed to answer that? "I've... been good, actually," I reply, injecting a cautious optimism I don't feel. "Better than usual. It's the best I've felt in years, honestly."

It's a carefully curated half-truth. Ever since I stopped taking their drug, I *have* felt the best I've ever felt. It has also, terrifyingly and exhilaratingly, allowed my body to begin to change, making the chronic pain finally disappear. Yet, a new, equally unsettling sensation has emerged in its place—a persistent, almost unbearable pressure building deep within me, as if my body is coiling for another profound, unknown transformation.

My response seems to lift his spirits. He breaks into a genuine smile. "That's wonderful to hear, Devika. Maybe... maybe we can even postpone that visit to the specialist."

The relief is immense. Now, I just need to work out what this unnerving pressure truly means. I really hope it just means I need to... shift, now and then. I don't think I can handle any more shocking surprises.

"I spoke to your headmaster today," John then says, his voice tinged with renewed concern. "He mentioned that, despite everything, you've been performing exceptionally well. He also filled me in on the missing children." He pauses, his gaze serious. "Given your exams are approaching, it's vital you don't miss any more school. Just remember, please, no one is allowed to go anywhere alone."

"Okay," I reply softly.

"And if you ever feel uneasy, Devika, staying home is always an option," he offers. "We can also... connect you with a nearby community. A group of our friends. They have children your age. You may discover some new friendships there."

A rising tide of sheer, unadulterated panic grips me. My heart accelerates. The notion of this 'community' looms like a dark, threatening cloud. It feels, with a chilling certainty, like a pack of wolves waiting to ensnare their prey. *If I go there, will I ever come back?*

Just as I struggle to formulate a response, a voice surges, unbidden and frantic, within my mind.

'*NO! Devika! Don't let them take you there!*' Kracis shrieks, her urgency an icy tidal wave that makes me physically jump in my seat, a startled gasp escaping my lips. Then, to my utter astonishment, she suggests something I've fleetingly, terrifyingly, thought about myself. '*Maybe… maybe you should think about running away, Devika. From all of this. Then I can truly help you.*'

The thought, echoing my own nascent fears, sends a perverse thrill of abject fear and intoxicating freedom through me.

I can't answer her. My involuntary jump doesn't go unnoticed—both John and Sarah give me concerned stares, casting quick glances at one another.

"I… I would prefer to stay in school, actually," I interject quickly, a little too loudly. "As you've both pointed out, getting good grades is crucial for a bright future, isn't it?"

John nods thoughtfully. "You're absolutely right, Devika. But please, if you ever need a break, just know that visiting our friends could be a very refreshing change of pace. Very good for you."

As he speaks, I catch a glimpse of Sarah's face. Her eyes have narrowed. She seems… less enthusiastic about the idea. The chilling snippet of conversation I'd overheard weeks ago floods back to me. Sarah hadn't wanted *this* to end sooner than planned. John had even said she'd become… attached to me.

Eventually, the tense dinner concludes. I escape back to my room, the door clicking shut like the entrance to a besieged fortress. The moment the door clicks shut, Kracis appears, her presence vibrating with nervous energy.

'*Devika, you must not let them take you there,*' she urges, her tone a desperate plea. '*You mustn't! If you do, I… I might never see you again. And they could... they could hurt you. Badly.'*

My heart races. Unable to speak, I rummage for a fresh sheet of paper and a pencil. My hands tremble as I scratch out a reply.

'Kracis, don't worry. I won't go there. I promise.'

'Okay, Devika. Okay,' she sighs in my mind, though the worry still clings to her voice. *'But I am genuinely, deeply concerned about what will happen if they manage to take you to their pack grounds.'*

A new need compels me. I erase my message and write again, pressing softer this time so it's easier to rub out. *'Thank you, Kracis. For caring. Are you okay? You seem... different tonight.'*

Kracis's shadow-form darts restlessly around the room. *'I... I think I am changing, Devika. Being with you... your blood... it is helping me to remember. To feel. It is... strange. Unsettling. But also... strangely freeing.'*

A peculiar warmth envelops me, a sense of shared strangeness. Yet, an undeniable unease stirs. What does it mean for her to be *changing*?

'I had better let you get on with what you normally do,' she adds reluctantly. *'Just know that I will always be around. But please, Devika, consider what I said. Consider getting out of here. Soon.'*

I nod slowly as her form begins to fade. I start to write, *'Thank you, Kracis. And I will,'* but I rub it out before she can perceive it. Some thoughts are too dangerous to even commit to paper. Just before she vanishes completely, I catch a fleeting glimpse of what appear to be... faint features. A hint of bone structure, the barest suggestion of eyes, something more substantial lurking beneath her usual amorphous exterior.

A bubble of intense curiosity swells within me. The next time I see Cat, I need to ask her about Shades, about what these changes might mean. In that moment, I realise with a startling clarity that a deeper connection is forming between us. It feels... strangely similar, in its intensity, its unspoken understanding, to how I feel about Clare.

My best friend. And a demon. My world is becoming a very strange place indeed.

Chapter 24:
Chains, Forged and Broken

When I swing open the front door the next morning, a sharp, chill breeze greets me, carrying the damp, earthy scent of freshly cut grass and something else… an undercurrent of ozone, like the air before a storm. Standing by our gate, a dark silhouette against the pale morning sky, is Liz. Her face is drawn, her composure tinged with concern. My heart gives a sickening lurch, then begins to race. *Why is she here? And why is she here alone?*

Just as my thoughts begin to spiral, a gentle hand lands on my shoulder, pulling me back with a jolt that almost makes me yelp.

"It's just me, sweetheart," Sarah says, her calm tone not quite masking her own tension. Of course, it still makes me jump out of my skin.

I let out a shaky breath. "Mum! Please don't sneak up on me like that; you nearly gave me a heart attack!"

"Sorry about that, dear," she chuckles, a strained sound that falls utterly flat. Her gaze shifts past me to Liz, and the warmth in her expression falters. "Hey, Liz. I really do appreciate you doing this," Sarah adds, her gratitude feeling too forced.

"My pleasure, Mrs Lorcan," Liz replies, offering a polite smile that doesn't reach her eyes.

"What's going on?" I ask, the words clipped, irritation bubbling in my chest.

Sarah takes a deep, deliberate breath. "I called Liz's mother this morning," she says, her tone matter-of-fact. "We've arranged for

Liz to be here for you every school day. She'll walk with you to your meeting point with Clare and Tom until this whole… messy situation… blows over."

Her words settle heavily in the tense air. A suffocating mix of white-hot anger and cold, creeping fear coils in my gut. I cross my arms tightly. "Why?" I protest, my voice rising. "Nothing is going to happen between here and where I meet Clare. It's a short walk!"

"We just want to be cautious, Devika," Sarah insists, her eyes attempting a soft, pleading look I no longer trust. "And besides, having your best friend along might make you feel a bit better, don't you think?"

Best friend. The words are a bitter mockery. We're more like frenemies in some unspoken cold war. It's like they've deliberately forged another chain, heavy and cold, and clamped it firmly around my ankle, adding to all the others weighing me down.

"Okay," is all I manage to grit out. There's no point arguing. I start walking, brushing past Liz at the gate without a word. I feel her eyes on me, then on my mother. More proof, if any were needed, that they're all conspiring against me.

We traverse the dew-kissed park in an uneasy, crackling silence. As we approach the wrought-iron gate where I meet Clare and Tom, Liz suddenly halts. Her entire demeanour shifts, quiet contemplation replaced by a fierce determination.

With a strength that is both surprising and deeply unsettling, she seizes my right arm, her grip like steel. The sheer force she uses is jarring, far more powerful than I'd expect from a girl her size. It's just more chilling, undeniable proof that she is not entirely human.

"Dev, what the hell is your problem?" she demands, her voice taut.

I feign ignorance, shrugging casually. "Don't know what you mean, Liz."

Her eyes narrow, sharp and piercing. "Don't act stupid with me, Devika. You know exactly what I'm talking about," she presses, her voice lowering. "You've got a big issue with me. I saw your reaction when your mother—who, by the way, is just trying to protect you—said I'd walk with you."

Now Liz is trying to add mental chains to the physical ones. Well, it's not going to work. Not anymore. I have to come up with something plausible.

"Honestly, Liz, is it safe for *you* to walk all the way to my house alone?" I say, trying to sound earnest. "You're putting yourself at risk. Tom lives much closer. It makes more sense for him to meet me. It's safer for everyone."

"For starters," she replies, her expression sceptical, "your parents don't know Tom's family. Or Clare's. They only trust my family."

How could she be so certain? "Fine," I say, trying to regain control. "Here's the deal. I'll ask Tom to meet me. You and Clare can walk together, since you live closer anyway."

She crosses her arms, shaking her head. "Your parents won't agree to that, Devika."

"I honestly don't care what they'll agree to anymore," I shoot back, a surprising surge of rebellion rising within me. "This is about everyone's safety. Not just mine. And I'm ready to fight for that." I stare her down, hoping I look more resolute than I feel.

When I don't back down, I see Liz's body seem to slump, a subtle deflation of her aggression. "Fine. Whatever," she says, her voice flat. "But something about you has definitely changed recently, Devika. You're... different."

Crap! A wave of pure panic surges through me. I am absolutely, monumentally failing at this. Drama class was never my forte, despite John and Sarah insisting I had to do well in it, just like in all my other classes. The way they push me so hard to do well at school is just another form of control, another invisible chain to keep me too busy to ever work out the truth of what they are. What I am.

"Maybe I'm just... maturing, Liz," I reply, my casual tone not quite landing. "Everyone evolves. To be honest, I've noticed you've changed, too. And I don't really feel the same closeness between us. It's like we're starting to drift apart." The words are out before I can stop them, a desperate gamble.

Her reaction catches me completely off guard. Raw fear and genuine surprise flash across her face. "I... I agree that people can change," she says slowly, her voice wavering. "But I... I feel deep within me, we're... we're destined to be friends. Forever." She adds the last part with a faint, forced smirk that fails to mask the desperation in her eyes.

Her words are a chilling threat. The idea of being bound to her for eternity feels less like a promise and more like a life sentence. Running away, as Kracis suggested, seems to be the only other escape. But could I truly handle that?

"Time will tell, Liz. Come on," I urge, starting to walk again.

As we near the gate, I spot Clare and Tom waiting. A visible wave of relief washes over their faces when they see me, but when they realise Liz is trailing in my wake, the atmosphere shifts. Clare looks worried, while Tom just looks utterly confused.

"Morning," I greet, forcing a casual note into my voice.

"Yeah, morning," Tom replies, his eyes narrowing on Liz. "Liz? Why are you coming from Dev's direction?"

"Well, for the record, Tom," Liz replies sharply, "Devika's parents called mine and specifically asked for me to walk with her. For safety."

"Really? That's... strange," Clare says, her voice tinged with a concern that mirrors my own. I can practically hear her unspoken question: *Is she spying on you for them?* The answer is yes.

"It's a bit out of your way though, isn't it, Liz?" Clare continues, crossing her arms.

"Yeah, well, it's what you do for a friend," Liz responds, her voice laced with a false sweetness that makes my skin crawl.

"Yes, and as we just discussed," I say, deliberately turning to

Tom. "Would you be up for…"

"Yes! Of course, I will!" Tom interjects enthusiastically before I can even finish. He shoots a small, triumphant smirk in Liz's direction.

"Thank you, Tom," I say with a genuine smile of relief.

"It just makes more sense, practically speaking, if Clare and Liz walk together and I walk with you," I say.

But Clare doesn't look happy. "I really don't think that's necessary," she says, her voice tight as she shoots a venomous glare at Liz. When her attention shifts back to me, her expression morphs into something that feels more like deep concern—or perhaps, disturbingly, even fear.

"Clare, please," I say, trying to sound optimistic. "For now, for all of our safety, this is our best option. Hopefully, it won't last for long."

Clare finally, reluctantly, relents. "Fine. Sure. Whatever."

Tom, on the other hand, is practically revelling in the new arrangement, a goofy grin plastered across his face. Maybe it's not the smartest choice, given his crush, but it's the lesser of two evils. The alternative—being alone with Liz—is something I'm definitely not ready to face.

The police presence around the school is significantly heightened. Uniformed officers stand at every entry point, their grim faces lending a palpable tension to the air. Yet inside, the atmosphere is eerily subdued. It was decided when we were sent home that the lower years would be kept home for a few days, as they feared the younger kids are more likely to wander off as they don't fully understand the situation. This has left the hallways unusually empty and silent today.

I find a strange, fleeting comfort in diving headfirst into my favourite subjects, the familiar routine a welcome distraction. However, I'm grappling with a pressing issue. The pressure within me, that coiled, restless energy I now recognise as the precursor to change, is like a physical weight. It's building significantly, amplified by the stress, the confrontations, the constant fear. The only way I can think to alleviate it is to shift. To let whatever is inside me out, even for a short while. But attempting this at home is impossible. I have to take a risk. I have to find a way to do it here, at school.

The school bathrooms give me a sliver of hope. They each have a larger, private cubicle for disabled students. Given the reduced student numbers, it seems like the best, perhaps only, chance I have. The real challenge is timing. I have to wait until the very end of the lunch break, when the corridors are quietest.

As luck, or misfortune, would have it, a sudden downpour forces us all indoors. The cafeteria is a cacophony of chatter, with Katie and Danny being the main topic of morbid fascination. The strain is visible on Tom's pale face; he knew Danny from the football team. He sits mostly silent, his food untouched.

My own stomach churning, I hastily push my barely-touched food around my plate, shovelling some of it into my mouth. I have to concoct a plausible excuse for a bathroom escape. The pressure is becoming almost unbearable. I know, with a certainty that borders on panic, that I have to act swiftly, before something… snaps.

Setting down my fork with a clatter, I rise abruptly. "I'll… catch up with you guys back in class," I call over my shoulder, my heart hammering.

"Where are you going, Dev?" Clare asks immediately, her brow furrowed with suspicion.

"Just… popping to the bathroom," I reply, attempting to keep my voice steady. "Be right back."

"I can come with you," she offers instantly, her eyes wide. *The new rules.*

"No! No, it's okay, really. I won't be long," I insist, forcing a tight smile as I make my hasty exit.

I don't head to the nearest bathroom. Instead, I veer off towards the far end of the maths block, where it should be deserted. When I finally reach it, I push the door open cautiously and check each of the standard cubicles. Empty. With a sigh of relief, I slip into the larger disabled cubicle and bolt the door.

I take a few deep breaths, then hastily take off my jumper and starchy white shirt. I leave my bra on, hoping it won't be an issue. I try to focus, to remember how to let the change happen. The last time was largely uncontrolled.

I can feel the power thrumming inside me, a restless, captive thing. I focus on it, running the intention through my mind: *I want to change. I need to shift.* Nothing happens. Frustrated, I focus harder on the insistent pressure and then, startlingly, I see it—a door in my mind's eye. It's intricately carved, ancient-looking, and pulsing with a faint, internal light. Intrigued, without a second thought, I mentally open it.

An overwhelming, almost euphoric sensation washes over me, like a crushing weight being instantly lifted from my soul. The relief is dizzying. The first thing I notice is the distinct, almost ticklish feeling of movement in my back. Then comes a sharp, pulling change in my mouth. My canines elongate, sharpen. I have to force my lips apart slightly to avoid the newly emerged, razor-sharp fangs piercing my bottom lip.

In a dizzying whirlwind of disbelief and burgeoning awe, I turn, craning my neck to glance over my shoulder. And there they are— massive, magnificent wings unfurling from my back, the slate grey feathers casting a vast, imposing shadow in the cramped space. The sight is both utterly terrifying and profoundly, breathtakingly surreal. A part of me still wishes for the ethereal, feathered wings I'd seen on the reaper that night, but these are undeniably impressive. Powerful.

I'm relieved to find that the world around me remains unaffected. My vision is normal, not showing the raw, unfiltered essence of things. I couldn't shake the deep-seated anxiety that comes with the thought of seeing people's souls, their auras—how it might irrevocably skew my perception. People make mistakes; those missteps don't inherently define them as bad people. Take Kracis. Despite her demonic heritage, she exudes a surprising kindness, a protectiveness. Her past doesn't encapsulate who she is choosing to be now. I don't want to dismiss the genuine light in others just because their souls momentarily flicker in shades of grey.

I'm so lost in these complex, unsettling thoughts that I don't hear the distinct sound of the main bathroom door creaking open.

Chapter 25
The Shape of the Secret

"Dev? Devika, are you in here?"

A hesitant, familiar voice ricochets off the tiled surfaces, making me jump. Suddenly, before I can respond, I hear a sharp exclamation from just outside my cubicle.

"What the hell is that? Is that… feathers?"

Panic, pure and undiluted, surges through me. My mind scrambles. I instinctively reach for that mental door, finding it much quicker this time. I forcefully envision it slamming shut. Miraculously, it closes with shocking ease. In a matter of terrifyingly swift moments, my wings retract, vanishing back into my body. My fangs slide back smoothly into my gums.

"Hey! What's going on in there? It sounded like… like wings were flapping! Huge ones!" Clare's voice, sharp with shock and dawning suspicion, pierces through my anxious thoughts.

The adrenaline coursing through my veins makes that mental door tremble. I have to stay calm. I steady my breath. "Hey, Clare! Uh, I'll be out in just a minute. What… what brings you all the way down here?"

There's a moment of charged silence. "I… had forgotten we aren't allowed to go anywhere alone," she says, her tone a confusing mix of concern and relief. "I started to worry when I couldn't find you. But seriously, Dev, what did I just see? And hear? Was that… you?"

Her questions hang heavy and accusatory. *Crap, crap, crap! How do I explain this away?*

"Devika… you really do have wings?" Clare asks then, her voice suddenly laced with an unexpected, almost breathless mix of childlike curiosity and genuine excitement. "Because if you do, that's… that's actually kind of cool, you know?"

At her astonishing words, a fresh wave of disbelief washes over me. Without thinking, I fling the cubicle door open. The cool air rushes in as I stand there, horrifyingly aware that I'm only in my bra. Her eyes widen, taking in my state of undress. For a long, suspended moment, I can't determine her expression—worry? Fear? Disgust?

"Clare, I… I don't know what you mean," I reply weakly, my heart racing like a runaway train.

"Devika, am I your best friend, or not?" she presses, her voice trembling with an undeniable urgency, with hurt. The simple, direct question resonates with the profound weight of our entire friendship. I see a desperate plea for honesty in her eyes that makes my heart ache with guilt.

I'm torn, agonizingly, between the terrifying truth and the paralysing fear of losing her. My panic surges, a tidal wave of dread making my legs tremble so uncontrollably I fear they'll buckle. My stress levels, already dangerously high, shoot through the roof.

And then, the absolute worst-case scenario unfolds.

Clare takes a sharp, involuntary step back. The expression on her face is contorting into one of profound disbelief and dawning fear. Her mouth falls open in a silent, horrified gasp. In that terrible moment, I see the bright, trusting light in her eyes dimming, and it feels as though my own heart is shattering along with our bond.

I try to stop it, but it's too late. The wings, my monstrous, magnificent wings, burst back out, unfurling in all their shadowy glory. My fangs emerge much quicker, more aggressively, a primal, fear-triggered response. The sharp points push painfully against my lower lip as I clamp my mouth shut, trying to hide them, trying not to scare her even more.

As if it couldn't get any worse, Kracis suddenly materialises between us, her imposing figure now somehow clearly, terrifyingly visible to Clare. Her shadowy hands transform into wickedly sharp claws, her fingers elongating into tapered points that I know from painful experience are razor sharp.

'Devika! You are in grave danger!' Kracis states, her mental voice urgent, cutting through my panic. *'We need to flee! Now! Before she has the chance to expose you! Or... or I could handle the situation myself. Permanently.'*

The unspoken threat sends a fresh wave of ice through my veins. "No!" I cry out, my voice hoarse. "No, Kracis, you won't do anything! Clare... Clare won't expose me! Will you, Clare? You wouldn't!" I implore, pouring every ounce of my fading hope into the question.

Clare stands frozen, her eyes darting between Kracis's threatening form and my enormous wings. Kracis shifts protectively in front of me, raising her clawed hands. Clare flinches.

"Clare! Are you okay? Please... say something! If you don't, I... I might have to run," I urge, my voice laced with desperation.

The silence stretches, taut and unnerving, until my words finally seem to break through her shocked stupor. She blinks rapidly. "No! No, Dev, please... please don't run," she pleads, her voice shaky but clear, her eyes wide with a worry that seems to outweigh her fear.

A massive, shuddering wave of relief washes over me. Kracis's presence somehow steadies me. I feel my mental barriers strengthening, that internal door becoming more solid, allowing me, with a surge of will, to reclose it once more. My wings retract, folding back into me, their slate grey colour fading like mist.

Once they vanish, Clare finally meets my gaze, her expression now filled with an overwhelming, consuming curiosity. "Why... why didn't you tell they were so beautiful, Dev?" she asks, her voice steady but edged with disappointment.

"I... I was scared, Clare," I admit, the words a whisper.

"Scared? Scared of me? Why?"

"Clare, I... I'm not human. Not fully. Of course, I was scared!" I reply, the full weight of that truth finally spoken aloud. I fumble with my discarded shirt, my hands trembling so violently I can't manage the buttons. Clare, noticing me struggling, hesitantly steps forward. She gently slaps my fumbling hands away and, with surprising tenderness, starts to button up my shirt for me. I feel incredibly vulnerable, exposed, and utterly unworthy of her kindness.

"Devika," Clare says softly, finishing the last button. "I would never do anything to harm you. You have to know that." I see a flicker of that initial fear in her eyes transform, shift, into something deeper—perhaps awe, perhaps understanding.

'Devika, you must learn to conceal your wings from ordinary human eyes,' Kracis interrupts our fragile moment. *'I was not aware you even possessed the ability to reveal them so openly. One usually requires a special sight to perceive them; humans can't see most of the paranormal world.'*

How would I know? I say frustratingly to myself. *It's not like I've had any guidance.*

"What... what is she saying?" Clare asks, her gaze fixed on Kracis.

"She... she said that normally, humans shouldn't be able to see wings."

"Oh! Yeah, I think I've read about that. Glamours, or something?" Clare muses. "Okay, I think I understand."

"Well, at least someone does," I mutter.

'How did you manage to access your change so deliberately?' Kracis inquires.

"There's... a door. In my mind," I explain, unsure of how much to divulge.

'Are there any... markings? Any symbols, on this door?' Kracis presses.

I close my eyes, seeking that inner sanctum. When I find the door, an image, startlingly clear, flickers to life upon its surface—a breathtakingly detailed rendering of a pair of majestic wings, just like my own. I mentally reach out, and the image shimmers, simplifying into a stark, clean outline, like the imprint on my back.

"Devika? What's going on?" Clare asks, pulling me from my trance.

"I... I think I just figured out how to hide my wings," I finally say.

"Really? That's amazing! You should try it! Right now!"

I shake my head firmly. "No. It's too risky. Someone could walk in. We've been in here for ages."

Clare's face falls with disappointment. I look at her crestfallen face. I need to ask her for my own state of mind, for absolute reassurance if she is really okay with me being the monster I know I am. "Clare. Seriously. Are we... are we good? Will you keep my secret? All of it?"

"Yes! Yes, of course, I will! You idiot! You're my best friend!" she replies fervently. She attempts to give me a hug, but Kracis moves in between us, pushing Clare away from me.

"Kracis, it's okay. She isn't a danger to me," I reassure my guardian.

'*Okay, Devika,*' Kracis replies, her mental voice tinged with a faint hint of something like... sadness? With a fluid, almost mournful motion, she melts back into the shadows.

In an overwhelming rush of emotion, Clare flings herself at me, her arms wrapping around me in a fierce hug. She starts to laugh, a wild, shaky sound muffled as she buries her face in my neck. "You silly, silly bitch," she whispers, her voice thick with tears and laughter.

"I'm so sorry, Clare," I choke out, my own tears finally falling. "I was just so scared you wouldn't be able to handle it all at once." I cling to her, feeling the tight, painful knot of anxiety in my stomach finally begin to unravel.

"You know you can trust me with anything, Dev," she reassures me, her voice strong despite her own tears. She pulls back slightly, her gaze intense. "On that note… is there anything else you want to share? Any other massive, life-altering secrets?"

I sigh, a shaky sound. "Not that I can tell you right now. But… yes. I do have fangs as well. Just so you know."

"Yeah, I know about the fangs. You didn't hide them very well when you were yelling at Kracis," she replies, a watery smile touching her lips. "But otherwise… that's fair enough. I get it."

"I'm really, really glad you know, Clare. I've felt so incredibly, desperately lonely," I admit, wrapping my arms around her again. I pull away quickly, self-consciously wiping the moisture from my eyes.

But Clare is crying freely now. "Hey, hey, there's no need to cry," I say softly, my heart aching for her.

I grab my discarded jumper, pulling it on, then reach for my bag. "Come on," I say, gently tugging her arm. "Let's wash your face. If we don't get back to class soon, Liz is definitely going to come looking for us."

"Yeah," Clare sniffles, wiping her eyes with her sleeve. "That's the absolute last thing we need." A small, watery smile breaks through her sadness.

A soft chuckle rolls off my lips, and Clare soon joins in, her own laughter mingling with mine. The crushing weight of our worries seems to lift, if only for a moment, thanks to the enduring, now irrevocably altered, strength of our friendship.

"I really hope this woman, Cat, works something out soon, Dev," Clare says, her voice serious again as we make our way to the door.

"Me too, Clare. Me too," I reply. "At least I have Kracis watching my back. And now that you're in on my not-so-little secret… everything feels like it'll be so much easier to handle."

My words hang in the air, a fragile blend of anxiety and overwhelming relief. I hope, with every fibre of my being, that her presence, her acceptance, her unwavering light, can pierce the oppressive darkness that has been steadily building inside me. It feels, with a certainty that is both surprising and incredibly liberating, like one of the many heavy, invisible chains that have been shackling me for so long has finally, blessedly, been removed.

Catherine M. Clark

Chapter 26:

The Walls Close In

As Clare and I step out of the bathroom, the dimly lit corridor feels suddenly ominous. Just as we start walking, I catch a fleeting glimpse of a figure—a girl—vanishing around the far corner. It's just a flash of dark hair and a navy-blue jumper, but it leaves an unsettling lurch in my stomach. My heart, already thrumming, begins to race with a fresh, sharp anxiety. *Was someone lingering outside? Did they overhear us?* The thought twists into a cold, hard knot. My mind immediately, terrifyingly, conjures the image of Liz.

"Did you see that?" Clare whispers, her voice tight with a shared panic.

"I did," I reply, trying to inject a calm I don't feel. "But let's not jump to conclusions. It could have been anyone." *But it felt like Liz.*

"I just really hope whoever it was didn't hear anything important," she says, her teeth worrying her bottom lip.

"Me too," I admit, my gaze drawn back to that corner, which, I note with another jolt of unease, is the direction one takes to head towards our form class.

Suddenly, Clare playfully but firmly slaps my arm. "Hey! Stop that right now."

"Stop what?" I snap, my nerves frayed beyond endurance.

"You started to bite your nails again, Dev," she points out with a look of worry.

I sigh, a ragged exhalation of defeat, glancing at my offending hand. "Sorry, Clare. I guess all of this is just really getting to me."

"Don't let it," she urges, her tone turning unexpectedly serious. "You have me. And Kracis. And don't forget Cat. I promise you, Dev, we'll do our absolute best to figure out a way to keep you safe. We will."

A cold wave of realism washes over me. "Clare, please don't make promises you can't keep."

"Doing my best is the best promise I can make, Dev. I might not always succeed, I know that. But I will try my hardest. Always. Okay?" She looks at me so earnestly with a fierce, unwavering determination shining in her eyes.

"Okay," I say, a lump forming in my throat. I pull her into a quick, awkward side hug, immensely grateful. Knowing I'm not completely alone is a small, but deeply comforting, mercy.

As we step into our classroom, a wave of relief washes over me—we aren't the last ones to arrive. I quickly scan the faces, but no one gives us a peculiar look. We make our way to our usual seats at the back, spotting Tom and, to my immediate unease, Liz. Their eyes lock onto us the moment we approach. I notice an unusual, almost unnatural spark of... happiness?... on Liz's face that sends an icy shiver down my spine. This morning, she was hostile. This sudden shift feels deeply wrong.

Once we take our seats, my heart sinks as Tom, oblivious, breaks the silence. "I thought the three of you were together in the bathroom."

"What do you mean, Tom?" Clare asks, her expression shifting instantly to open alarm.

"Liz went to find you both. She said you'd been gone for ages. She only got back in here a minute or so before you two did," Tom explains, confused.

"Well, I didn't find them, did I? So I just came straight to class—sue me," Liz interjects, her tone airy, almost aggressively nonchalant. But the unnatural, knowing gleam in her eyes, the slight, smug upturn of her lips, feels utterly, terrifyingly wrong.

A cold, sickening certainty floods me. *It was Liz.* What did she overhear? Had she been standing outside the bathroom door, silently eavesdropping? As raw panic courses through me, I mentally replay our entire exchange. Strangely, I recall each detail with a chilling clarity my memory never had before. Clare shoots me a quick, terrified look from the corner of her eye, her knuckles white where she grips the table.

"What's the issue, guys?" Tom inquires, looking confused as he always does.

"Nothing!" Clare replies quickly as Mrs Davison enters the classroom, her brisk footsteps indicating to the class to stop our chatter.

My mind, however, is a million miles away from Shakespeare for the rest of the day. I steal furtive glances at Liz, trying to gauge her expressions for any hint of what she might know. The gnawing uncertainty is eating away at me. The one glimmer of fragile hope is the conspicuous absence of Kracis's familiar warning: 'Shifter coming.' If Liz had caught anything truly significant, wouldn't Kracis have alerted me? Perhaps she only caught a fleeting snippet. But even that feels profoundly ominous.

By the time the final bell shrills, anxiety is knotted so tightly in my stomach at the thought of returning home that I feel physically sick. The others—Clare, Tom, and a conspicuously quiet Liz—keep pace beside me, their collective silence a strange comfort.

As we pass the brooding woods, bright yellow police tape flutters eerily from the trees, a stark reminder of the threat lurking nearby. I catch sight of uniformed officers combing slowly through the underbrush. For the first time in days, I don't feel like I'm being watched from within those shadowed depths. Perhaps whatever malevolent presence was prowling there has finally gone. Or perhaps, more chillingly, it's simply biding its time.

When we reach the park gate, Clare pulls me into a quick, warm embrace. "It will be okay, Dev. We'll figure this out," she murmurs, her words a soothing balm. She turns to Liz, a new urgency in her tone. "Come on, Liz."

"What?" Liz replies, her gaze distant.

"The new arrangement? We have to walk together now," Clare insists, frustration creeping into her voice.

"Oh. Right. But I really should walk Dev back home," Liz counters, her excuse flimsy.

"Liz!" Clare responds, her voice sharp with exasperation. "That makes no sense! Tom lives near Dev. If you don't come with me, I'll have to walk home alone. Are you really going to be that selfish and put other people at risk?"

After a long, charged moment, Liz grudgingly relents, muttering a barely audible, "Fine," before turning and walking off at a brisk clip. Clare rolls her eyes, gives me a quick, apologetic shrug, and sprints to catch up.

"Liz is acting really strange today, isn't she?" Tom remarks as we push open the creaky iron gate.

"She really is," I agree. "And… thanks again for coming with me, Tom."

"It's no trouble at all, Devvy. I'm glad to help," he says, offering a small, encouraging smile.

"Well, I appreciate it," I reply. "Just… stay safe yourself, once you leave me, okay?" Tom really is a genuinely nice guy. Maybe… maybe in another, simpler life, I might have risked our comfortable friendship for something more.

"I will, Dev. I promise." On impulse, I slip my arm through his, placing my hand lightly on his forearm. The simple action seems to light up Tom's face with a surprised, boyish delight I've never seen before. It's… sweet.

The park is unnervingly quiet. The usual cheerful sounds of children and dogs are conspicuously absent, leaving an expectant stillness in their wake. The heavy, unseen weight of the missing children looms over everything like a dark cloud.

When we finally reach the gate leading to my street, I pause. Turning to Tom, I mumble a hasty goodbye, but he lingers, an uncharacteristic hesitation in his eyes. For a brief, heart-stopping second, he edges closer, his gaze dropping to my lips. I have the sudden, overwhelming feeling that he's going to kiss me. My mind screams, *Please don't! Not here! Not in full view of my house!*

Just as suddenly, he moves back, a faint blush colouring his cheeks, and says a quick, flustered goodbye. As I watch him leave, he gives a shy wave, casting one last lingering glance over his shoulder. A sharp pang of... guilt? Regret?... comes over me, swiftly followed by the confusing, traitorous wish that he *had* kissed me. *Damn it, Devika! What is wrong with you? My life is in danger, and now I'm suddenly starting to like that Tom has a massive crush on me?* My priorities are clearly shot to hell.

I stand at the crossroads, my home on one side, a slim, terrifying chance of freedom on the other. With a deep, shuddering breath, I steel myself and start the lonely walk, each step heavier than the last, utterly uncertain of what awaits me behind that familiar, yet suddenly threatening, front door.

I let myself into the house and immediately hear the unmistakable sounds of Sarah bustling in the kitchen. Today, I feel a strange, detached resolve. I don't rush upstairs. I'm going to face whatever is coming, head-on.

Pushing open the kitchen door, I see Sarah methodically putting away groceries. "Need any help, Mum?" I ask, trying to keep my tone casual.

"Hey, darling! That would be wonderful, thank you," she replies with a bright, overly warm smile.

I begin sorting through the shopping bags, my hands moving automatically.

"How was school today, dear?" she inquires, her voice filled with that cloying, maternal concern I now know is utterly fake.

"It was... almost back to normal," I answer. "But the school still felt very empty."

"Hopefully, this whole unpleasantness won't go on for much longer," she says with breezy, unfounded optimism.

"I hope not," I say softly. Seizing the moment, I decide to share my news. "Mum?"

"Yes, dear?"

"I wanted to thank you for arranging for Liz to meet me. But it doesn't make much sense for safety. Liz lives closer to Clare, so it's more logical for them to walk together. And if Tom walks with me, it's safer for everyone. So… I went ahead and changed it today. Tom will be meeting me from now on." I deliver the speech calmly, factually.

I can see the gears turning in her mind. Her eyes narrow. She doesn't look happy. "Is that the only reason, Devika?"

"What other reason could there be?" I ask, screwing up my eyes in exaggerated confusion.

"A reason like… you might actually like the boy, perhaps? You know how we feel about boyfriends, Devika. You need to wait until you're at least eighteen." Her tone is teasing, but edged with a serious warning.

"No! Of course not! He's just a friend!" I insist, a hot rush of indignation washing over me. But then, traitorously, the fleeting image of Tom being my boyfriend sends a strange, warm energy coursing over my body.

She shifts uncomfortably, a flash of annoyance passing over her features. "Well, in any case, when the time is right, *we* will introduce you to someone nice. Someone suitable."

The moment the words escape her lips, I recognise the profound, unintended truth they reveal. My heart leaps with the silent, triumphant urge to shout, *Yes! I bloody knew it!* It's a small, crucial victory. She just confirmed, in part, what Cat warned me about.

Feigning nonchalance, I play along. She averts her gaze. "Anyway," she says, her back now partially to me, "we would still prefer Liz to be the one. But… I guess we can see how it goes with

Tom. For now."

"Okay. I was just trying to think about everyone's safety."

"You're right, dear. We just... don't know him well enough. And your father will undoubtedly think you're doing this for... other reasons."

In my distraction, I stumble headfirst into a conversational minefield. "Well, if you'd ever let my friends come over, even just once, you would have had a chance to get to know him properly," I blurt out, instantly, bitterly, regretting the words. I squeeze my eyes shut. *What have I just done?*

"You know why we don't allow your friends over, Devika," Sarah's voice is suddenly cold, sharp. "This is our home. Our private space. Not some teenage hang-out."

"I know, Mum. I'm sorry. I'm just feeling a bit overwhelmed."

"That doesn't give you the right to challenge our rules. Our decisions are made for your benefit."

"I get it. I just... thought you'd want me to feel... happy," I blurt out, the raw words tasting like ash.

Sarah turns to me, a strange, fleeting sadness in her eyes. "Of course... *I* want you to be happy, Devika. Of course I do. But... are you saying that you're not?"

I notice her emphasis on the 'I' instead of 'We.' Having already opened this dangerous door, I feel compelled to step through it. "I often feel a deep, aching sense of loneliness, Mum. We don't spend any real, quality time together outside of school. But I suppose, as you've often reminded me, it's not unusual for teenagers, is it?"

Her expression turns sombre. "I'm... truly sorry to hear that, Devika. It must be... very difficult. But... it won't be for much longer now, will it? Till we m..... I mean, I'm confident you'll find new friends. In the future."

Something about the way she stumbled—*Till we m...*—makes my blood run cold. My mind instantly, terrifyingly, fills in the blank:

Move. It sounds like it's going to happen really soon. That's twice now she has seriously messed up.

I fall into a heavy, brooding quiet as I finish putting away the shopping. I can feel her eyes flickering towards me, her constant, oppressive presence making me acutely uncomfortable. Once we're done, I turn to leave. "I'm going to go and change. And read for a bit."

"Okay, dear. I'll call you when dinner is ready," she replies, her tone attempting a casualness that feels utterly false.

I make my escape. The moment my bedroom door closes, I climb into my cosiest pyjamas, craving the sweet, temporary oblivion of sleep. Yet, a different, darker, more desperate plan is already beginning to simmer just beneath the surface of my thoughts.

Chapter 27:
The End of All This

After a dinner thick with unspoken tension, I retreat to my room, leaving the door slightly ajar. I need to listen. For phone calls, for hushed conversations, for anything that might reveal what they know. I pray, with a desperation I haven't known I possessed, that things don't somehow manage to get any worse.

About an hour later, as I lie on my bed, feigning sleep, a familiar, jarring sound breaks the heavy stillness—a notification ping from a mobile phone downstairs. I focus intently, mentally saying the strange phrase Cat taught me, the one that activates the stealth ward she placed on me. With a deep breath, I creep silently towards my door, repeating the arcane incantation like a protective mantra.

I hear John's voice, low and urgent. "Sarah, it's Liz. She needs to speak to us. Now!"

A cold, terrible moment of tension fills the air. My worst fears are about to be confirmed.

"I... I'd better go up and check that her door is properly closed, then. So we can talk in private," Sarah replies, her voice tinged with a matching concern.

My heart hammers. I spring into silent action, pushing my door completely closed and scrambling back onto my bed. I snatch up my book, but the words blur, swimming on the page.

In the oppressive stillness, I hear the ominous creak of the stairs. Moments later, I sense movement just outside my door. Someone walks past, their footsteps unnaturally soft, pausing for a heart-stopping, eternal moment. My breath catches. Then, the footsteps carry on, and I hear their own bedroom door open and softly close.

Not long after, the footsteps return, descending the staircase. My mind is a maelstrom of terrified questions. I set my book aside with trembling hands and creep silently, like a phantom, toward my bedroom door. Cautiously, I turn the cold metal knob, cracking it open just a fraction. Heart pounding, I sink to the carpeted floor, crawling just outside my door into the shadowed alcove of the landing. From this precarious position, I pray I can catch every damning word.

I hear John's voice, grave and concerned. "Liz? What's up? Has... has something happened?"

I can't hear her response, only a low murmur. John's ensuing silence stretches for an unbearable eternity. Just as I feel the walls closing in, I hear him speak again.

"Thank you, Liz. That's... very helpful. Let us know if you find anything else out tomorrow, won't you?" His voice drops to a low, conspiratorial whisper that sends ice snaking down my spine. "It looks like... it looks like we will be moving to phase two. Early."

A tense, pregnant silence follows, before John continues, his voice now devoid of any warmth. "She's hiding things from us, Sarah. Just like we suspected. Liz overheard her talking to Clare in the bathrooms today. Talking about a 'secret.' And something about people called... Cat, and Kracis... being 'in her corner.' Liz has already checked; there's no one in their entire year group, or the one below, with those names."

Panic, raw and visceral, seeps into Sarah's voice. "Oh, John! What do we do now? If her... her change... has already happened, even with the meds... do you really think she would confide such a monumental, dangerous secret to Clare, and not to Liz?"

John's tone grows sharp with anger. "Liz also mentioned that Devika's been acting very strangely around her recently. Being evasive."

The mounting dread in Sarah's voice is palpable. "Do you... do you think she's somehow figured it all out? That Liz is... with us?"

"I don't know how she could have," John admits, his voice heavy with grim resignation. "But maybe... maybe it's time, Sarah. If she has indeed gained her power, it could be increasingly difficult, if not impossible, to keep her under our control for much longer."

His cold, clinical words hang in the stale air, heavy with horrifying implications. I lie there, frozen, immobilised by sheer terror.

"Honestly, John, do you really believe this is the best approach?" Sarah urges, her voice a desperate mix of fading hope and rising desperation. "Perhaps if we were just a little more truthful with her? About some of the more... palatable aspects? She has a deep fascination with the paranormal. If we told her the truth, that she was adopted—that we, too, have our own deep connections to the paranormal world—she could even see the move to the pack grounds as an exciting new adventure."

"Sean would never allow that, Sarah, and you know it. He would never consent for us to confess anything significant before we get her safely to him. She will be kept in that... special room they've prepared. The one that suppresses all magic. And she will, eventually, find out the truth—that we took her, stole her, from that human foster family. When she does, do you honestly think she will be remotely willing to cooperate? What the pack is truly planning for her, Sarah, it isn't a pleasant future. That's precisely why it was agreed she could enjoy her childhood—before she is inevitably expected to fulfil her designated role in our pack's destiny."

"But she hasn't truly been enjoying it, John!" Sarah insists, her voice cracking. "Just today, she confided in me about her profound loneliness!"

The crushing weight of their conversation, the stark tensions between their duties to this monstrous 'Sean' and their twisted obligations to me, seems to be pulling them in opposing directions.

"Too bad," John's voice is cold, utterly devoid of emotion. "We have had to be strict with her. To keep her contained. It's been almost impossible to get hold of magically gifted children in recent years. She is one of the very first we've managed to secure in over a decade. We have to make our pack strong again, Sarah. Strong enough to win. By re-introducing powerful, controllable magic into our bloodlines. War is coming. And if we want to finally take over, it needs to happen soon." His tone makes me not recognise the man I blindly, naively, thought was my father. He is a stranger. A monster.

"I know all that, John. But… I've come to genuinely care for her," her voice trembles with unshed tears and helpless fear.

"There isn't another way, Sarah. And you need to accept that. The current situation at her school is the perfect excuse for taking her out permanently. So, this weekend's planned trip to the pack grounds… it will be the end of all this. The end of her life as she knows it," he says, his tone imbued with an unsettling, absolute finality.

"Does… does it truly have to be so soon?" Sarah pleads. "It will be such a terrible shock."

"NO! Sarah! It's too late for that!" His voice is firm, cold, unyielding. "I will call Sean first thing in the morning and let him know it's time. Then, I will notify the school that she won't be returning next week. Or ever."

The crushing, inescapable weight of his words, of their devastating decision, crashes down on me, threatening to shatter my already fragile sanity.

"Okay, John. Okay. But please… don't shout at me like that. She might hear you," Sarah whispers, her voice small, defeated.

Overwhelmed, my mind reeling, my body trembling, I retreat silently back into the sanctuary of my room, shutting the door firmly behind me. I flick off the main light, plunging the space into a deep, comforting shadow. I crawl onto my bed, open the drawer to my bedside table and remove three pills and hide them within my pillow case till morning, while leaving the medication pot on the bedside table so it looks like I've taken them in case one of them decides to look in on me, then I lay down and pull the duvet high over my head.

As I nestle deeper beneath my duvet, shrouding myself in a self-imposed darkness, tears finally begin to flow. Hot, silent, and unstoppable, they stream freely down my face while my pillow muffles the quiet, choked sobs, blend with the hushed, indifferent sounds of the sleeping night—a poignant, heartbreaking melody of utter devastation, profound betrayal, and a crushing, soul-deep helplessness, and I finally cry myself to sleep.

Catherine M. Clark

Chapter 28:
A Desperate Sort of Hope

What I heard last night, the cold, hard facts of their betrayal, shattered whatever fragile remnants of hope I had been foolishly clinging to. When I awake this morning, the world grey and unwelcoming, a plan, stark and terrifying, begins to form in the ruins of my mind. I need Cat now more than ever, but with no other options on the bleak horizon, my only chance lies in following Kracis's desperate advice. I must make a break for it. I have to run.

I tell myself that as long as Kracis is by my side, I will somehow be okay. The vast, crushing uncertainty of that conviction looms over me, a suffocating blanket, but I push it aside, focusing fiercely on what little I can actually control.

A cold resolve settles in my gut. I grab my battered school rucksack and start to pack, my worldly belongings pitifully few. I roll a couple of my most comfortable T-shirts into tight cylinders. Next, a faded pair of jeans and a handful of underwear. Finally, my trusty, battered Pumas—I know I'm going to need their comfort for whatever horrors are to come.

As I reach for my favourite book, I feel a momentary, deceptive sense of solace. It's just paper and ink, but it represents a small, portable corner of normality. With everything loaded up, I take a deep, steadying breath.

Now, I just need to find a moment to talk to Kracis, to let her know I'm ready.

Luck, for once, seems to be on my side. The weather is bad—a grey, drizzling curtain of rain—so I can wear one of my warmer, bulkier jackets without raising suspicion. I pick up my rucksack, which looks noticeably more stuffed than usual, yet, strangely, it feels no heavier than it normally does with just my schoolbooks inside. *Another unsettling sign of the changes coursing through me.*

I carry it in my right hand, draping my folded waterproof jacket over my arm to conceal the tell-tale bulge. With my heart hammering, I leave my room. At the bottom of the stairs, I surreptitiously set the rucksack down beside the shoe rack and casually lay my jacket over it. This is a significant risk, but I have no other choice. My escape has begun.

Breakfast is an uncomfortable, charged silence. I sit at the table, a large, untouched bowl of cereal in front of me. It feels as if Sarah's eyes are fixed on me, cold and calculating, scrutinising my every move. I can't shake the gnawing anxiety about when, or if, I might eat again. I have to devise a plausible excuse to escape school early. Any delay could have irreversible consequences.

As I finally make my way to the front door, the usual "Bye, Mum!" slips from my lips. My heart pounds as I notice Sarah, a silent shadow, trailing closely behind me. *This has to be it,* I think, a cold dread gripping me. *They know.*

"Devika," she begins, her voice soft, yet tinged with an urgency that sets my nerves on high alert. "Before you go, I just wanted to let you know that we're planning a little trip this weekend. To visit some old friends. It'll be a bit like camping, but much nicer—we'll be staying in lovely, cosy wooden cabins. There will be plenty of other children there too, so hopefully, you'll make some wonderful new friends." Her eyes, those deceptive windows, brim with a manufactured sadness that, for a fleeting, treacherous moment, actually tugs at my heartstrings.

The feeling evaporates instantly, consumed by the cold reality of what I now know. My mind races, replaying the horrifying litany of their plans. Cat's words echo in my mind: *a baby maker. A broodmare.* John all but confirmed it last night. A shiver traces my spine at the thought of what will happen when they discover I'm not the witch they expect me to be. If I fail to meet their inhuman expectations, it will ultimately end in my demise—or perhaps something even worse.

For a horrifying, guilty moment, I wish I could be Katie, free from this suffocating mess.

"Okay, Mum," I hear myself say, forcing a bright, eager smile that feels like a grotesque, painful rictus. "That... that sounds interesting. Will you tell me more about it when I get home?"

I know this is what she wants to hear. And it works. Her face transforms, a soft, relieved glow overtaking her features—a genuine smile I haven't witnessed in ages.

"I will, honey. Of course, I will. Now, you have a good day at school," she replies, her voice warm. The relief in her posture is almost palpable as she returns to the kitchen.

The moment the door shuts, a massive, shuddering wave of relief surges through me, so potent my knees almost buckle. I grab my rucksack, hide it again with my jacket, and take one last, lingering, hateful glance at the house that has, for sixteen years, felt like a well-disguised prison.

When I step into the damp morning air, I spot Tom waiting patiently by a lamppost across the street. I'd texted him in the pre-dawn gloom, telling him not to knock, under any circumstances. Seeing him there brings a surprising sense of comfort and, to my utter confusion, a slight, betraying flutter in my heart. A genuine, unforced smile finally breaks through my anxious expression.

"Hey, Dev."

"Good morning, Tom! Thanks again. I really, really appreciate this."

"My pleasure, Devvy," he replies, his tone friendly and

unsuspicious.

We begin our walk. As we approach the park, I slip on my jacket and hoist my deceptively light rucksack onto my back. I really must be getting stronger.

"Wow, Dev! What on earth do you have in there?" Tom exclaims, his eyes widening. "It looks like you've packed for a week!"

"Oh, um… just some extra textbooks for coursework," I lie. "And I caught my toe really badly last night, so if my school shoes start to hurt, I brought my Pumas to change into."

"Wait, how'd you do that?" he asks, his expression clouding with concern.

"Yeah, well, I wasn't paying attention," I admit with a sheepish smile. "I was off in my own little world and caught my big toe right on a kitchen chair. Idiot."

"Ouch! I totally get that," Tom agrees sympathetically. Once we're well out of sight of my former home, I slip my arm through his again, the familiar contact surprisingly reassuring. This time, however, I do it with a subtle, ulterior motive, angling us slightly left, towards the less-frequented edge of the park near the woods.

Tom, of course, notices immediately. "Hey, Dev, why are we heading this way? The gate's over there."

I take a deep breath. "Tom, I'm really sorry about this, but I can't explain right now. I need to avoid Liz until we get closer to school. There's been so much police presence… I thought it might be safer to cut through the woods this morning, just to get ahead of them. Is… is that okay with you?"

For a long, tense moment, he just stares at me, his brow furrowed in perplexity. I can see the gears turning. "Sure, Devvy. Yeah, I get it," he finally says, his tone a careful mixture of understanding and concern. "To be honest, I've noticed you and Clare haven't exactly been on the best of terms with Liz lately."

With a sigh, I reply, "We really aren't. She's… done something that's utterly betrayed my trust. But it's complicated, Tom.

I can't say more right now." A sharp regret shoots through me. I hastily add, "Maybe one day Clare will share everything with you."

As soon as the words are out, I regret my lack of caution. His expression shifts, his eyes narrowing with a new, unwelcome hint of suspicion. Nonetheless, to my relief, he holds his tongue. We continue toward the corner of the park that borders the dense, dark woods.

Upon reaching the edge, a familiar, prickling anxiety washes over me. I scan the tree line, searching for any sign of Liz. My heart races. When I discern no trace of her, a fleeting moment of fragile serenity envelops me.

"Are you okay, Dev?" Tom asks softly.

"Come on," I urge, my voice a little too breathless, glancing back through the trees as we take our first hesitant steps into the wild, untamed woods. "Let's hurry, try and get a head start. I have a horrible feeling Clare is going to be really, really upset with me for this."

"Honestly, Dev, I wouldn't worry about Liz too much," Tom says with a dismissive shrug.

"Right now, I don't care about Liz. I just need to avoid her."

"I hope you will tell me why, as for Clare, don't worry, I'm sure she will understand," Tom says, though he softens it with a teasing smirk. "You might have to do some serious grovelling with her, though."

"I have a horrible feeling you're right," I sigh.

As we venture deeper, the path becomes less distinct, and a sudden, inexplicable chill runs through me. The air here feels different—dense, heavy, almost… watchful.

A faint, wispy voice speaks directly in my mind: '*Devika… you should not be in these woods. It is… not safe here for you.*' Kracis's connection seems to be growing weak again, distant. She'll need more of my blood, and soon.

I have to respond. "We will be fine, Kracis," I insist, forcing a confident smile.

"Of course we will, Dev," Tom replies, his brow furrowing in confusion.

"Yes. We will," I repeat, more for my own benefit. "Though… I did kind of expect to see some police still combing through here," I add, a genuine unease in my voice.

"I'm sure they're nearby somewhere," Tom says, though his own apprehension is becoming more evident. "They'll be furious, though, when they see us wandering about out here."

"I'm sure they will be," I echo, my heart now racing for entirely different reasons.

We make our way deeper into the woods. An unsettling, prickling sensation grips me, halting my steps. It feels, with a chilling certainty, like unseen eyes are tracking my every move. Doubts bubble up—have I made a grave mistake? My eyes sweep the gloomy wood floor, desperately searching for anything that might explain the gnawing feeling of being hunted.

Then, in a single, heart-stopping moment, two things happen catastrophically.

Kracis's faint, strained voice pierces my mind, but Tom's sudden, sharp exclamation immediately drowns it out. All I catch before her weak connection severs is the single, ominous, terrifying word: '*Danger*!'

"Dev! What's that? Over there!" Tom exclaims, his voice sharp with alarm.

Following his pointing finger, I squint into the dense shadows. At first, I see nothing but tangled branches and decaying leaves. "I… I don't see anything, Tom," I say hesitantly, a cold knot of dread forming in my stomach.

"Right there! Look! Partly concealed by that big holly bush!" he insists, a raw urgency in his words.

I strain my eyes. And then I notice it. Something pale. Something still. My heart skips a beat, then thuds painfully as a fresh, sickening wave of dread pools within me.

Without hesitation, Tom charges recklessly towards the

object. I stand frozen, my feet like lead. When he reaches it, he uses his foot to roughly push the concealing bush away. In an instant, his brave demeanour shatters.

"NO!!!" he cries out, a raw, agonised sound that tears through the unnatural stillness. The air leaves my lungs in a silent, horrified gasp.

"NO! NO! NO!" he repeats, his voice cracking as he sinks to his knees in the mud, utter despair washing over his pale face.

Panic, cold and absolute, envelops me. The horrifying realisation strikes me like a thunderclap. I already know, with a soul-crushing certainty, what he has unearthed. I run towards him, my paralysis broken by a surge of adrenaline. When I reach his slumped form, I see my worst fears confirmed.

It's Danny. Or what's left of him. So, so pale. His eyes, wide and staring, are like polished stones, frozen in an expression of unimaginable fear.

I grab the back of Tom's jacket, tugging hard. "Tom! Come on! We need to get out of here! Now! Please!"

"No! I'm not leaving him! We need to call the police!" Tom sobs, frantically searching his pockets for his phone.

"Tom, we need to leave! Right now!" I say, tugging harder. I put all of my rapidly increasing, unnatural strength into pulling him to his feet. Suddenly, shockingly, he shoots up off the ground as if he weighs nothing, his body momentarily airborne, before crashing back down, hard, onto the unforgiving ground. He lands awkwardly, sickeningly, on his outstretched arm.

I stumble backwards, the unexpected lack of resistance unbalancing me, but I manage to stay on my feet. I race back over to where he lies, moaning in pain. He turns towards me, his face contorted in agony, cradling the arm he fell on. I gasp in sheer, unadulterated shock. I hurt him.

"Tom! Oh my god, Tom, I'm so sorry! I didn't mean to!" I cry, the words tumbling out, my voice laced with crushing guilt.

"How... how did you do that, Devvy?" his voice trembles with a volatile mixture of disbelief, pain, and a dawning, undeniable concern. Then, the look in his eyes shifts, hardens, and turns, just a little, to one of unmistakable fear.

That single, fleeting look, that tiny flicker of fear directed at me, hurts me to my very core, more than any physical blow ever could.

"I... I don't know," I stammer, my voice shaking. The full, crushing weight of utter despair crashes down on me. Hot, shameful tears stream down my cheeks as I sink to my knees in the damp earth beside him. My meticulously crafted plan, my desperate bid for freedom, has unravelled. Spectacularly. Horrifically. All that matters now is getting Tom to safety.

"Tom, please," I plead, my voice cracking, "we have to get out of these woods. Now. Your arm—do you... do you think it's broken?"

His gaze flickers to his injured arm. "I... I'm not sure," he replies, his voice strained. "But we still should call the police. For Danny. They'll send an ambulance for me, too."

"No, Tom! Please, believe me! We need to get out of here! We are in terrible danger!" I plead again, my heart hammering. "Whatever did this to Danny... it could still be lurking nearby! We can't risk it!"

A long, agonising silence envelops us. "All the better to get the police here soon, then, isn't it?" Tom says, his voice grim but resolute. He painstakingly pulls out his mobile with his good hand and, his face pale with pain, begins to dial 999.

I collapse back onto the damp ground, the last vestiges of my strength deserting me. The invisible chains that bound me, the ones I so naively thought I could escape, seem to tighten with every agonising second. But then, just as I'm about to surrender completely, a tiny, desperate flicker of defiance ignites within me. *Unless.*

I wait till Tom has finished telling the authorities where we are and what we found before I say, "Tom... I need to leave," I urge, my voice trembling but resolute, a new, desperate plan forming. "This is my only chance to escape them. I'm so, so sorry." I struggle unsteadily to my feet.

"What are you talking about, Dev?" Tom replies, his face a mask of confusion.

"There's danger all around me, Tom. My parents—they're not my parents. They're not who you think they are. They... they kidnapped me, Tom. When I was just a baby," I blurt out, the horrifying truth tumbling out in a torrent.

His jaw drops, shock rendering him momentarily speechless. "Are... are you serious, Devvy? How can you know something like that? That's... insane!"

"A distant relative. She tracked me down. She had proof. It led me to find other clues about who I am. But she warned me getting me away from them might take a long time. They've kept me isolated my whole life, Tom."

"I can't believe this. Your parents... they love you. I've seen it."

"Because she showed me irrefutable proof, Tom! And they don't love me. They need me. There's a huge, terrifying difference." My eyes dart nervously to the grey horizon as the distant, mournful sound of approaching sirens begins to echo in the cold air. "I'm so sorry, Tom. So, so sorry. But I have to go now—before I lose my only chance. Forever."

"You can't just run away, Dev! We can tell the police! They'll help you!" His voice rises, sharp with panic.

"No, Tom. They can't," I insist, my heart pounding as I slowly back away. I need to retrace my steps, then veer off in a completely different direction. Away from the school. Away from my home. Away from everything.

Just as I turn, poised to make a desperate, blind dash into the dense thicket, a vast, monstrous shadow looms large, impossibly large, from behind a towering oak tree just a few feet away. It doesn't resemble anything remotely human. My breath catches, a silent, terrified scream lodging in my throat. Kracis, my shadowy guardian, simultaneously emerges from the deeper shadows on my other side, a menacing, protective presence.

In that single, heart-stopping instant, I can't tell if Tom is reacting to the newly appeared monster or to the sudden, shocking manifestation of Kracis, but the raw, unadulterated terror in his voice, in his wide, disbelieving eyes, is unmistakable as he screams, his voice cracking.

"RUN, DEV! RUN! NOW!"

Chapter 29:
A Monster Like Me

I stir slowly, a profound shiver of disorientation washing over me as the last terrifying images from the woods resurface. I remember Kracis, my brave, shadowy guardian, lunging with fearless abandon at the monstrous creature. I loved her for her sheer, selfless bravery in that instant. But the monster countered her valiant effort with contemptuous ease. Its razor-sharp claws lashed out. I can still see Kracis, all fierce determination, suddenly, horribly, crumpling as she was struck, again and again. Vicious gashes, deeper than any physical wound, formed on her ethereal body. Within those terrible, shimmering wounds, I saw a strange, almost psychedelic sight—pure light and deepest dark twisting and contorting violently, as if her very soul was at war with itself. Then, a blinding, searing white light enveloped me, and everything faded to an absolute, terrifying black. The last thing I remember is the haunting sight of Kracis falling, her form smoking and dissolving like a dying campfire brutally snuffed out.

As my senses gradually return, a terrifying realisation dawns on me. I can't move. Not an inch. Sheer, animalistic panic grips me as I discover my hands and legs are tightly, painfully bound. Fighting the rising, suffocating tide of fear, I blink my eyes open. My vision is frustratingly muddled, like looking through dirty water. Slowly, painfully, my surroundings take hesitant shape. A foul, cloying smell invades my nostrils—a putrid blend of pervasive dampness and the unmistakable, metallic tang of old blood. The stench makes me gag, a violent cough racking my body.

With each blink, my vision grows a fraction clearer. I'm imprisoned in a cave. Its walls are rugged and uneven, carved from stone that seems to absorb the light. The air is thick and heavy, clinging to my skin. To my left, an endless, impenetrable void stretches out. To my right, a chaotic array of dry sticks and brittle leaves forms a crude, makeshift nest, as if for some giant, prehistoric bird.

A warm, orange glow flickers in the centre of the cavern. A crude fire crackles and spits, casting long, dancing shadows across the uneven floor, creating an atmosphere that is both deeply eerie and perversely enchanting.

A subtle movement catches my attention. I turn my head slowly, every muscle protesting, and there, slumped heavily against the cold stone beside me, is Tom. He looks dishevelled, his breathing shallow and irregular. A fresh wave of acute, painful guilt surges within me. I need to find a way to free us before *it* returns.

I am too late.

Even as the desperate thought forms, I hear a faint rustling, like dry scales brushing against stone—a sound that sends an icy shiver of pure dread down my spine. I turn my head slowly, fearfully, toward the source of the sound. The monster begins to materialise from the suffocating darkness at the cave's edge.

I take a moment, a single, suspended heartbeat, to truly consider its grotesque features. It is a true, unadulterated monster, ripped from the pages of the darkest nightmares. Its scales have a shimmering, iridescent sheen, reflecting the firelight in hues of sickly green and oily black. A long, thick, muscular tail, easily twice the length of its torso, trails behind it, undulating with a sinuous, serpentine grace as it slithers closer.

With each inch it approaches, the chilling realisation of its overwhelmingly snake-like characteristics strikes me harder. Its piercing, intelligent yellow eyes are vertically slit, glowing with a malevolent intensity. But it isn't just the hypnotic eyes that captivate my unwilling attention; atop its vaguely humanoid head is a writhing, seething mane of glossy black snakes, hissing softly, their forked tongues flicking constantly. It reminds me of the ancient tales of Medusa, the infamous Gorgon whose very gaze turned mortals to stone. My heart hammers against my ribs. I know, with absolute certainty, that I have to look away. Now.

I sit frozen as its slithering halts directly in front of me. An awkward, suffocating silence presses down on my chest. Finally, it speaks, its voice surprisingly smooth, yet deeply menacing. "You are awake, then. You cannot hide that from me, little morsel. I can hear your heart racing, a frantic little drum. Open your eyes, child. Look at me."

Panic seizes me. My eyelids clamp shut even tighter. I shake my head vehemently.

Without warning, it strikes me. A hard, vicious slap across my face sends my head spinning. Against my will, my eyes spring open from the shock and pain.

"That is better, yes? Now, look at me," it commands again, its voice laced with a playful, sadistic tone that chills me to the bone.

Despite my paralysing fear, a single, trembling question tumbles from my lips. "Won't I… turn to stone if I look at you?"

The creature responds with a deep-throated belly laugh that reverberates through the stale air. "I am not Medusa, you silly, ignorant child. I am a Lamia," it says, its voice dripping with a condescending mockery that is somehow more terrifying than rage.

"Oh," is all I can choke out. "So… I won't turn to stone?"

"Of course not, you utterly foolish child! How do you not even know what I am? You are a part of my world. And your… parents… they are a part of it too—except, of course, you are not truly one of them, are you? Not really. And just so you know," it adds, its yellow eyes glinting with malicious pleasure, "I also thoroughly, and quite satisfyingly, destroyed your pathetic little shadow minion out there."

Its casual, cruel words hang in the stagnant air. *Kracis... gone?*

"My... my what?" I respond weakly.

"Your shadow demon, child," the Lamia replies, a cruel smirk on its thin, reptilian lips.

"Oh... her?" I whisper, a surge of unbearable, aching sorrow washing over me. "Have you... have you really killed her?"

"She? It is a *thing*, child. Not a 'her'," it shoots back dismissively.

"She *is* a her! And she was my friend!" I retort, a surprising surge of protective anger flaring within me.

"Too bad for you, then. You are not going to be needing her services any longer," the Lamia taunts.

"What... what are you going to do to us?" I manage to ask, raw fear creeping back into my voice.

Before it can answer, Tom stirs, his eyelids fluttering open. Sheer panic sets in as he takes in the horrifying sight of the Lamia looming over us. He tugs violently at his bonds, a sharp, agonised cry escaping his lips as pain shoots through his injured arm.

"Tom! Tom, don't! Don't hurt yourself!" I exclaim.

His wide, terrified gaze locks onto mine. The raw, naked fear within them is a fresh stab of guilt twisting in my gut. "This is all my fault."

"Dev... Dev, it's... it's not your fault," he manages to say, his voice rough with fear. But deep down, I know the truth. I am to blame. Completely.

"Oh, but of course, it *is* her fault that you are here, little human boy," the Lamia hisses. "I was merely... passing through when I sensed her power emerging. Uncontrolled. Untamed. A power which is... strangely familiar to me. Yet, at the same time, not so much. It is... peculiar," it says, almost to itself.

"Dev... what... what is it talking about?" Tom asks, his body now visibly shaking. "And what *is* it?"

The Lamia turns its hypnotic gaze slowly toward him, hissing again, a low, menacing sound that makes him flinch violently. "I am not an IT, little boy! I am a powerful, ancient Lamia. My name," it adds, its tone both regal and deeply threatening but clearly very feminine voice, "is Pherohsa."

"I... I think I've read about your kind," Tom stutters, a horrified realisation dawning on his pale face. "You're... the type of demon who feeds on children, aren't you?"

"It is curious that the little human boy holds more knowledge of our world than you do, sweet girl," Pherohsa taunts, turning its condescending gaze back to me.

"Devika! What is she saying?" Tom asks again, desperation evident in his voice.

Fear grips me. I keep my mouth clamped shut.

"Boy," Pherohsa declares, its voice dark and mocking, "she is like me. She is not human. Not anymore."

"I'm nothing like you! You're a monster! A killer!" I spit, my anger flaring uncontrollably. But even as the words leave my lips, the undeniable truth of her statement settles deep within me, a cold, heavy stone. *I am a monster, too. If she's right, if I'm truly like her, then Katie and Danny's blood is on my hands. And now, perhaps, Tom's.*

Pherohsa strikes me again, a vicious backhand this time.

"Leave her alone!" Tom shouts, his voice surprisingly strong. "I don't care what she is! She is still my friend!" His words echo in the oppressive silence, unwavering, defiant.

"Deluded, foolish child," Pherohsa sneers. "It does not matter anyway. As you will not be around to care for very much longer." A slow, horrifying smile spreads across its reptilian face, a smile I know I will never be able to unsee.

A knot of pure terror tightens in my stomach. "Please... please let him go," I implore. "You can keep me. Do what you want with me. But please, I beg you, just let him go." The fact that he still sees me as his friend, as someone worth defending, fuels my desperate plea.

"No," it replies simply, its tone dripping with a cold, cruel delight. "He, my dear, is going to be my... appetiser. My little starter.

And then, sweet, powerful girl, I am going to *savour* you. I am going to drain every last, precious ounce of that nascent power from you. I can feel it, you know. Lurking just beneath your skin, potent and wild and utterly, irresistibly alluring. It is going to make me stronger than I have ever been before. I might even," it adds, its yellow eyes gleaming with sadistic pleasure, "be generous enough to keep you alive for a little while afterwards. So I can continue to savour the unique taste of your blood."

Its chilling, mocking laughter echoes through the dimly lit, oppressive space. I shudder violently. I know, with a certainty that chills me to the bone, that I would do anything to make sure Tom doesn't suffer the same horrific, bloodless fate that befell Katie and Danny.

This was not the day I had envisioned. I had dreamed of breaking free. Yet here I am, shackled and terrified in another prison that feels just as hopeless as the last. "If I truly possess all this power you claim I have," I declare, attempting a confidence I am far from feeling, "then you don't need Tom. Just let him go." Then an idea sparks in my mind, "If you dare to harm me or Tom," I warn, my voice steady despite the fear twisting in my gut, "My protector will find you. And she will destroy you."

Its reptilian eyes narrow. "If I were to release him, little fool, he would undoubtedly go straight to your kind. Then those self-righteous, interfering witches, and perhaps even your shifter guardians, would come after me. I am a powerful, ancient being! I have as much right to exist as they do!"

"I wasn't referring to them!" I snap.

"Then who, dear child? Who could possibly instil fear in one such as I?"

A desperate gamble forms in my mind. "Hecate," I say, the conviction in my voice surprising even myself. "You need to fear Hecate."

To my utter shock, Pherohsa's arrogant expression falters. It actually slithers backwards a little. "Hecate? Hecate is *dead*. She perished long, long ago," it retorts, though its voice is laced with an undeniable uncertainty.

"No. You're wrong. She is very much alive. And she runs the Underworld now. And I am blood-related to her. If you hurt me, she will come for you. And she will not be merciful."

A dawning, horrified realisation appears in Pherohsa's gaze. "Ah... now I understand the extraordinary power I sense. You harbour an angel's pure essence, yes... but there is something far darker lurking within you as well. You are a formidable child. A rare prize. But Hecate? I do not fear her. She is bound by ancient laws that strictly prevent her return to this mortal world."

"I've encountered her in this world. Recently," I insist.

"Really?" it queries, its incredulity palpable. "If she is indeed alive, and has truly, recklessly, set foot here... then I can spread the word. Her unauthorised presence would lead to... severe consequences. For her."

Panic surges through me. *What have I just done?* In my desperate, stupid gamble, I have just posed a grave, potentially fatal, threat to Hecate's own existence.

"Don't listen to her, Dev! The police will locate us soon! They have to!" Tom urges, his voice strained.

"Oh, but they won't, little boy," Pherohsa interrupts with a cruel smile. "Powerful, ancient wards protect this cave. No one will perceive anything amiss. And sound is effectively muted."

The tiny, fragile flicker of hope I had been clinging to vanishes, snuffed out like a candle. I sag weakly against the cold, damp wall, the full, horrifying reality of our inescapable situation crashing down on me.

Pherohsa's chilling, triumphant laughter echoes through the small, oppressive cave, a harsh, grating sound that seems to mock our despair, painting the very walls with the dark, encroaching shadows of our impending, inevitable doom.

Pherohsa takes us completely by surprise, slithering with terrifying speed towards Tom. It grabs him roughly by the front of his torn school shirt and hauls him effortlessly up to a dangling position. I look up in fresh, horrified shock and see long, needle-sharp fangs, like ivory daggers, appear in its previously almost human-looking mouth. Before I can scream, before I can even process what is happening, it sinks them, with a sickening, tearing sound, deep into the left side of Tom's vulnerable neck.

I scream then, a raw, desperate sound, "NO! STOP IT! LEAVE HIM ALONE!"

It just ignores me, its eyes closing in reptilian ecstasy as it begins to drink his blood, a low, guttural purring sound emanating from its throat. After a horrifyingly short, yet eternal-seeming time, it lets go. He drops to the unforgiving ground like a discarded puppet, cries out weakly in pain, and then just whimpers, a small, pathetic sound.

"Tom! Tom, are you okay?" I beg, desperately trying to move towards him, my bonds holding me fast.

"I… I think so," he struggles to reply, his voice faint, weak, sounding terribly, unnervingly sleepy.

A strange, alien feeling suddenly washes over me, like a dark, insidious fog creeping into my mind—cold and yet… alluring. At first, I try to ignore it, my concern solely for Tom. But then, my mouth begins to water uncontrollably, an embarrassing flood of saliva, and a sickly sweet, almost intoxicating scent fills the air. My nostrils flare involuntarily as I try to pinpoint its source. It seems to be emanating from my right. From Tom.

My eyes dart past his slumped form. Suddenly, my gaze falls, as if drawn by an invisible force, upon his neck, upon the dark, glistening blood welling from the fresh puncture wounds. The sight, the scent, of his blood sends a powerful, undeniable, primal urge coursing like wildfire through my entire body. My own fangs, sharp and aching, descend without my conscious bidding, a painful, stretching sensation in my gums. My very muscles try to move, to lunge towards Tom, completely, terrifyingly, uncontrollably.

I am instantly disgusted, horrified, sick to my very stomach at my own monstrous, predatory reaction. Struggling with every ounce of my willpower, I wrench my head away, squeezing my eyes tightly shut, trying desperately to block out everything—the sight, the scent, the overwhelming urge—to regain some semblance of control over this new, monstrous part of me.

After what feels like an eternity, an agonising internal battle, I manage, somehow, to suppress this terrifying, vampiric part of myself. My fangs, with a painful reluctance, retract. But the shame, the horror, of what I almost did, lingers heavily, poisonously, on me. *What the fuck was that?* I scream silently at myself. *I have fangs, I know I'm supposedly part vampire, but Cat said the reaper side of me should suppress that! If there was even a remote risk of this, I should have been warned.*

I am in luck, in a twisted, horrific way. The Lamia, after feeding on Tom, seems sated, almost lethargic. It curls up with a contented sigh on its makeshift bed of sticks and leaves and, to my utter astonishment, appears to go to sleep. Tom, weakened by blood loss, his breathing shallow, drifts off into a fitful slumber. In the quiet, oppressive darkness of the cave, fresh tears stream, hot and silent, down my face as I curl up into a tight, protective ball. I am grateful, with a shame that burns, that Tom didn't witness this horrifying side of me, didn't see me as a true monster, too. And also, perversely, terrifyingly, grateful that I was so securely bound that I couldn't possibly have acted on that horrifying, overwhelming feeling that had hit me with the force, the seductive allure, of a full syringe of heroin.

Catherine M. Clark

Chapter 30:
My Friend, My Victim

I stir, a dull ache throbbing behind my eyes, as I feel someone gently shaking me. When I finally manage to pry open my sore, gritty eyelids, the dim, flickering firelight of the cave slowly swims into focus. It's Tom. He's leaning over me, his face pale and drawn.

"Are you… okay, Tom?" I ask, my voice thick with sleep. I have no idea how much time has passed.

"Sorry… sorry to wake you, Devvy. But I… I can't handle being alone right now," he says, his voice alarmingly slurred. He looks terribly ill, his skin almost translucent, and he's speaking as if he's had far too much to drink.

"Are you sure you're okay?" I ask again, growing concerned. "You look really unwell, Tom."

"It… it fed on me again. While you were asleep," he says, his words slow, difficult. "Guess I'm… suffering from blood loss." He sways then, a weak, boneless movement, a strange, disconnected chuckle escaping his lips.

I struggle against my bonds, managing to shift to a more upright position as Tom slumps heavily against my side. "Where… where is she?" I whisper, fear coiling in my stomach.

"She… she left the cave. Some time ago. That's all I know."

"Good," I say, a flicker of desperate hope igniting within me. "Let's see if we can get you free." My voice is surprisingly steady as I reach for his hands, my fingers fumbling, feeling for the knots that bind his wrists.

"Dev..." he calls, his voice faint.

"Yes, Tom? What is it?" I reply, sensing a new weight behind his question.

"Are you... are you really... not human, Devvy?" His eyes, clouded with pain, search mine, filled with a desperate, childlike curiosity.

I pause, taking a deep, shaky breath. The truth feels heavy, dangerous. "I... I think I'm part human, Tom," I finally admit, the words tasting like ash.

"Okay... so... so what else are you, then?" he presses, his eyebrows furrowing in a valiant effort to concentrate.

"Cat... Cat believes I am part... either angel or reaper... and... and something else as well. Something... darker."

Tom's eyes widen, a flicker of awe cutting through the fog of his pain. "Really? Angel? Reaper? Do you... do you have wings, then?"

"Yes. Yes, I do," I whisper. "They're a kind of... slate grey colour."

After a brief, loaded silence, he speaks again, his voice soft, raspy, revealing a profound hurt. "Why... why didn't you tell me, Dev? Before all this? You know I would have kept your secret safe. I've always been there for you, Devvy. Always. We... we also used to talk for hours, remember? About how we would love to become paranormal beings ourselves. Together. Just you and me, and Clare. Against the whole stupid world."

A deep, ragged breath shudders through me. "I really wanted to believe you would be okay with who I am, Tom. I really did. But I was so terrified. I only uncovered the real truth a few weeks ago. The people who kidnapped me... they've been drugging me, Tom. Systematically. Since I was twelve. They did it to try and suppress this other side of me. And all the while, they fabricated that cruel story about me having a rare genetic disorder." My voice trembles, the full, horrifying reality of my stolen life crashing over me.

"That's... that's absolutely unbelievable, Dev! Monstrous!" he exclaims, his weak voice trembling with a protective fury.

"They're not ordinary people, Tom. They're wolf shifters," I reply, leaning in closer as I continue to try to untie him. "At least, that's what Cat told me. I've heard them mention a pack. And pack lands."

"Who... who told you all this, Devvy?"

"This woman. Named Cat," I say. "Well... her real name is Hecate."

"Wait... you mean... like the goddess Hecate?" he asks, his eyes widening further in profound surprise. "The one they associate with magic and witchcraft? This... this is getting really serious now, Dev! Seriously paranormal!"

"Exactly. One and the same," I affirm, a hint of awe in my own tone. "She's actually really nice, Tom. Powerful, but... kind. I just wish she could have helped me escape all this bloody mess sooner."

"Why didn't she, then?"

"She said if she simply took me away, the police would come looking for me. For a missing child. I'd always be in hiding. Plus," I add wearily, "she thought she had more time. Until I turned eighteen, and she was busy with something else."

"I'm so sorry, Devvy. So sorry you've had to endure all of this. Alone," Tom interjects, his expression a heart-wrenching mix of concern and helpless frustration. "Clare had no idea, did she?"

"Well... Clare actually caught me yesterday," I reply, and a shadow passes over his pale face. "You know I've been having funny turns, well, it was my wings wanting to come out from being suppressed for so long? I knew I had to take a risk. I used the disabled bathroom stall to let my wings out. I thought I was alone. But Clare walked in and saw them sticking out over the top of the door."

"Wow! I wish I could have witnessed that! Did Liz see it too?" Tom asks, his eyes wide with a childlike intrigue.

"No, thank god. But Liz... Liz is a shifter too, Tom. Like them. She's been working for my supposed parents all along. To keep tabs on me. And that's why I had planned to run away. Today."

Tom's eyes go wide again, this time in sheer, uncomprehending disbelief. "Wait... what? Are you saying that Liz has been complicit in your kidnapping? All these years?"

"Well... not during the very early years, I don't think. But for the most part? For the last few years? Yes."

Tom pauses, processing my devastating words. Then, his gaze snaps back to me. "Hold on, Dev. Did you just say you were actually planning to run away? Today?"

"Yes. Liz squealed on me to them. My 'father' was going to call the school today, pull me out permanently. After that, they were planning to take me to their pack lands. This weekend. For... for breeding." The word tastes like poison.

Tom's jaw drops in stunned, horrified shock. And then he says something so out of character it's almost comical. "Fuckers."

I can't help it. A small, hysterical chuckle escapes me. This whole situation is utterly, dangerously insane.

"What's... what's so funny, Devvy?" Tom asks, a curious, weak smile playing on his own pale lips.

I chuckle softly again. "You. You always seem to have a way of making me laugh, Tom. Even now." Just then, my traitorous stomach lets out a loud, incredibly embarrassing, hungry rumble.

Tom's weak laughter fills the air. "I guess you're as hungry as I am, then."

"I really am," I admit.

He shrugs weakly, a glint of his old mischief in his tired eyes. "Well... I don't think she plans on feeding us. We might have to donate a finger to each other. You know. To keep us alive."

"Eww, Tom!" I shiver involuntarily, though his gruesome joke does make me instantly forget about being hungry. My disgusted reaction seems to make him happy; he smiles, a genuine, if faint, smile.

My fingers have been working furiously at the thick ropes binding his hands, but the bloody cords are twisted so tightly that every painful attempt feels utterly futile.

"No luck then?" Tom asks, watching me struggle. "Still can't get me untied, huh? Sorry, Dev."

"Let me see if I can get *you* loose instead," he says then, his weak voice laced with a surprising, new determination. I notice he isn't slurring his words quite as much.

"I'm not going to leave you here, Tom," I reply firmly.

"If I can free you, Devvy... then you can go. Go and get help," he urges, his tired eyes locked on mine with an intensity, a selfless bravery, that makes my throat ache.

"I won't leave you, Tom. No matter what," I insist.

In a sudden, completely unexpected movement, Tom catches me off guard. He swings his bound arms up and over my head, somehow managing to wrap them surprisingly tightly around my neck, pulling me close with a desperate strength that takes my breath away. Time seems to warp and slow. His warm, shallow breath brushes softly against my skin. In that single, lingering, charged moment, our eyes lock. Then, he leans in and smashes his mouth against mine in a swift, clumsy, desperate kiss that sends an unexpected, dizzying rush of pure, unadulterated electricity coursing like wildfire through my entire body.

It confuses me, shocks me, yet, at the same time, it ignites every single dormant nerve in my being. The kiss is utterly, overwhelmingly electric. It lingers, a phantom pressure, a burning warmth, long after he pulls away, leaving me breathless, shaken, and, for some strange, inexplicable reason, yearning for more.

The kiss ignites a violent, chaotic storm of emotions within me—desire, fear, confusion. It is a desperate, unexpected lifeline in this desolate hellhole. A tiny, incandescent spark of human connection. His scent, a heady blend of clean, rain-washed air and his own unique, boyish musk, envelops me like a warm cocoon. In my daze, Tom pulls me even closer, pressing my body against his, forcing my head to rest on his shoulder. I can't help it; I bury my face into the warm curve of his neck and breathe him in, deeply, greedily.

Because I am so completely distracted, I forget, for one critical, fatal moment, about something very, very important. As Tom holds me, an insatiable, terrifying hunger—an alien urge—suddenly, violently, overtakes me. That same sweet, beautiful, intoxicating smell from before, the one that had horrified me, now lights up my senses, consumes me. My fangs, sharp and aching, extend with an alarming, uncontrollable speed. Before I can even comprehend what is happening, I sink them, with a guttural, predatory growl I don't recognise as my own, deep into his neck. Right into the same vulnerable spot where Pherohsa had fed.

The taste of his warm, metallic blood as it hits my tongue is pure, unadulterated, horrifying ecstasy. It courses through me like liquid fire.

I hear Tom scream then, a choked, gurgling sound of sheer, unimaginable agony, but it feels distant, muffled, unimportant compared to the overwhelming euphoria washing over my body. I can't stop. I can't control the primal urge compelling me to take more, and more, and more of this sweet, intoxicating nectar.

A massive, unimaginable surge of raw, untamed power courses through me as I pull in even more of this beautiful, irresistible drink. It is like a blinding light spreading from him directly into me, filling every inch of my being. On the fringes of that overwhelming power, I can sense his emotions. Raw terror. Desperation. But also… a strange, resigned acceptance. A giving in. It feels like his essence. His soul.

Just as the rush threatens to consume me completely, a tiny, nagging voice, a flicker of my own fading humanity, whispers urgently in the back of my mind, reminding me that this is wrong. That I am hurting him. Killing someone who trusts me. I almost stop—until the intoxicating power surges again, stronger this time, washing away all doubt, all resistance.

I am suddenly, violently, yanked backwards by an unseen force. The solid, unforgiving rock of the cave rushes up to meet me with a sickening, bone-jarring thud. A dizzying whirlwind of confusion swirls in my rapidly clearing mind. It feels as if every single nerve in my body has simultaneously ignited, sending an incredibly exhilarating surge of raw power through my veins, making them feel like they are literally on fire. Strangely, miraculously, it doesn't hurt. It envelops me in a new, pervasive wave of blissful, intoxicating warmth.

'Devika! What have you done?'

The voice, sharp and accusatory, echoes loudly in my mind, a haunting familiarity to it that sends fresh shivers of icy dread down my spine.

'Devika! Can you hear me? I am so sorry, but... I need a little of your blood. Now. If I am going to be strong enough to help you.' The urgency in the familiar voice is profound. I feel a cold, yet strangely comforting, touch wrap gently around my arm. My mind feels adrift, untethered.

Then, as if breaking through a thick fog, I hear another voice—a faint, weak, yet achingly familiar whisper. *'I... I forgive you, Devvy. I... forgive you.'* The precious, heartbreaking words linger, pulling me, slowly, painfully, back to a horrifying, devastating reality.

With a sudden, violent jolt, I snap out of my trance. The first thing my newly focused eyes lock onto is Kracis. Her shadowy form is somehow more solid, more defined, her grip firm yet comforting around my arm as she draws a small amount of blood. I register the act with a detached calm. My only real, overwhelming concern is the miraculous sight of her. "Kracis! You're alive! Oh my god, I thought it killed you!"

She separates herself from my arm. She looks... different. Her shadow, her very essence, looks lighter, less dense. For the first time, I can clearly see more of her underlying features, the faint, ethereal outline of her face, her long, dark hair. The terrible gashes on her form are slowly, miraculously, repairing themselves before my very eyes.

'You need to break free from these bindings, Devika. Now,' Kracis urges, her mental voice steady, strong, unwavering. *'I know it*

feels overwhelming, but you have the strength to do this. Now more than ever.'

"Kracis! We can't waste time! We need to get Tom out of here! Before she returns! Can you release us?"

'Devika...' Kracis's voice is soft, tinged with an infinite sadness. *'Tom... Tom is gone. You need to free yourself. While you still can.'*

"What do you mean, he's gone?" I look over to where he is lying, still and silent. He must have just fallen asleep again. I move clumsily towards him, intending to wake him. I shake him gently, then more urgently. Nothing. My trembling hand touches his cold cheek. I look down at his face and rear back with a choked, horrified gasp.

His face is so, so pale. Utterly drained of all colour. And his eyes... his eyes are wide, staring, empty white orbs. Just like Danny's. Just like Katie's.

"She... she killed him," I whisper, my voice hollow, stunned with a fresh, devastating wave of grief.

'Devika... what is wrong with you? You did that to him,' Kracis says, her mental voice flat, devoid of accusation, yet heavy with an undeniable, heartbreaking truth.

"What? I... I wouldn't... I could never..." but even as I stammer the denials, the horrifying, repressed images come flooding back. The kiss. The scent of his blood. The uncontrollable urge. The fangs. The feeding. The ecstasy. The power. I gasp again, a raw, tearing sound of pure horror, and fall backwards, scrambling desperately away from him, away from what I've done. In my frantic struggle, the bindings around my ankles, weakened perhaps by my earlier struggles, suddenly snap free.

'I am so sorry, Devika. So very sorry. You just need to break the bindings around your wrists now. And then we can go.'

I panic, truly panic, at the full, horrifying realisation of what I have done. I want to be sick. I want to scream. I want to die. How could I have lost control so completely? "What have I done?" I sob, the words a broken, desperate prayer.

'You do not have time for this, Devika! You need to go! You need to run! Before it is too late!'

I keep trying to scramble further away from Tom's still, lifeless body, and as I do, I unthinkingly break the remaining bindings around my wrists with a surge of newfound, horrifying strength. And then, in that single, devastating moment of freedom, of utter self-realisation, something inside of me—something vital, something human—finally, irrevocably snaps, as I remember, with a fresh, chilling wave of horrific clarity, just how good his blood tasted. Just how incredibly, wonderfully good it had made me feel.

'That's it, Devika! You're free! Now, you need to run! I will try to stop it from coming after you.'

As I cry, silent, racking sobs for Tom, for myself, for everything I've lost, Kracis's urgent words finally sink in. And what broke inside of me, that cold, empty, newly awakened part of me, starts to take control. A chilling, unnatural calmness descends. "No," I say, my voice surprisingly steady, devoid of its earlier terror. "No, you're not. I do not want to lose anyone else. You need to go to Cat. Now. And tell her everything that happened here." I pause, a new, desperate, and perhaps insane, plan forming in my fractured mind. "The safest place for me right now… is to go home. And just… hope that Cat can get me out. Later."

'I cannot leave you here, Devika! Not alone!' she protests as I slowly, deliberately, climb to my feet.

As my tears for Tom finally subside, replaced by a chilling, all-consuming anger, a burning desire for… something… I then say, my voice now as cold as the cave walls around us, "Go to Cat. Now. Or I swear to whatever gods are listening, Kracis, I will never speak to you again."

Kracis looks… torn. But ultimately, heartbreakingly, resigned. *'Fine, Devika. But… it will take me longer than normal to reach her. I am still injured.'*

"Go, then! Now!" I command, my voice a harsh, unfamiliar rasp.

She slowly, reluctantly, melts back into the deepest shadows. I then turn, my heart a cold, heavy stone in my chest, and run, not blindly, but with a new, terrifying purpose, for the dark, gaping entrance of the cave. I am glad, in a strange, twisted way, that Kracis will not see what I hope, what I intend, will happen next. As I hope, with every fibre of my newly awakened, monstrous being, to get my revenge.

Chapter 31:
The Coldest Kind of Quiet

As I near the shadowed mouth of the cave, the exit a dark promise of escape, I hear it again—the faint, dry shush of something large and scaled brushing over cold stone. I round a sharp bend and there she is: Pherohsa, moving swiftly in my direction. She hasn't spotted me yet. With the astonishing, unnatural speed I now possess, I hit her with the full force of my weight, my shoulder colliding hard with her side. Her reptilian eyes widen in shocked realisation, but she has no time to react. She goes flying sideways, hitting the rough wall of the cave with a sickening crunch.

I stumble but regain my balance. Without a backward glance, I run, bursting out of the oppressive darkness into the light. A vibrant, almost frantic energy courses through me; running feels almost effortless, fluid, despite not having had a proper meal in what feels like ages. Tears, hot and stinging, still stream unchecked from my eyes, blurring my vision, but the crushing disgust, the self-loathing of what I did to Tom, never slows me down. In fact, the horror of it urges me on, pushes me to run faster, my legs moving with an unyielding, mechanical determination.

I sense an instinctual, inexplicable pull to veer sharply right. I pivot without thought, pure adrenaline surging through me. A guttural, inhuman roar echoes from behind me. Pherohsa, enraged and likely injured, is now in hot pursuit. Just as I hoped. Just as I planned.

My heart races as I urge myself even faster. The trees thin out ahead, and then, abruptly, I break through the tangled boundary of the woods and emerge into the wide, open expanse of the park. I angle my desperate flight toward the gated entrance near my street, but just as freedom seems within my grasp, I hear the violent snap of branches as the enraged Lamia bursts through the tree line. She is gaining with alarming speed.

Desperation fuels my final efforts. Just as I think I might not make it, an unexpected, unseen force jolts violently through my back. In an instant, I am launched into the air, my feet leaving the ground as I soar upwards into the cold morning sky. I am flying.

I glance to my right. My slate-grey wings are beating powerfully, a fierce, driving intensity propelling me forward. Any other time, I might have revelled in this incredible freedom. But not now. The familiar, red-brick landscape of my home rushes rapidly, unnervingly, toward me.

As I descend, I land with surprising, unnatural softness on the familiar concrete doorstep. With a final, soft flutter, my wings retract seamlessly into my shoulder blades. I take a single, precious moment to catch my ragged breath, the terrifying thrill of the chase still coursing like electricity through my veins.

I have no time to waste. I immediately start beating frantically on the front door with both fists. I pray they answer in time. Within seconds, the door swings open, revealing a man I don't immediately recognise. Tall, stern-faced, wearing… a police uniform? I don't hesitate. I push forcefully past him as he reflexively tries to block my path.

"Help!" I scream into the shocked stillness of the hallway.

"Miss! Miss! You can't just do that!" the man says, his voice firm, his hand going to his radio. Only then, as my eyes adjust, do I fully register he *is* a police officer. In my house. *Why?* I turn instantly to flee, ducking into the living room just as the kitchen door flies open with a crash.

"Devika! Is that you?" John exclaims, his voice a guttural, unrecognisable snarl of pure, unadulterated anger that sends an icy chill down my spine. He looks ready to kill me.

"Is that your daughter, sir?" the officer asks, his voice regaining some professional composure.

"Yes! It is!" John snarls, his eyes blazing with a cold, murderous fury as he storms into the living room, Sarah right on his heels, her own face a mask of pale, tight-lipped rage.

"Right. I need to call the station," the police officer says, fumbling for his radio again.

"Whatever!" John spits, rounding on me, taking another menacing step forward.

Any second now. My instrument of revenge should appear. I watch, my breath held tight, as John charges furiously towards me, his jaw clenched, his hands balled into white-knuckled fists.

"Where the hell have you been? With that boy?!" he roars.

"We... we were taken," I choke out. "He's... he's dead." The last bit, admitting Tom's death aloud, is impossibly hard, tearing at my shredded soul.

My words pull John up short. He freezes, confusion warring with his rage. "What do you mean, he's dead?"

Just then, I hear it. A chilling, reptilian hissing slicing through the tension. I look past John and Sarah towards the hallway. "I know everything," I say, my voice surprisingly steady. "I hope you both enjoy my revenge."

The confusion on their faces deepens. Just as Sarah opens her mouth to respond, they both abruptly shift their attention behind them. A look of sheer, animalistic panic overtakes their furious expressions.

The police officer's eyes widen in stark terror. Before he has a fraction of a chance to react, a monstrous, shadowy figure materialises in a horrifying blur of impossible movement. Pherohsa. She towers over him. With lightning speed, she lunges and slices her set of razor-sharp claws viciously across his unprotected neck. A gruesome arc of bright red blood sprays against the wall. The officer collapses, gasping, as darkness mercifully closes in around him.

A primal, savage growl erupts from John and Sarah. Sarah immediately crouches, her body beginning to contort, to ripple, as she violently transforms into a monstrous beast.

"Sarah! Don't! Not yet!" John begs, his voice trembling with a desperation I have never heard.

"I can't control it, John! I have to!" Sarah snarls back, her voice already deepening, her clothes stretching and tearing.

John's own hands are morphing, his nails elongating into sharp claws. As Pherohsa slithers confidently into the room, she laughs, that same chilling, mocking sound from the cave.

"Give her back to me, mutts," Pherohsa hisses, her yellow, reptilian eyes fixed on me.

"She belongs to us! Leave now, creature, or face your demise!" John roars back.

Pherohsa uses the distraction to her advantage. With blinding speed, she lashes out with her thick, muscular tail, sending John flying across the room. He collides heavily with the wall right next to me, the brutal impact making the entire structure tremble.

Sarah lets out a low, pained whimper. But amidst the chaos, I see something extraordinary. In place of my deceitful captor now stands a magnificent, terrifying creature—a giant wolf, easily the size of a small pony, her thick, lustrous fur shimmering like a living tapestry of molten white and rich browns. It is both utterly fearsome and, in a strange, primal way, breathtakingly beautiful.

My fleeting admiration is short-lived. The Lamia strikes the wolf viciously across the face, causing blood to spray from her muzzle. In that same instant, John, recovering with unnatural speed, leaps from the wall and tackles the Lamia, their movements becoming a tangled, savage blur of claws and coils.

Sarah, in her massive wolf form, staggers back onto her feet, dazed. As the two other monsters fight, her amber gaze falls upon me. I see conflict warring within her intelligent, animal eyes. She lets out a low, distressed whimper and begins to make her way towards me, her posture strangely submissive. A fresh, burning surge of visceral anger consumes me.

"Stay away from me, you bitch!" I spit, my voice raw with hatred.

Sarah's wolf form whimpers again but continues to move closer.

"I said stay away from me!" I repeat, my voice shaking with pent-up emotion. "I know what you had planned for me! I heard you! I would rather die! Anyway," I add, a cold, cruel satisfaction twisting inside me, "I'm not even what you think I am. I'm not the prize you thought you had."

The cryptic revelation finally makes her stop. A deafening, agonised scream tears through the air. John is thrown across the room again, crashing into the far wall with a final-sounding thud. Blood spurts from multiple, grievous wounds. In that instant, Sarah, her hesitation forgotten, ferociously attacks the Lamia again, leaping onto her back. Her powerful wolf jaws clamp down on the Lamia's arm. With a horrifying tearing sound, the arm is ripped clean off at the shoulder. But just as victory seems within grasp, Pherohsa uses Sarah's momentary distraction to strike back, grabbing the giant wolf by the thick fur of her neck. Her powerful, serpentine body coils rapidly, constricting, crushing the life out of Sarah in mere agonising moments. Her magnificent wolf body goes horribly limp, dropping heavily to the floor.

Fuelled by a final, desperate surge of rage, John, somehow still alive, rises unsteadily one last time and charges, roaring, at the Lamia. With one last dying movement, he slashes her face and chest with his claws. Blood pours from Pherohsa's new wounds as she staggers back. John falls heavily to the floor, motionless. Pherohsa stands swaying over his still body. She had, somehow, used his final lunge to her advantage, striking him lethally in the back with her claws, piercing his heart from behind. Now, she stands, bleeding, swaying, yet impossibly triumphant.

I watch, numbly, my emotions a tangled, chaotic mess. Part of me feels a strange, unwelcome flicker of pity for John. But another, larger, darker part of me, the part that had tasted Tom's life force, feels a cold, twisted joy at Pherohsa's bloody victory.

As she turns slowly, painfully, to face me, her piercing yellow eyes locking onto mine, I can't deny the overwhelming fear that courses like ice water through my veins. I am now in the presence of a deadly, wounded, enraged creature that could still easily end my own life. Yet, I can't look away. I can't move. She is a predator in every sense of the word, and I can't help but admire her in a twisted way.

The Lamia, Pherohsa, finally reaches me, starts to sway and collapses just inches away. She has lost a catastrophic amount of blood. I watch on, detached, numb. I hope, with a strange, cold certainty, that she has just enough strength left to kill me as well. After what I did to Tom, I don't deserve to live.

"Once... once I drain you... little prize..." Pherohsa rasps, her voice weak, bubbling with blood, "I should... heal enough..."

"Come on then," I say, my own voice surprisingly steady, almost inviting. "Get it over with."

A faint, gleeful smile spreads across her blood-streaked face. She begins to slowly drag herself the final few inches toward me. I deliberately sink to the floor, my knees hitting the blood-sticky surface, making it easier for this dying monster to reach my neck.

As she settles in front of me, her laboured breathing loud in the silence, she leans in, her voice barely a ragged whisper. "Why are you letting me do this, child?"

I take a deep, shuddering breath. "Because I'm a monster, too," I whisper, the words raw, broken. "After what I did to Tom... I feel like I deserve this. I deserve to die."

"Fair... enough..." she replies, a flicker of what might have been understanding in her dimming gaze. With deliberate, agonising slowness, she places her single remaining, clawed hand on my shoulder, its surprising warmth grounding me in this final, horrifying moment. As she begins to trace her sharp claws towards my neck, I recall with chilling clarity how she moved in the exact same way with Tom.

I don't know what comes over me then. A survival instinct? A final act of defiance? Just before her fangs can sink into my neck, my own right hand flies up, seemingly of its own accord. Sharp, needle-like claws, long and thick, erupt instantly from my fingertips. I plunge them, with shocking, unnatural force, deep into her throat. She freezes, her remaining eye widening in utter disbelief, and then, slowly, she falls sideways to the floor. As she does, my claws slide wetly out of her neck, followed by a torrent of dark, viscous blood.

I watch, stunned into silence. *When did I get claws?* Then, a faint, familiar voice whispers gently in my head. '*Now forgive yourself, Devvy.*' The voice... it's Tom again. His last, lingering echo. He somehow made me save myself. But it doesn't matter. I can never forgive myself.

I look at the horrific carnage. The blood-soaked living room, the four dead bodies. Even if I wanted to go on, the rest of John and Sarah's pack is still out there. They will hunt me down.

I only have one choice left.

I stand up numbly, stepping over the grotesque bodies, and make my way to the kitchen. I open the knife drawer and grab the sharpest, longest blade. Clutching it tightly, I head for the stairs. The front door is still wide open; I quickly, mechanically, close it and head up. In the main bathroom, I place the gleaming knife on the side of the bath and put the plug in the drain. I turn on both taps.

I return to my bedroom, stripping off my blood-splattered school uniform and change into clean leggings and a hoodie. On autopilot, I sit at my dressing table and apply thick black eyeliner and layers of mascara. A final mask. I tear a clean piece of paper from my sketchbook. My hands tremble only slightly as I write:

'*I was kidnapped as a baby by a secretive group. I discovered their chilling plans for me when I turn eighteen, which is why I took the steps I did today. The individuals behind my abduction are dead downstairs, but I know there are others. One is a man named Sean Lorcan, who is part of their pack. Additionally, there's Liz, a classmate, who was manipulated into keeping tabs on me. I can't shake the feeling she was just a pawn. Furthermore, the person responsible for the tragic deaths of Katie, Danny, and Tom is also lying lifeless downstairs in this house.'*

With the note resting heavily on my bed, I return to the bathroom. I turn off the hot water tap, leaving only the cold running. I step deliberately into the rapidly filling bath and slide down. The water is barely lukewarm. I pick up the knife and place it carefully on my lap, hidden beneath the rising water. When the bath is almost full, I turn off the tap.

I lean back and grab the knife firmly. I don't hesitate. I am a monster. I don't deserve to live. I cannot, will not, take the chance I will end up with the pack. Whatever snapped inside me earlier won't let me choose life.

I dig the sharp blade deep into the soft flesh of my left forearm and drag the unforgiving steel tip firmly towards my wrist. The pain is sharp, intense, a welcome, grounding distraction. As my warm, dark blood pours freely, turning the clear water red, I feel the crushing stress, the unbearable weight of existence, finally begin to leave.

I switch the knife to my left hand, repeating the action on my right arm. As I finally, weakly, drop the blood-slicked knife into the crimson water, I lean my head back against the cold porcelain. I close my eyes and consciously, deliberately, let myself succumb to the heavy exhaustion creeping over me. The darkness is beckoning, and I am finally, utterly, ready to embrace it.

But then, just as oblivion begins to claim me, I feel it—a strange, insistent pressure building just to my left. I hear a door slam loudly downstairs, followed by muffled male voices shouting. It's enough, just barely, to jolt me back towards a fading reality. I try to open my heavy eyelids but find myself unable to move. *They're coming for me,* I think, with a final flicker of dread. *The wolves… they found me after all.* Then, a strange, unexpected wave of relief washes over me. It isn't the wolves.

"This is the police! Is there anyone in the house?" a strong, demanding voice calls from downstairs.

No, I think dimly, the darkness creeping in, consuming my vision. I feel that strange pressure build again, stronger, and with a monumental effort, I try one last time to open my eyes.

All I can see is a minuscule, shimmering patch of soft, ethereal light, suspended in an overwhelming sea of blackness. Dark, billowing clouds of what looks like pure shadow swirl gracefully around a central point. Suddenly, a door, seemingly crafted from darkness itself, springs open. Time seems to pause as the black smoke parts, revealing a figure. The most exquisite, beautiful man I have ever laid eyes on steps calmly, purposefully, through the impossible doorway.

As he emerges fully, spectacular, enormous black wings unfurl majestically from his back, their countless feathers gleaming like polished onyx. They are even more breathtaking than the pristine white wings of the reaper I saw take Mr Harding's soul. My mind, sluggish, fading, forms a final, dawning realisation. *This stunning, terrifying, beautiful figure… he must be my reaper. Come to collect me.*

The thought washes over me like a soothing tide. It is a moment of utter, unexpected serenity. I close my eyes for the final time, surrendering willingly, gratefully, to the deepening, welcoming darkness. *This,* I think with a final flicker of consciousness, *is my punishment. And my release.*

Nathaniel

As I step through the shimmering, unstable portal hastily

conjured by Hecate—her power strained even from across the veil by the urgency of Kracis's fragmented, desperate message—a rush of cool, strangely vibrant air envelops me. Before me lies a scene that shatters my grim expectations—a dimly lit, ordinary human bathroom, yet filled with an unsettling, palpable tension.

I had braced myself for an immediate, violent confrontation. But this... this is quiet. Terribly, unnervingly quiet. My immortal heart races as I strain my enhanced hearing, deciphering the chaotic, muffled sounds from the floor below. Frantic shouts—human voices, police—calling out about... bodies?

And then I see her.

Lying there, small and still, in the rapidly cooling water. The sight shocks me profoundly. The sight of this young girl, barely more than a child, lying pale and lifeless in a bath rapidly filling with her blood... it throws me completely off balance. Then, my instincts kick in. I feel multiple presences—the police—pounding up the wooden staircase.

I reach swiftly into the bath, the cold, blood-tinged water shockingly tangible, and slide one arm carefully around Devika's back, the other beneath her knees. As I gently pull her slight form from the water, her blood soaking instantly into my clothes, and as soon as my skin makes contact with hers, I feel it—another presence. Faint, flickering, but undeniably there, residing within her. I lift her carefully, cradling her surprisingly light body against my chest, and as I move instinctively towards the still shimmering plane door, I simultaneously probe her gently with my power.

I feel a strange resistance just before I step back through the fading portal. I focus my senses. There is indeed another soul, or rather, the fading echo of one, tethered within her failing life force. She is sharing her body, her essence, with another. Its fragile presence is draining away at an alarming rate. My protective instincts kick in, urging me to grasp that fragile spirit before it vanishes forever.

As I grapple with the urgency of the moment, a desperate,

fading whisper pierces through the tension, echoing seemingly from within the girl herself. '*I… can't keep her alive much longer… hurry…*' The voice, male, young, is a heart-wrenching mix of weakening fear and fierce determination. It ignites a fire of resolve I haven't felt in centuries.

I waste no further time. I step back quickly through the now rapidly destabilising plane door as the heavy, panicked footsteps of the humans are about to burst through the bathroom door. The portal closes silently, thankfully, behind me just as the door is flung open. I don't have to worry about being seen; they are only human. Once I had her securely in my arms, I instantly cloaked us both, rendering us utterly invisible as they rushed into the blood-filled room.

Other books by Catherine M. Clark

The Harper Legacy Series

No Witchin Way – Book 1
Dark Intentions – Book 2

Ava the Destroyer Series

The Mission – Book 1

Book 2 in this series will be the final book in the Bloodlines & Chains series.

You can contact the author via the following means:
Email: authorcatherinemclark@hotmail.com
TikTok: www.tiktok.com/@catherine.m.clark
https://www.facebook.com/groups/themoontree/

Printed in Dunstable, United Kingdom